MEETING ETHAN

"What's your name?"

"Ethan."

In all the ways I have fantasized about meeting Ethan, it was never like this. I thought I would recognize him instantly. I imagined him shorter. I pictured his hair darker, his features more chiseled, his teeth white, straight, and evenly spaced. We'd both be dressed elegantly, certainly not wearing old sweatshirts and baseball caps. I never imagined we'd be breathing in the greasy fumes of bacon or the sugary scent of syrup. I assumed I'd be sipping Chianti or champagne, not slurping hot chocolate. Sometimes I even envisioned fireworks in the distance exploding in a star-filled sky, not sand trucks whizzing by a diner window on a dismal gray day.

I never figured out exactly what I would say, but I knew it would be something corny like "I knew you would come" or "You were worth the wait." And he wouldn't think it was weird. He'd know exactly what I was talking about.

Here in the actual moment, though, I just stare across the table and try to repeat his name, but it gets stuck in my throat.

"Let me guess. Your ex-boyfriend's name is Ethan?"

Not my ex-boyfriend. My future husband. For just a moment, I consider saying it aloud, telling him about Ajee and her prediction, but then I imagine him sprinting for the exit before I can get all the words out.

"It's my favorite name," I finally say.

Waiting for Ethan

Diane Barnes

LYRICAL SHINE
Kensington Publishing Corp.
www.kensingtonbooks.com

LYRICAL SHINE BOOKS are published by

Kensington Publishing Corp.
119 West 40th Street
New York, NY 10018

First Electronic Edition: September 2015
eISBN-13: 978-1-61650-788-6
eISBN-10: 1-61650-788-8

First Print Edition: September 2015
ISBN-13: 978-1-61650-789-3
ISBN-10: 1-61650-789-6

Printed in the United States of America

To Steve: Surely if I had known someone like Ajee, she would have said, "Steven with a V."
To Mom and Dad: I love you.

ACKNOWLEDGMENTS

This book began as a challenge to participate in National Novel Writing Month and has since gone through several iterations. I might not have started it if Julie Peterson hadn't encouraged me to participate. Thank you, Julie, and thanks to everyone who has read part of any version.

I must express special gratitude to Alan Hurvitz, who offered constant support through every draft. Heartfelt thanks also to my writing group at the Hudson library, especially Tiana, Neville, Martha, Amanda and Steve. You helped me maintain my confidence throughout the entire process.

My instructors at Grub Street, Lisa Borders, Michelle Hoover and Stuart Horwitz, as well as fellow workshop participants asked key questions early on that helped me work out the story. A huge thank you to Laurel King and my classmates at the Worcester Art Museum who were ambitious enough to read an entire draft and provide valuable feedback.

As I was writing this novel, I had the great fortune to attend a writing workshop taught by Elizabeth Berg. In addition to meeting my literary idol Elizabeth, I met seven other extraordinary women who made me feel like a rock star every time they critiqued my work. Thank you Ann, Barb, Celia, Carol, Lynda, Molly and Vicki.

Susan Timmerman, thanks for letting me run ideas by you on our walks and for your never-wavering interest in my characters and story. Tricia Brown, thanks for lending your keen eye.

To my agent Liza Fleissig, THANK YOU for helping make my dream come true, but more than that, I really appreciate how responsive and kind you've been through the entire process, even before you read my manuscript and decided to represent me. To the readers at Liza Royce

Agency, thank you for liking my manuscript enough to bring it to Liza's attention.

Finally, thanks to my family, the one I was lucky enough to be born into and the one I was smart enough to marry into. I am grateful for your support throughout the process and your understanding every time I said, "I can't today. I'm writing."

Chapter 1

2012

"Neesha Patel's grandmother ruined your life." That's what my mother says when I point out the obituary. She mutters to herself in Italian, glances at the picture in the newspaper, and then goes right back to making the list of things she wants me to check on when she and my father make their annual exodus to Florida later that day. I slide closer to her on the couch and begin reading the article out loud:

> *Satya E. Patel (known as Ajee), 92, of San Antonio, TX, formerly of Westham, MA, died Wednesday. She is survived by her son, Dr. Kumar Patel of San Antonio, TX, her grandson, Dr. Sanjit Patel of San Antonio, TX, her granddaughter, Neesha Davidian of Canyon Lake, TX, and five great-grandchildren . . .*

At the mention of the great-grandchildren, my mother looks up from her notepad and frowns. Finally, I think, she's going to show some sympathy for the Patels. I even think I see tears in her eyes. "It sounds like both Sanjit and Neesha have children." I nod, trying to picture my old friend with kids, but all I can see is a lanky fourteen-year-old girl with a long dark ponytail and a mouthful of wires. "Their grandmother is the reason I'll never have grandchildren of my own." Although her words sting, they don't shock me. I am thirty-six and single. My mother long ago abandoned all hope of me ever getting married and having a family, and for this she blames the deceased, a woman I haven't seen since I was fourteen.

"What's going on in here? You're supposed to be packing." My father appears at the bottom of the stairs, dressed in a golf shirt and holding the driver I gave him for Christmas two weeks before. He can't get to Florida fast enough to start playing again.

"Neesha Patel's grandmother died."

My father raises his eyebrows. "Recently?"

"Last week."

"She must have been well over a hundred. She was ancient when she lived here."

"The paper says she was ninety-two."

My father rubs his chin. "That means she was only sixty-nine or seventy when they moved to Texas?"

"Right, Dad. Your age. Ancient."

"I'm only sixty-seven, Gina, and I feel like I'm twenty." He steps away from the stairs and takes a halfhearted swing with his golf club. "It's being active that keeps me so young." He winks. "May I?" He points at the paper, so I hand it to him.

My mother sighs. "Why did they even bother to publish her obituary in the Westham paper? They haven't lived here for almost twenty-five years. People don't remember her."

I glare at my mother. "Mom, everyone remembers Ajee. She was a hero in this town."

My mother rolls her eyes. "She was a nosy old woman, Gina. That's all."

I stand and walk to the living room window. The Patels' old house is directly across the street. The Murphys live there now, but someday Neesha will be back. Her grandmother said so. She said it the same day she told me I would marry a man named Ethan.

As we load the last of the suitcases into my parents' car, Mr. and Mrs. Murphy make their way across the street. My father mutters something incomprehensible under his breath. Mr. Murphy makes a beeline up the driveway and heads straight to me. "Gina." He hugs me tightly as if he hasn't seen me in ages. "Are you still on the market?" I nod. "What's wrong with young men today? If I were just a few years younger . . . But don't you worry. Every pot has a lid." He passes on similar pearls of wisdom every time I see him, which is about once a week when I visit my parents.

Mrs. Murphy follows about four steps behind her husband and zeroes in on my mother. She waves a picture in the air above her head. "I just have to show you my grandson before you leave, Angela." She reaches the passenger door where my mother is standing and hands her a snapshot of a newborn baby. "Born yesterday. Isn't he beautiful?"

My mother looks at me pointedly, and I feel my stomach begin a gymnastic act. How is it possible that Kelli Murphy, the seven-year-old sniveler I babysat for, is a wife and parent, while I'm not only single but haven't had a meaningful date in the last three years?

My mother turns her attention to the photo and then smiles at Mrs. Murphy. My father looks at his watch. He wants to be in Virginia in bed by 10 p.m. because he has a 7:30 tee time tomorrow morning.

"He's a big boy," Mrs. Murphy says. "Nine pounds, six ounces."

"He's beautiful," my mother says.

"He looks like me," Mr. Murphy adds. "Spitting image."

My mother laughs. My father opens the driver's side door.

"They named him Ethan." By the look on my mother's face, you would think Mr. Murphy just said his grandson was named after Bin Laden.

"That's a great name," I say. My mother won't make eye contact with me.

"It's an old name that's come back around," Mrs. Murphy says.

My father leans into the car, puts the keys into the ignition, and starts the engine.

"We have to get going," my mother says. "Congratulations on your grandson."

The Murphys wobble back down the driveway, and my dad jumps into the driver's seat. My mother hugs me. "Strange we should hear that name on the same day we learn of Ajee's death," she says. But I don't think it's strange at all. It's a sign from Ajee. *Don't worry*, she's saying. *Your Ethan will be here soon.*

As the car starts to pull out of the driveway, my mother opens her window. "Gina, if some nice man asks you out this winter, promise me you'll say yes, no matter what his name is."

Chapter 2

1987

The news vans were parked up and down both sides of Towering Heights Lane. Television cameras pointed toward the top of the stairs leading to the Patels' front door. A mob of reporters holding microphones stood on the lawn at the bottom of the steps calling Ajee's name. From the bushes where Neesha and I crouched, I saw the Patels' front door swing open and watched Ajee step outside and wave. She was wearing a purple and gold silk sari and a matching headband to keep her salt-and-pepper hair off her well-lined face. The clothes were a stark contrast to the Levi's, Izod shirt, and tennis sneakers she had been wearing an hour earlier. I was pretty sure my mother was watching the commotion from our living room window, and I could imagine her snickering when she saw Ajee's outfit. "That woman is such a fraud," she would say to my father. Since the day Ajee arrived in Westham and predicted Neesha and Sanjit's mother would not return from the hospital, my mother had no tolerance for Ajee and her so-called gift. It didn't matter that Ajee had been right and Mrs. Patel died in the hospital. In fact, that only seemed to make my mother's resentment worse.

The media had been stationed in our neighborhood all week. Before today, though, their attention was focused on the Colbys, my next-door neighbors. On Tuesday afternoon, six-year-old Matthew was playing in the sprinkler with his mother and three-year-old sister, Lisa. Mrs. Colby took Lisa inside to use the bathroom, and when she returned five minutes later, Matthew was gone.

The police investigated around the clock for five days and had no leads. On the sixth day, the Patels returned from their vacation. Within minutes of finding out what had happened to Matthew, Ajee was sitting on the Colbys' front lawn cradling the sprinkler. My mother and I watched fascinated from our driveway. Dr. Patel came racing out of the Patels' house. "What are you doing?" he shouted at his mother. "Get up now."

The Colbys' front door opened, and a police officer stepped outside. Ajee stood. "The boy was taken by a woman in a gray Oldsmobile. She lives in Rhode Island and is a friend of the father."

Dr. Patel buried his head in his hands. "She thinks she has psychic abilities."

Mr. Colby appeared at the door. "Tell him about your friend in Rhode Island," Ajee hissed.

Dr. Patel grabbed Ajee's arm. "I sincerely apologize," he said as he led his mother back to their house.

Later that day, though, Matthew was found unharmed at the home of a woman who lived in Rhode Island and drove a gray Oldsmobile Cutlass Supreme. Until three months before the abduction, she worked with Matthew's father.

The police credited Ajee with the tip that brought Matthew home safely, and the media that had been staking out the Colbys' house turned their attention to the Patels. Ajee basked in it. She stood at the top of the Patels' landing with her hands clasped together in front of her stomach, explaining the origins of her gift. "I began experiencing visionary images at a very young age. I can't explain why or how it happens; it just does." She paused. "When I touched the sprinkler, I saw the woman and the car. Who knows why these things are so?" She shrugged.

A redheaded reporter whom I had seen on Channel 5 for years raised her hand. I struggled to recall her name. Cindy maybe? "So you need to touch something for your power to work?"

Ajee nodded. "Usually." She descended to the bottom of the stairs and extended her arm to the reporter. "Give me your pen."

Shelly Lange? No, that wasn't her name.

The reporter handed her the pen. Ajee closed her eyes and rolled the writing instrument between her hands. The only sound was the clanking the pen made as it crossed over her rings.

Terri Vance. That was the reporter's name.

After what seemed like several minutes, Ajee opened her eyes and gave the pen back to Terri. "You will quite enjoy the West Coast."

Terri's expression was blank. "I have no idea what you're talking about."

Ajee smiled, turned her back to the reporter, and climbed to the top of the landing. She spun to face the crowd again and looked directly at Terri. "Soon. You will understand soon." She scanned the crowd with her eyes. "If the rest of you want readings, you will need to make appointments."

A few weeks later, the redheaded reporter, Terri Vance, announced on the air that she had been offered and accepted a job with the ABC affiliate in San Francisco. "You may remember," she said. "The psychic of Westham predicted I would enjoy the West Coast. At the time I had no idea what she was talking about." The name stuck. Ajee became known as the psychic of Westham, and her business took off.

Before all the media attention, she gave one or two readings a week. Now she was conducting four or five a day. One afternoon Neesha and I decided we wanted to see what went on during these readings. Before Ajee's two o'clock appointment, we snuck downstairs to the Patels' basement and hid in the large closet directly across from Ajee's "reading parlor." That's what Ajee called the area. In reality, it was a section of the cellar partitioned off with a curtain.

When we first entered the closet, Neesha froze, noticing her mother's clothes still hanging from the racks. She reached for a green wool sweater that I remembered Mrs. Patel wearing often and put it on even though beads of sweat were running down her forehead. We were thirteen. Neesha's mother had been dead for six years, and I still hadn't figured out what I could do or say to make her feel better at times like this, so I said nothing.

As we took our positions on the floor, we heard footsteps on the stairs and a voice we didn't recognize followed by Ajee's. Soon Ajee was sitting at her reading table with a client, a blond woman named Mary who was the teller at my parents' bank. Mary sat erect in the chair with her arms folded across her chest. Ajee, dressed in the sari she wore at her press conference and the only sari she owned as far as I knew, leaned forward with both elbows on the table and her chin resting on the backs of her clasped hands watching Mary.

The smell of cedar in the closet was overpowering, so I pushed the door open a crack more to bring in fresh air. The sound of the squeaking hinges reverberated throughout the basement. Ajee's head turned toward the closet. Neesha and I both leaned away from the door. After several seconds, Ajee refocused her attention on Mary.

"Let me have your watch," Ajee instructed.

I watched Mary unclasp the watch and hand it to Ajee. She cradled it in her hands and held it in front of her heart. She closed her eyes and didn't move for several seconds. Behind me, I heard Neesha take a deep breath. When I turned to look, I saw she was holding her breath. She looked so ridiculous with her puffed-out cheeks trying not to laugh, that I laughed, causing Neesha to snort.

"What was that?" Mary asked.

I pulled the closet door shut. Neesha and I slid back into the row of clothing. A moment later we heard the *flip-flop* sound of Ajee's sandals slapping the cement floor approaching the closet. The door flew open, and Ajee jerked her head inside. She looked at us with a half smile and then suddenly yelled, "Scram!" Giggling, Neesha and I ran upstairs. Later, when Ajee emerged from the basement, she fanned three ten-dollar bills in front of us. "Laugh all you want, girls, but that woman paid thirty dollars for my information."

The next day, when she caught us spying again, she wasn't as amused. "What I do is a business. It is serious. There is no room for little girls spying. How can I get you to stop?"

Neesha and I looked at each other and grinned. "Tell us our fortunes," we said in unison. Until that day, Ajee had always refused, saying we had to wait until we were older.

Neesha went first. Ajee instructed her to hand over her bracelet. It was made of thick white rope, and I had one that matched on my wrist. We had bought them the previous summer on Cape Cod. With some effort, Neesha removed the bracelet and handed it to Ajee.

Ajee immediately dropped it. "Sometimes it is better not to know the future."

"You promised," Neesha said.

Ajee cleared her throat. "Very well." She picked up the bracelet and closed her eyes. "You will like this," she said, opening her eyes. "The handsome boy will kiss you before summer ends."

The handsome boy was Josh Levine, the neighborhood cutie. I had to admit, I hoped Ajee was wrong. I didn't want Josh kissing Neesha. I wanted him to kiss me.

Ajee closed her eyes again. She opened them a few moments later, and she looked as serious as I had ever seen her. "You will move away before the start of high school, and you will not return again until you are an adult with children of your own. Yes, you and your family will own this very house."

I felt my heart racing. High school was just a year away. Neesha couldn't move. She was my best friend.

Neesha looked at me and shook her head. "She's just trying to scare us."

Ajee reached for Neesha's hand and held it for several seconds. "I am sorry, dear one, but it is what I see."

Neesha popped up from the seat. "Your turn, Gina." She looked pointedly at her grandmother. "Be truthful."

I sat, and Ajee instructed me to give her my bracelet. I pulled it from my wrist and handed it to her. She spun it around her index finger and closed her eyes. "You will visit Italy before high school starts." She was quiet for a second and then frowned. "You will break your arm before school starts again."

"Ajee!" Neesha screamed.

"I am only telling you what I see." Ajee opened her eyes. I must have looked scared because she reached for my hand. "Bella," because of my dark hair and eyes and olive complexion, she thought I looked more Italian than American and often addressed me by the Italian word for "beautiful." "Do not worry. I will tell you the name of your husband. You will like that, yes?"

I nodded enthusiastically, sure she was going to say Josh Levine. Who cared if Neesha got to kiss him? I was going to marry him. Mrs. Josh Levine. Gina Levine.

Ajee looked right into my eyes. "Ethan."

Ethan? Confused, I pulled my hand from hers. "I don't know anyone named Ethan."

"You will not meet him for many years. You will get tired of waiting. You will doubt that he will come, but he will. You must wait. You must wait for Ethan."

Within days of Ajee making those predictions, Josh Levine kissed Neesha, and I fell off my bicycle and broke my arm. Still, I might have ignored her instructions to wait for Ethan if not for what happened Labor Day weekend. To celebrate getting my cast off, I went to the beach with the Patels. Neesha, her brother Sanjit, and I were playing in the waves most of the day while Ajee and Dr. Patel were rooted in beach chairs reading. In the late afternoon, Ajee walked down to the water and called for us. "I want you to get out of the water now," she said. "I have a very bad feeling."

Sanjit splashed her and swam away. Neesha followed. I stood on the shoreline with her. "Come, Bella. It is not safe." At the same time, Neesha and Sanjit called for me to come back in the water.

"Sorry, Ajee," I said. I turned and started walking to them. In front of me a father lifted his small daughter onto his shoulders and she dove off. I took several steps to the right to avoid them. The water I was walking through became eerily still. I took another step, but this time when I tried to put my foot down, I could no longer touch the bottom. I turned back to look at the shore and realized I was out much deeper than I thought, much deeper than I was comfortable with. I had somehow been carried out beyond Neesha and Sanjit. I tried to swim toward the shore, but felt myself getting pulled farther and farther away. I moved my arms as fast as possible. I kicked my legs as hard as I could. It made no difference. Instead of going forward I was being pulled backward. The people on the beach got smaller. My arms and legs became heavy. I no longer had the strength to move them. I gasped to catch my breath and could taste salt water filling my mouth. My heart, which had been beating frantically, seemed to stop as I felt myself sinking beneath the surface. Everything got black and quiet.

I came to lying on the beach while the lifeguard pumped my chest. A crowd with worried expressions peered over her shoulder down at me. Someone nearby was crying. I coughed, and water spurted out of my mouth. The lifeguard stopped pounding. She sank from her knees to her butt and wiped her forehead with the back of her hand. The crowd clapped.

"You got caught in a riptide. I pulled you out," the lifeguard said.

"Thank you," I murmured.

"Swim out of a rip current. Parallel to the shore. Never against it." She seemed to be addressing the entire crowd.

"You're okay now," Dr. Patel said. I hadn't noticed he was kneeling to my right. "But you scared us." Behind him, Sanjit, with tears streaming down his face, held Neesha's hand. Her usually dark face was white. Next to them, Ajee repeatedly tapped her bare foot on the sand. "I warned you. Why didn't you listen?" she mumbled. She came and sat next to me, taking my hand into hers. "You girls have to listen. I know things."

"We will. From now on," I promised, knowing I would never speak truer words.

Chapter 3

Neesha and I spent most of eighth grade trying to figure out how Ajee knew the things she did. We'd sit at the kitchen table pretending to do our homework while we studied her cooking at the stove. She hummed a lot. We'd follow her into the living room and watch her while she watched television. She'd scream at the characters on *General Hospital*, telling them they were stupid. We volunteered to go to the grocery store with her. She ate a bag of Doritos as she shopped and always discarded the empty bag before getting to the cash register. Her breath would smell like nacho cheese, and her fingers would be covered with orange powder that would inevitably get smeared on the money she gave to the cashier, but she never got caught. As closely as we scrutinized her, we found nothing that explained how she could see the things she did. When we asked her, she would only shrug.

While we believed in her powers wholeheartedly, as each day of eighth grade passed with no word that the Patels would be moving or I would visit Italy, we let ourselves believe that Ajee could sometimes get it wrong. On the last day of the school year we believed we were in the clear and that Neesha would be attending Westham High with me that fall. We planned to celebrate the beginning of summer vacation with a trip to the Westham Creamery. Ajee promised she would take us there after dinner, and Neesha and I were planning to split the Gut Wrencher, a monstrous six-scoop ice cream sundae with three different kinds of toppings. I had just finished dinner and was in the backyard playing badminton with my mother. I was camped under the birdie, waiting for it to come down, when out of the corner of my eye, I saw Neesha racing into our backyard. I figured she was there to collect me for our trip to the creamery. I hit the birdie back at my mother, but she didn't return it because she was looking at Neesha. "What's wrong?" she asked. That's when I noticed Neesha's blood-shot eyes and the tears streaming down her face.

Neesha tried to speak, but she couldn't catch her breath. My mother put her arm around Neesha and walked her to the picnic table to sit down. "Calm down, honey," she said.

The only other time I had seen Neesha cry was when her mother died, so I was certain something horrible had happened to Ajee, Dr. Patel, or maybe even Sanjit. I stayed glued to my spot by the bad-minton net because I didn't want my suspicions confirmed. Like by staying where I was, I could somehow change what had happened.

"Gina, run inside and get Neesha a drink of water and some tissues," my mom instructed.

I took my time inside the house. When I returned several minutes later, my mother was hugging Neesha, who was no longer crying. "Here," I said, handing Neesha the glass and tissues.

She looked up at me. "Ajee was right," she said. "We're moving to Texas. My dad is going to be the chief neurologist at a hospital there."

I looked at my mother, who nodded with a somber expression.

"When?"

Neesha blew her nose before answering. "The end of July."

I could taste the hot dog I had for dinner bubbling back up in my mouth. "But what about high school? We're supposed to be in the same classes."

"I know," Neesha said. She was crying again, and I could feel my eyes watering up, as well.

"I'm sorry, girls." My mom gave us each a small smile. No one said anything else. The only sound in our backyard was the crickets chirping.

A few minutes later, the jingling of keys broke up the silence as Ajee burst around the corner. When she saw us at the picnic table with our tear-streaked faces, she came to a screeching halt and smacked the palm of her hand against her forehead. "You are still crying," she shouted, looking at Neesha. "If you do not stop soon, the tracks of your tears will carve deep grooves into your face. You will be four-teen years old, and you will be as wrinkled as me."

I could feel my mother stiffen next to me. "This is hard on the girls."

Ajee waved her hand in the air to dismiss my mother's comment. "Nonsense. Leaving everyone and everything I knew in India. That was hard."

My mother exhaled loudly. I imagined she was counting silently. Usually when she lost patience with me, she counted out loud.

Ajee turned to me. "Are you ready for some ice cream?"

My stomach hurt. "I'm not really hungry."

Ajee sat down on the picnic bench next to me. "I tried to prepare you girls for this last summer." She patted my knee. "People come into your life. People leave your life. It is the way it is, Bella. By the time you are my age, you will be used to it."

My mother stood. "You girls can write each other and talk on the phone, and Neesha, you're welcome to come back and visit us anytime."

"I will," Neesha said. She sounded like she meant it, but I knew it wouldn't happen because Ajee's last prediction for Neesha was that she wouldn't return until she was an adult with children of her own.

I looked at Ajee. She stood. "I am getting ice cream. Who is coming with?"

The Patels left for Texas on July 30, the hottest day of the summer. My parents and I stood at the end of our driveway and waved goodbye as their blue Cadillac rolled down Towering Heights Lane. Ajee was riding shotgun, and she gave a thumbs-up as the car passed. Behind her, Neesha extended her arm out the open back window like she was reaching for me. Sanjit stuck out his tongue and then gave a quick wave in the back windshield. Dr. Patel tapped the horn two times, and seconds later the car was out of sight.

The next few days I moped around the house. My mother volunteered to take me shopping, to the beach, or to the movies, but I refused, content to stay in my room in my pajamas all day. Finally, one August evening, my parents burst into my room with big smiles on their faces. My father fanned three envelopes in front of me. "Guess what these are?"

"Tickets to Italy," I answered.

He looked accusingly at my mother. "I didn't say a thing, Dominick," she said.

"Ajee told me I'd be visiting Italy before high school," I responded.

"Well, get packing," my father said. "We leave in three days."

When we returned from Italy, five letters from Neesha were waiting for me. Through the first three years of high school we corresponded regularly and talked on the phone at least once a month. Senior year we promised each other we'd both go to Boston College and be roommates. We mailed our applications on the same exact day, and for the next few months our letters to each other were mostly about how we would be reunited soon. In March when I received my acceptance letter, I called Neesha.

"I got in," I shouted.

My enthusiasm was met by silence and then a clearing of the throat. "Me, too, Gina, but I've decided I want to go to school in Texas to be near my high school friends."

"Wait, what?"

"I don't want to move away from my friends again. It was hard enough the first time."

"You'd rather be with your Texas friends than me?" Even as I asked the question, I knew there was no way it could be true.

"Yeah, I guess that's what I've decided," she said.

It felt as if she had swung a wrecking ball through my heart. We were both silent. "Sorry, Gina," Neesha finally said. "But I'm a Texas girl now."

After that, our letters and phone calls became fewer and farther between, and then one day they just stopped. Through the years, I often thought about picking up the phone and calling her. A few times I'd even start to dial, but then I'd remember how she chose her Texas friends over me and I'd put down the phone.

Chapter 4

2012

Sunday morning, the day after my parents left for Florida, I awake at 6:45 and lie in bed staring at the ceiling and listening to the constant drip from the bathroom sink. I have asked my landlord to repair it ten times, and each time he has told me he will stop by. I even tried to fix it myself, but only succeeded in making it worse. I bet when I meet Ethan, he will hear it dripping, and without me even asking, he will retrieve the toolbox he keeps in the trunk of his car and fix it.

At 7:15 I give up trying to fall back to sleep and get out of bed. Usually on Sunday mornings my mother's phone call wakes me from a dead sleep at 8:15. "Gina, just calling to see if you would like to go to Mass with me and Dad?"

I have said yes only once, but that one time was enough to make her hopeful enough to keep calling every week. Today, I am thinking that I would like to go to church with my parents. I'd even be willing to put up with my mother's critique of my clothing. "That sweater is too baggy, and your slacks are at least one size too big," she'd say, shaking her head. "I don't understand why you spend so much time working out and then hide your beautiful figure underneath clothing that swims on you." She'd give me a few minutes' reprieve before starting in on my hair. "Women your age shouldn't wear their hair so long, and why do you straighten it? People pay good money for curls like yours." Then she would mutter to herself in Italian, and the only words I'd be able to make out would be "That daughter of mine. What am I going to do with her?"

Yes, at 7:30 in the morning I am already so bored that I would be willing to put up with all that today, but of course I can't. My parents are somewhere on Interstate 95 heading south toward sunny, warm Florida, orphaning me in cold, gray New England for the next four months.

By 7:45 I have flipped through every channel on TV without finding anything that interests me. I hate Sundays in the winter. They are endless. When I finally meet Ethan, I imagine he will wake up before me and sneak down to the convenience store for the paper. Then he'll walk around the corner to the bakery for fresh blueberry muffins and piping hot coffee. We'll sit at the kitchen table for the better part of the morning, him reading the articles out loud, his voice distinguished like a prominent newscaster.

By 9:30 I'm showered, dressed, and going stir-crazy. I think about going to the ten o'clock Mass here in Clayton but quickly reject the idea. I never feel more alone than I do in a crowded church where I am surrounded by families. I don't care what "Dear Abby" says. Church is no place to meet someone. I swear, I am always the only single person there.

The last time I went to church by myself was about three months ago. Father Moynihan was celebrating Mass. His voice is soft and monotonous, making it very hard to pay attention. The baby with the couple next to me started crying. I turned to look and noticed the mother and father appeared to be at least ten years younger than I was. A few rows ahead, a teenage boy repeatedly poked his sister, who was probably about twelve. The mother shot the boy a harsh look. I guessed she was my age. My heart pounded faster. When it came time to give the sign of peace, I turned around to shake hands with the people behind me, and a pregnant woman much younger than me extended her arm. I felt my heart miss a beat. To my right, a woman my age with tween girls offered me her hand. I felt a tightness in my chest. By the time the parishioners were lining up for communion, I had confirmed that all the parents with infants and toddlers were much younger than me and all the mothers and fathers with teenage kids were my age. I was running out of time. I tried to take a deep breath, but a sharp pain ripped through my upper left side. I could feel my heart jumping in my chest and sweat dripping down my back. The woman next to me tapped me on the shoulder. I hadn't noticed it was our row's turn to line up for communion. I leaned back in the pew to let her pass. She stared at me with wide, open eyes. "Are you okay?" she asked.

I nodded, but when the row was empty, I fled to the side aisle and out the back door. Convinced I was having a heart attack, I drove straight to the emergency room. I told the man at the registration desk I was having chest pains. He rushed me into the examining room, where a heavyset blond nurse took my vitals. My heart rate raced to nearly two hundred beats per minute. The doctor gave me medication to slow it down. After, he told me that I had experienced a panic attack. I haven't been back to church since.

Now, alone in my apartment, I think of Ajee. I wish I had asked her if Ethan and I would ever have kids. Of course, when she told me about Ethan, I never imagined there was a possibility we wouldn't. I think about Neesha being married and having kids. I wonder what they're like. Then I think of the day the ambulance took Neesha's mother away and how she never came back, how I always felt so powerless to make Neesha feel better. I decide I will send a sympathy card for Ajee.

I bundle up in my ski coat, hat, and gloves and set out to walk the two blocks to the drugstore. The only person I see is a woman running in shorts and a T-shirt. Her face, nose, and ears are bright red. I notice a steady stream of breath escaping her mouth as it hits the cold air. *Hey, it's seven degrees!* I want to shout. *Smarten up.* She must notice me watching her because she looks up and smiles. Now I feel bad for wanting to yell at her.

I spend over an hour in the drugstore looking at sympathy cards. I read every card there, and the one I end up selecting is the first one I looked at. The teenage girl at the cash register is talking to a boy her age who is leaning over the counter toward her. The boy, wearing a Clayton High letter jacket with the number seventeen and the name Ryan stitched on the sleeve, has jet-black hair and bright green eyes. He is exactly the type of boy I would have fallen for in high school. He moves out of the way so I can buy the card and taps the counter next to me with his fingertips while I remove my money from my wallet. Out of the corner of my eye, I see the cashier smile at him. There are no other customers in the store, and I suddenly feel like I'm intruding on their alone time. I give up looking for exact change and hand over three dollar bills.

On the walk back to my apartment, I think about my high school boyfriend, Kyle Nolan. For five months, Kyle tried to convince me to go all the way, and for five months I resisted. Six days before the prom, he broke up with me to take a date who was a sure thing. I remember we were sitting in his parents' station wagon in my driveway. There was something wrong with the catalytic converter, and the car smelled like rotten eggs. I was trying not to breathe in the fumes. Kyle stared straight ahead at my garage. "We're all staying at the Sheraton. Unless you tell me that you are going to stay there with me, and, you know, do it, I think I should take someone else."

I let out a deep breath and clenched my hands into tight fists, thinking about all the times Kyle had told me he loved me. How I had meant it when I said it back to him. I had even been planning to sleep with him on prom night. Idiot. "Who are you going to take?" My voice was much softer than usual.

He kept staring straight ahead. "Jodi Learner."

Jodi had slept with seven of the starting nine on Westham High's baseball team. I tried to think of something clever to say. Nothing came to me, but later that night as I unsuccessfully struggled to fall asleep, I came up with three great lines. I got out of the car, slammed the door, and stomped up the driveway, all the while hoping that Jodi would give Kyle one of the several sexually transmitted diseases she was certain to have.

The night of the prom I stayed home alone watching *Designing Women* reruns. Even my parents had plans that night. When *Designing Women* ended, I called Neesha in Texas. Ajee answered the phone and told me Neesha was out with friends. Ajee must have sensed that I was upset because she asked me what was wrong. I told her about being dumped days before the prom.

She clicked her tongue. "Oh Bella, I am so sorry."

"Thanks, Ajee." I felt stupid I'd told her.

"Bella, if it makes you feel any better, Ethan did not attend his prom, either."

"How do you know that?"

She laughed. "I just know things, Bella."

"Well, when will he be here? When will I meet Ethan?"

"That I do not know, but you must wait."

* * *

Once I get home, I stare blankly at the inside of the sympathy card, trying to think of something to write. I feel my grip on the pen tightening as nothing comes to me. I decide it will be easier to compose the message on my computer and transcribe it to the card. I open a Word document and stare at the blinking cursor on the empty white screen. "Dear Neesha," I begin. Dear? I backspace and delete the words. They're too formal. "Hey, Neesha, bet you're surprised to hear from me?" Too casual. I try again and settle on "Hello, Neesha," and then delete the "Hello" and go back to "Dear." Now what? I get up, walk to the kitchen, pour myself a glass of water, and return to my desk. Five minutes later, I still haven't typed another word. I return to the refrigerator for an apple. Ten minutes later, when I toss the core into the trash, the only words on my screen are still "Dear Neesha."

How can it be so hard to think of something to say to someone I talked nonstop with until the age of fourteen? We used to sit next to each other on the bus on the way home from school, walk home from the bus stop together, and the minute we got inside our houses, we'd call each other. "How in the world can you have anything left to say to her?" my mother would ask. But there was always more because whatever thought popped in my head came out my mouth to Neesha's ears. I have never confided with anyone else as much since.

Okay, Gina. This shouldn't be so hard. Offer condolences about Ajee. "I was sorry to learn of Ajee's passing," I write. "I always found her enchanting, and you and she are part of my best childhood memories." I read it back to myself—a little corny, but it will do. What else? Of course, ask about her husband and children. "I imagine your husband looks like a grown-up version of Josh Levine," I write. Will she even remember who Josh Levine is? Of course she will. He's the first boy she ever kissed.

How do I end? "I hope you'll write back, Gina." No, that's almost like begging. "Love, Gina." Love, we haven't spoken in almost twenty years. I decide to go with "Your old friend, Gina Rossi." Under it, I add my e-mail address. Then, before I lose my nerve, I walk the few blocks to the post office to mail the card.

Chapter 5

Since my parents left for Florida three weeks ago, I have been working twelve-hour days. I am a senior editor at TechVisions, a leading market research firm in New England. All day long I fix other people's mistakes so that our clients never know the analysts whom they pay six figures to solve their business problems don't know the difference between *it's* and *its*; *their*, *there*, and *they're*; *sight*, *site*, and *cite*; and so on. Our customers want to know how their markets will perform and where they'll be able to earn the biggest market share. Honestly, I think they would have better luck getting this information from someone like Ajee, who would probably charge a lot less and make more accurate predictions.

I'm pretty sure the analysts just make up their forecasts. Last spring, for example, one of our top analysts boldly declared the technology market was over the worst of the economic slump. Based on this advice, TechVisions hired twenty-five new employees. Two weeks before Christmas the market was still underperforming so TechVisions laid off 30 percent of its workforce and surrendered 50 percent of its office space. The analyst who inaccurately predicted the rebound got to keep his job. Eight of ten editors did not. Luci Chin and I are the lucky ones who survived, and by lucky I mean that since the day pink slips were handed out, Luci and I have been forced to share an office the size of a bathroom stall and do the work of ten editors.

Luci is thirty-nine and has never worked anywhere but TechVisions. Five years ago when I was interviewing for my job, I had to meet with her before being hired. As I sat in the windowless conference room waiting for her, I envisioned a bookish Chinese woman. Instead, a tall, thin Caucasian woman who looked like she should be walking a fashion runway in Paris sauntered into the room. "I'm Luci Chin," she said, extending her hand. "Nice suit." She sounded exactly like the waitress at the Chinese restaurant down the street from my apartment. I desperately searched her features for a hint of something that would reveal she was partially Chinese, but her long auburn hair, bright green eyes, and pale complexion led me to believe she was all Irish. I was so confused by the dichotomy between her name, accent, and appearance that I couldn't concentrate on the questions she was asking. Finally she slammed her hand on the desk. "What the matter?" she asked, sounding more Chinese than ever.

"I'm sorry. You just look so Irish."

A strand of hair had fallen across her eye. Instead of swiping it away with her hand, she blew it back in place before speaking. "My accent's pretty good, isn't it? It's an imitation of my mother-in-law. I love doing that to people." She laughed.

I gave her my best look of disapproval, but I was trying really hard not to laugh. "How old are you?"

She laughed but didn't answer.

Two years ago Luci and her husband, Kip, divorced. We all assumed she'd go back to her maiden name, Corrigan. I swear the only reason she hasn't is so that she can keep playing her childish prank on new employees.

When Kip and Luci separated, she called in sick for a week. When she returned to work, she was no longer wearing her rings. "Is everything all right with Kip?" I asked.

There wasn't a hint of emotion in Luci's voice when she answered, "Kip moved out and is no longer an acceptable subject of conversation."

"What happened?"

"That's between Kip and I."

"Me. Between Kip and me." Sometimes I just can't help myself.

Luci rolled her chair back from her desk so hard that it hit the wall behind her and stormed out of the office. We've barely talked about Kip since.

Despite her reluctance to talk about herself, Luci is the best friend I have had since Neesha moved. In fact, sharing an office with her is much how I imagine sharing a room with a sister would have been. Today, when I get to work, I notice a keyboard stained with coffee in the trash next to Luci's desk, yet Luci sits behind her computer, typing away. When I look at my desk, I see that my keyboard is missing. "Give me back my keyboard."

"Just go to IT and get a new one." I walk to her desk and rip the keyboard cord out of the monitor. Luci picks up the keyboard and hugs it tightly to her chest. "Just go to IT."

I yank on the cord. "You go!"

Our manager, Jamie, walks in on our argument. "Gina's trying to steal my keyboard," Luci whines.

"It's my keyboard."

Jamie ignores us. "Cooper Allen submitted a report that needs to be at Apple by three today. Which one of you has the bandwidth?" Luci points at me, and just like that, I'm stuck with the rush job.

I'm so engrossed editing the report that I don't notice what's happening outside until just after 1 p.m., when Luci stands before me, dressed in her coat, hat, and gloves. "It's snowing really hard." She uses her keys to point to the window behind me. "I'm leaving before it gets worse. You should, too."

I turn toward the window. Luci's right. Flakes the size of cotton balls pour from the sky, and a thick white blanket covers the ground. Honest to God, I have no business living in New England. I hate snow, and I especially hate driving in it. I should be in Florida for the winter with my parents.

"They're predicting seventeen inches," Luci says.

The forecast I heard this morning was two to three inches, but I can see that there is already at least four or five inches out there. Imagine being a meteorologist and everyone knowing when you screw up at work? Of course, if I was wrong as often as our local meteorologists, I certainly wouldn't have a job anymore. "I'll leave as soon as I finish editing Cooper's report."

"Well, be careful." Luci leaves without offering to help. That's Luci Chin, my best friend.

Three hours later, the snow comes halfway up my shins as I trudge through the parking lot to my car. Only two other vehicles remain. They are both SUVs that will have no problem negotiating the snowy roads. My sporty little Mazda, on the other hand, was not designed to be driven in conditions like this. It's supposed to be driven with the top down on a road that parallels the ocean.

I hear a *beep*, like someone is unlocking a car, but I don't see anyone. A moment later, one of the SUVs in the parking lot starts. There is still not another soul around. A few minutes later, as I remove the last of the snow from my car, I see a short man wearing a pea coat and gray floppy ski hat walk out of the building. As he gets closer to the running SUV, I realize it's Cooper Allen. He sees me and freezes in his tracks. He doesn't wave. He doesn't say anything. He just stares. Most of the analysts don't have great social skills. I wave, and he approaches me.

"You're not going to try to drive that in these conditions?" He points to my car, which is quickly getting covered in snow again. "You'll never get out of the parking lot." The analysts are paid a lot of money to have opinions and are therefore never shy about expressing them. "You should have left hours ago. What were you thinking?"

They are also pompous and condescending. I really don't enjoy talking to most of them. "I was thinking I had to finish editing your report."

He kicks at the snow on the ground with his boots. "So this is my fault?"

"There's no fault to be had. There's nothing wrong."

"I'll give you a ride." He takes a few steps toward his SUV. "Come on."

Honestly, I'd rather walk than be stuck in a vehicle with an analyst, so I ignore him and get in my car, intending to drive away, but my wheels just spin and the car doesn't move. Cooper watches with his arms folded across his chest and a smug look on his face. I'll be damned if I let him give me a ride home. He'll probably lecture me the entire way about how impractical my convertible is. I turn the steering wheel a few times, and the car lurches forward. I wave to Cooper and make my way to the exit.

My two-mile drive to Route 128 takes fifty-two minutes, and the highway is no better. In addition to worrying about maintaining traction in the snow, I have to dodge abandoned cars. A little less than an hour later, I barely make it off the exit ramp. The last several miles of my commute are on surface roads flanked with mini-malls and restaurants. Usually lines of slow-moving traffic clog these roads, but today the streets are eerily quiet. I drive for a minute or so before meeting a steep incline. My car gets stuck near the very start of the climb. I press on the gas and can feel the wheels spinning fiercely on the snow and ice without making contact with the pavement. I try everything, but the car only slides sideways. I see one other car on the road now, a black SUV behind me. The driver leans on the horn and maneuvers around me.

During the next fifteen minutes, only two other vehicles drive by, but neither driver looks in my direction. I take out my cell phone and try to figure out who to call. None of my friends live close by, though. For a moment, I wonder if I could possibly walk the rest of the way, but then I notice how loud the wind is howling and immediately decide against it. Five minutes later, a blue Jeep Cherokee going the other direction drives past. I make eye contact with the driver. A few moments later, the same Jeep pulls in behind me. A man wearing a dark skullcap, gray sweatshirt, and big black gloves runs with his head down toward my car. As he gets closer, I notice big red stains that look like blood on his sweatshirt. He knocks on my window. I am debating whether I should lower it when he opens my car door. In my head, I hear my mother's voice telling me to always lock my car doors.

The slow-falling big snowflakes from earlier in the day are gone, replaced by pellet-like snow falling at a much faster rate. The wind gusts and blows snow directly into the man's face. He leans into my car to get away from the piercing snow pellets. "How far do you have to go?" When his eyes meet mine, they open wide and the color drains from his face. He looks like he's seen a ghost or something. He squints and rolls his head like he's trying to work out a neck cramp.

I lean away from him. "Just up the street and around the corner."

He nods. "Even if I get you out of here, you won't get far. The conditions are worse up ahead." He shields his eyes with his hand and looks up and down the street. Finally, he points to a small convenience store. "Let me try to get your car off the road and into that parking lot."

I hesitate, but I don't see that I have any other option. I step out of the car. Immediately a blast of drifting snow assaults my face. The stranger with the bloody sweatshirt climbs into my driver's seat. I stand to the side, pull my hood as far forward as it will go, and shove my hands into my pockets while watching the tires spin, throwing snow in all directions. The car inches forward and back. The wheels change direction, and again the car inches forward and back. After this occurs several times, the car accelerates forward, and the stranger drives it to the parking lot of the convenience store.

He runs back through the snow to where I am standing, shivering and wet. "Get in the Jeep and I'll give you a ride." Before I can answer, he opens the driver's door. "Come on before you freeze to death." I can't believe I'm getting into a car with a stranger in a bloody sweatshirt. I know better.

Empty coffee cups, soda cans, and candy wrappers litter the inside of the Jeep. A toolbox with the name GREGORY written in black Magic Marker across the top sits on the passenger seat. I pick it up to move it, but he reaches for it. "That's heavy. Let me get it." As he takes the toolbox, his gloved hand brushes my thigh. I feel a chill run up and down my spine. The sensation takes me by surprise, but then I rationalize that it's not unusual that I would feel a chill. I've been standing outside in the middle of a nor'easter, for crying out loud.

My cell phone rings. I pull it from my coat pocket. "Where are you? I heard the roads are awful." All the way in Florida, my mother's up to speed on Boston's driving conditions. That's my mom: always looking for something to worry about.

"Don't worry, I'm safe at home." I hang up. Gregory smiles. "My mother. I don't want to upset her."

He nods. "So your family thinks you're safe and sound at home. Meanwhile you're out in a nor'easter, relying on a stranger to get you home safely."

"What's that on your sweatshirt?"

He looks down at his chest and then looks me in the eye. "Blood from the last girl I helped." His eye contact does not waver. I swallow hard and take my phone from my pocket again.

"Relax, I'm joking." He smiles, revealing teeth that a cosmetic dentist would consider a gold mine. "I cut my hand at work." He takes off his big black glove to reveal a bandage between his thumb and wrist. "Sorry, I didn't mean to scare you."

His apology seems sincere, but still I'm not taking any chances. I dial Luci's number. Her phone goes straight to voice mail. "Hey, it's me. I got stuck on Route Thirty, but this very nice man named Gregory, driving a blue Jeep, a Cherokee, is giving me a ride."

I feel him watching me. I turn to look. His eyes, which are incredibly blue, sky-blue, are twinkling. I notice a long scar running vertically through his right cheekbone. It's sexy in a dangerous sort of way. He has a cleft chin. I can't decide if I think he's handsome or scary. If he got his teeth fixed, I would definitely go with handsome.

I put my phone away while he reaches into his pocket and takes out his. He presses a button. "I'm going to be late," he says. "I'm helping out a stranded motorist. She hasn't told me her name, but she was driving a red Mazda with the license plate 123456 and got stuck on Route Thirty. See ya in about an hour." He puts his phone back in his pocket and winks.

I laugh. "I'm Gina. I really appreciate your help."

"Well then, sit back and relax. I'm not going to hurt you. I'm trying to help." I realize that I literally have been sitting on the edge of my seat. I slide back until I reach the backrest and let out a deep breath.

There's an intersection with a traffic signal a few feet ahead. The light is green, and Gregory approaches it cautiously. A car appears from the other direction and starts to turn left in front of us, but the driver loses control. The car spins counterclockwise into our lane. Gregory swerves into the other lane to avoid a collision, and we end up sliding across the intersection. He mumbles something under his breath and steers back to the right side of the road.

He looks over at me. "Are you all right?" I nod. For the rest of the ride, Gregory keeps his eyes on the road and focuses on his driving. We finally make it to my apartment. I live in the top floor of a house that is divided into three apartments.

Gregory pulls into the spot on the driveway where I usually park and cuts the engine. "I really have to use the restroom. Would you mind if I came in?" He couldn't hurt me while he was driving, but alone in my house, he could do anything. God, I hate it that I have this thought. I can't help it, though. Growing up in a neighborhood where little boys are snatched from their front lawns on beautiful summer days will do that to you. Gregory notices my hesitation. "It's okay. I'm sure there's a gas station nearby. I'll figure something out."

The man has gone out of his way to be kind to me. "Of course you can come in." I open the door and get out of the Jeep. After hesitating for a moment, he opens his door and gets out, too. We trudge through at least a foot of snow on the walkway to the back of the house and then climb the snowy stairs that lead to my door. "Who's supposed to shovel the stairs and the walkway?" Gregory asks when we get to the top of the stairs.

"Me."

"You should probably keep a shovel at the bottom of the stairs."

"Actually, my shovel is in my car." I open the door, and he comes inside and takes off his boots. He throws his gloves on the table and heads toward the hallway with the bathroom. It's the only hallway, so it's pretty obvious that's where the bathroom is.

When he returns to the kitchen, he looks at the pictures of my family and friends on the refrigerator. "Your parents?" he asks, pointing to my mother and father. I nod. "Your mother is beautiful." My entire life people have told me I look just like her. I don't see the resemblance, other than the coloring and curly hair. "Do you live here alone?"

"Well, there's a family who lives on the other side of the house and a couple downstairs."

"But you live in this apartment by yourself?"

I nod reluctantly. Now he knows he can terrorize me and no one will be coming home to rescue me. Okay. That's a ridiculous thought. Calm down. "Do you want a drink or something to eat?"

"I'd love a cup of coffee."

As a single woman, there is no appliance I love better than my individual-sized coffeemaker, which allows me to brew my caffeine infusions one cup at a time. As I fill the water reserve and grab a pod from the cabinet, his phone rings.

After saying hello, the next thing he says is "You're kidding? Where?" Next I hear him say, "I'll be right there." He disconnects and puts his boots back on. "I have to go rescue another motorist in distress. Can I take the coffee to go?"

I give him a travel mug. He is out the door before I can thank him for the ride. I watch him descend the back stairs. He waves good-bye with his big black glove and disappears around the corner, leaving me looking down over the railing yelling "thank you."

Back inside, my apartment suddenly feels cold. I grab a blanket and a book and lie down on the couch. I turn the pages but have no idea what I'm reading. I can't stop thinking about Gregory's blue eyes and cleft chin.

Chapter 6

Friday morning I wake up at seven and call the weather hotline at TechVisions. The recorded message states that the company is closed due to inclement weather. I let out a "Yippee!" Same as I did when I was a kid and heard my town listed in the school closing announcements. I go back to bed, and a few hours later wake to the sound of shoveling on the stairway. Maybe my landlord is pitching in because the storm was so big? I throw on a pair of jeans, a sweatshirt, and my Red Sox cap and open the door. I have to look twice. Gregory is shoveling my stairs.

I stand silently watching him, not sure what to say and wondering why he's here. He finally notices me. "Good morning, Gina."

"What are you doing here?"

"Nice to see you again, too. I came to return your cup and remembered you don't have a shovel so I thought I'd help out." I notice the travel mug I gave him yesterday sitting on the railing. "Do you want a ride back to your car?"

It's stopped snowing, and the plows have been by a few times. I figure I can get my car home safely. "Yes, please." He finishes shoveling the stairs and walkway while I go back inside to get ready.

When we get to the convenience store where we left my car, we can't see it because it's buried by snow. Gregory retrieves two shovels from the back of the Jeep, and we both get to work digging out my vehicle. We shovel on opposite sides of the car in relative silence. About a half hour later, my car is free. Gregory and I stand awkwardly by the driver's door. "Thank you for your help," I say, extending my hand toward him. "I feel like I should do something more than just say thanks for all the help you've given me." As I'm talking, my stomach rumbles. I'm sure my face is already red from the cold and wind, so Gregory can't tell how embarrassed I am. I ignore the rumbling. "Can I pay you or something?"

He smiles. "Have breakfast with me, and don't you dare say you're not hungry."

We take separate cars to a small diner up the street. There are a few plow trucks in the parking lot but no other cars. We have our choice of seats and pick a booth near the window. The waiter, a twenty-something with a silver hoop through his nose, tosses two menus on the table and walks away without saying anything. One of the plow drivers watching the interaction rolls his eyes and shakes his head. "The food is better than the service," he promises.

When the waiter returns, Gregory tries to make friends by commenting on his nose ring. "Looks good. I'm thinking of getting one myself." He winks at me. "Did it hurt?"

"Just for a minute." The waiter studies Gregory, probably trying to figure out if he's serious about wanting a nose ring. "I don't think you could pull it off." He turns toward me. "You could get away with it."

I think he means it as a compliment, but still I'm insulted. I ignore his comment and order hot chocolate and chocolate chip pancakes. Gregory orders coffee and a western omelet.

"What's with you, Rossi?" Gregory says. "You order a kid's meal and drive a kid's toy for a car."

I never told him my last name. "How do you know my last name?"

"I know everything about you. For example, you have trouble sleeping." I stare at him, wondering how he could possibly know that. "Don't look so worried. There was a prescription bottle of sleeping pills on the sink in your bathroom."

"So, what's your story, Gregory? Why did you come back to shovel me out?"

He laughs. "Because I dig chicks who call me by my last name."

I stop to think about it. I saw Gregory written on his toolbox and assumed it was his first name. He's not in elementary school. It's not his lunch box. He wouldn't write his first name on it. "What's your name?"

"Ethan."

In all the ways I have fantasized about meeting Ethan, it was never like this. I thought I would recognize him instantly. I imagined him shorter. I pictured his hair darker, his features more chiseled, his teeth white, straight, and evenly spaced. We'd both be dressed elegantly, certainly not wearing old sweatshirts and baseball caps. I never imagined we'd be breathing in the greasy fumes of bacon or the sugary scent of syrup. I assumed I'd be sipping Chianti or champagne, not slurping hot chocolate. Sometimes I even envisioned fireworks in the distance exploding in a star-filled sky, not sand trucks whizzing by a diner window on a dismal gray day.

I never figured out exactly what I would say, but I knew it would be something corny like "I knew you would come" or "You were worth the wait." And he wouldn't think it was weird. He'd know exactly what I was talking about.

Here in the actual moment, though, I just stare across the table and try to repeat his name, but it gets stuck in my throat.

"Let me guess. Your ex-boyfriend's name is Ethan?"

Not my ex-boyfriend. My future husband. For just a moment, I consider saying it aloud, telling him about Ajee and her prediction, but then I imagine him sprinting for the exit before I can get all the words out.

"It's my favorite name," I finally say.

He shrugs. "I didn't pick it." He looks at me for a moment. "So, do you have a boyfriend?"

I shake my head. "How about you?"

"No, I don't have a boyfriend." He laughs. "I do have—"

The waiter interrupts. "Anything else?"

"Just the check, Smiley," Ethan says.

We both laugh as the waiter storms off. We stop giggling. Ethan continues to stare at me. Right into my eyes. He's staring so intently that I wonder if he can see through to the thoughts bouncing around my mind. I look down at my lap. Ethan reaches across the table and touches my hand. The contact is brief, but I feel as though I stuck my finger into an electrical socket. He grins, but it's different from his regular smile. It's a confident expression that, along with his intense eye contact, says *I know I'm sending shock waves through your body right now.* I feel myself leaning across the booth toward him. He bends forward toward me. "So, why are you single?" he asks in a lower voice.

Because I've been waiting for you. He touches my hand again, but this time he keeps his finger on it. "I just mean you must have guys swarming all over you." Now his finger traces a line on the back of my hand. "You're beautiful."

He thinks I'm beautiful! *Ethan* thinks I'm beautiful. I wish I could be cool and simply say thank you, but I don't trust myself to speak. My face feels like it's on fire, and I can feel my chest and neck getting splotchy. His finger slows, and he pulls it off my hand. I look down, expecting my skin to be singed it's burning so badly. I look at him again. He rubs the stubble on his face while giving me that confident grin of his.

The waiter approaches and throws the bill on the table without saying anything. Ethan reaches for it, but I am quicker.

"The girl's not supposed to pay, Rossi. Give me that."

I shake my head. "It's the least I can do after everything you've done for me."

"Well, next time's on me," he says.

I smile. There's going to be a next time.

Chapter 7

The next day the ringing phone wakes me from a deep sleep. The only light in the room comes from the glowing red numbers of my alarm clock, which reads 6:30. Considering how much trouble I had falling asleep last night, I should be furious, but I feel myself smiling as I reach toward the nightstand. Ethan can't wait to see me again. That's why he's calling so early.

I clear my throat and practice saying hello aloud a few times before picking up the receiver. I don't want to sound like I just woke up because then he might feel bad for calling so early. When I'm sure all the sleep has left my voice, I pick up and say hello as brightly as I can.

"Good morning, Gina." It's my father. Of course, it's my father. Ethan knows better than to call this early. Everybody else in the world knows better than to call so early on a Saturday morning.

"Crikey, Dad. Do you know what time it is?"

"I'm on my way to the course. I want to be sure everything is okay at the house. I saw pictures of the storm on TV."

"Everything's fine."

"When's the last time you were there?"

"I don't remember." Truthfully, I haven't been there since my parents left. But if something had happened, the Murphys would call. They don't miss a thing that happens on Towering Heights Lane.

My father sighs. "You haven't been there at all, have you?"

"I'll go today."

"Really, Gina. Make sure you do. It's the one thing we ask of you all year."

* * *

Traffic is light in the afternoon when I make the drive to Westham. I reach my parents' house in thirty minutes instead of the usual forty-five. This year, rather than hire a plow truck, my parents are paying the eighth-grade boy down the street to shovel. I was skeptical about their decision, and my skepticism was apparently justified. Let's just say I'd have a better chance of keeping my balance walking across a tightrope from my car to the front door than across the ice and snow blanketing the steep driveway and stairs. Miraculously I make it to the door without leaving an impression of my face in the snow.

Inside, the house is a bit cold, but everything appears to be in order. I make my way to the family room, where younger versions of myself smile back at me from various photos taken through the years. My mother refuses to take them down or update them with more recent pictures. "I'll replace them with pictures of my grandchildren," she says each time I suggest she remove them. So, as I do every year when my parents are away, I take the photographs from the wall myself and place them in a box, where they will stay until my mother returns.

I pause as I reach for the last picture. It's of six-year-old Neesha and me in a small plastic pool in the Patels' backyard taken before Ajee moved in. It's my favorite. Even with three or four bottom teeth missing, I have a huge smile, still too young to be self-conscious. Neesha, on the other hand, has her mouth closed, but already she has the mischievous expression that would become her trademark. Neesha's mom took the picture. It was before she got sick, or at least before the diagnosis. By the following summer, she was gone, and Ajee was a permanent fixture in the Patels' home.

During those first few weeks after Mrs. Patel died, I didn't want to leave my mother's side, afraid that she, too, might disappear. Neesha also preferred to be at my house, and my parents went so far as to replace my single bed with bunk beds to let her know she was welcome anytime. We were inseparable back then. No one would have ever believed we would lose touch. It's been almost a month since I mailed the sympathy card, and she hasn't responded.

I finish checking the house and then navigate the slippery slope down my parents' driveway. As I do, a red SUV pulls into the Murphys' driveway. The driver gets out and we make eye contact. Her hat is pulled down to her eyebrows, her coat zipped so high the collar reaches her lower lip. "Hey, Gina." She waves, and then immediately ducks her head and trots up the Murphys' front stairs. Before I can figure out who she is, she disappears into their house.

I refocus on plodding my way to my car but lose my balance and end up sliding to the bottom of the driveway on my back. On my ride home, I try to think of someone I can call to plow and sand at my parents'. And that's how I figure out who the woman is at the Murphys'. Patricia McAllister, whose husband, Sean, owns a landscaping/plowing company. In the business world, she's still known by her maiden name, Patricia Ryan. When the weather is nice, her name, face, and phone number appear on signs planted in front lawns of homes scattered throughout Westham and its neighboring towns. More often than not, those signs also say SOLD.

A Realtor appearing at the Murphys' house a few days after I meet Ethan can mean only one thing: Ajee's third predictions for Neesha and me are about to come true. I have to admit, I'm just as excited by the prospect of being reunited with Neesha as I was to finally meet Ethan.

Chapter 8

Monday I get to work ninety minutes early because I'm so excited to tell Luci about Ethan. I tried calling her all weekend long, but she didn't pick up her phone or return my calls. Other than my parents and Neesha, she is the only person who knows about Ajee's prediction. I told her a year ago at the company holiday party after my third glass of Chianti. She was trying to convince me to ask Cooper Allen to dance. "He's been watching you all night," she said.

I looked over at Cooper. He was across the room, sitting alone checking his BlackBerry. Luci nudged me in his direction, and I thought, *Why not?* Emboldened by liquid courage, I marched across the room. When I reached his table, he looked up from his phone and smiled. Until that moment, I had never noticed he had dimples. Beautiful dimples.

I tried to figure out what to say. *Cooper, would you like to dance?* Too formal. *Will you dance with me?* Desperate. *Let's dance!*

What I ended up saying was "Are you checking your work e-mail?" I was going for funny, a mock scolding. What came out was a mixture of disgusted and judgmental. His ears reddened and the dimples disappeared. I shook my head and hightailed it back to Luci.

"What happened?" she asked. I sank into my chair. "You are just terrible with men."

I nodded. "Doesn't matter. Ethan will be here soon. He has to be."

Luci lowered her glass to the table. "Who's Ethan? You've been holding out on me. I knew it."

I picked up Luci's glass and drained the remaining wine before telling her about Ajee and her predictions.

When I was done speaking, Luci leaned back in her chair and studied me carefully. "You actually believed her? You believe in fortune-telling?"

I rolled the empty wineglass between my hands. "I do. The one time I didn't listen to her, I almost died." I told Luci about getting caught in the rip current and almost drowning.

She fidgeted in her chair as I told her. When I was done speaking, she was silent for a moment. "Well, I guess I can understand why you would believe her," she said. "But it's not even like guys our age have that name. Why didn't she say Mike or Jim or Steve, for God's sake, so that you'd have a fighting chance?"

"Because my husband's name is going to be Ethan, and I'm not your age. I'm younger."

Luci stood. "I need another drink."

While I wait for Luci to arrive, I check my e-mail. I have one message from Cooper Allen sent at 5:45 this morning, which is probably a late start for him.

Maybe Cooper is writing to thank me for doing such a great job editing his rush job before the storm? I open the e-mail and see the message is actually to my manager, Jamie, and that I am CC'd on it. *"Attached is a report on the worldwide smartphone market. I would like Gina to edit this and all my research going forward. ca."*

Figures. It's just more work. I open the attached file. Cooper has written ninety-six pages on cell phone sales. Kill me now. The words *thank you* appear nowhere in his message.

In fairness, Cooper probably does believe he is rewarding me, because after all, who wouldn't be honored to work so closely with TechVisions' resident rock star? And I have to admit, in a twisted way, I am flattered. Cooper has high standards, and I apparently meet them—or at least my editing skills do.

Luci stomps into the office fifteen minutes later. "Good morning," I say as she hangs her coat on the back of the door.

"It's really not." She doesn't even look at me.

"What's wrong?"

Now she turns to me. "It's Monday, and we're back here." Usually Luci isn't so cranky, so I think there's more to her bad mood, but I also know not to push. She'll tell me when she's ready, or she won't.

That's Luci Chin. "I'm going to the café. Do you need anything?" She leaves before I answer.

A few minutes later Jamie comes to our office to talk about Cooper's message. We are finishing our conversation when Luci returns from the cafeteria. She is clearly annoyed that Cooper has hand-selected me as his editing guru. She slams her breakfast on her desk, sending a clump of scrambled eggs soaring into the air, and then yanks open her bottom desk drawer and grabs a bottle of hot sauce. With one aggressive motion, she twists off the cap and hoists the bottle in the air above her remaining eggs. "Like I haven't done an exceptional job correcting his grammar and spelling errors the past fourteen years." She punctuates each word with a violent shake of the bottle, so that by the time she's done speaking, there's more hot sauce than eggs on her plate. Jamie responds the way he always does. He turns his back and leaves. Luci shoves a forkful of the brown-yellow mush on her plate into her mouth, makes a face, and then flings the dish into the garbage.

Now her fingers pound her keyboard as she composes an e-mail to Cooper. She should be celebrating the news that she has one less analyst to work with, but because it's the first time at work that Luci's been passed over for anything, she doesn't view it as a positive thing. I have no idea what Luci is writing to Cooper, but I hope she's being careful.

Vice president of research on mobile devices, Cooper Allen is otherwise known as Mr. TechVisions. He used to use his middle initial, *T*, in his byline, but everyone joked that it stood for TechVisions instead of Thomas so he stopped using it. Still, I wouldn't be surprised to learn the company's logo has been branded on his backside.

He is the company's number-one revenue generator. The media loves Cooper almost as much as the board of directors does. He's the go-to guy for quotes about cell phones and other handheld devices and the companies that make them. It's not unusual to see him on the nightly news sitting in front of a desk, the TechVisions logo illuminated on a backdrop behind him, explaining in precise detail why the market is performing the way it is. I don't understand the media's fascination with him. I get impatient listening to him because he speaks so slowly, each word deliberately chosen.

Anyway, Cooper has a lot of influence in the company. He's not someone you want mad at you.

"What are you writing to Cooper?" I ask.

Luci looks over at me. "Just asking if he has a problem with my editing."

"Why didn't you return my calls this weekend?" I ask. "I have news. Big news."

Luci finishes typing before looking up. "Guess who else called me this weekend?"

I shrug.

"Kip." I'll never understand how Luci is able to convey so much disdain with a three-letter name. "He got engaged and apparently couldn't wait to tell me." Her voice cracks.

This is the most emotion Luci has shown about Kip since her divorce, and I'm not sure what to say. *Sorry?* No, that doesn't sound like nearly enough. "I, Luci, I'm sorry."

She sniffs. "I knew it was going to happen eventually. I just didn't think it would happen so soon."

I stand and take a step toward Luci's desk, intending to hug her.

She shoots me a look. "Sit down."

As I return to my seat, Cooper appears in our doorway. Luci and I stare without speaking as he enters our office and leans against the wall between our two desks. Cooper never visits. He sits on the fourth floor in the heart of Mahogany Row with all the other executives at TechVisions. His office is bigger than my apartment. The bathroom stall–sized office that Luci and I share is on the first floor, otherwise known as the basement, sandwiched between the loading dock and the mail room. That Cooper's down here standing in our office is disorienting enough, but that he's down here looking, well, almost handsome, is making me dizzy.

"Did you get a haircut?" Luci asks.

Clearly Cooper has not had a haircut in months. His dark hair, which is usually cut close to his head military recruit–style, is actually long enough so that it curls. I didn't notice this on Thursday because he was wearing a ski hat.

Cooper runs his hand over the top of his head. "No. Haven't had time for a cut. Been traveling a lot."

"It looks good." The words slip out before I have time to think about to whom I am saying them. Luci whirls around to face me and studies me silently with her head cocked.

I glance at Cooper. He immediately looks away. Small red circles appear on his cheeks. I wish I came with a Rewind button or there was a way to edit words once they'd been spoken. Cooper clears his throat and turns his attention to Luci. "I received your e-mail. It appears as if I've unintentionally offended you." He should come with a Fast-Forward button because he pauses after every word, like there's a period there. "I apologize. I think both you and Gina do an admirable job editing my research. I just believe it would be more efficient if the same person always edited it so that you can build a subject-matter expertise on the market and reduce the number of questions you ask."

Luci smiles at me. I know that smile; it makes me dread what her next words will be. "Are you sure that's the only reason you want Gina to edit your research?"

Cooper shifts his weight from leg to leg. "Yes."

"There's no other reason?" Luci continues.

"What other reason would there be?" Cooper asks.

"I don't know." Luci pauses to study her nails. "Maybe you want to work closely with Gina so that you can"—she looks up from her nails and smiles at Cooper. I think about crawling under my desk—"get to know her better." She winks at Cooper.

Cooper looks at me. I shrug, wishing I were invisible.

He clears his throat. "Luci, if you would like to edit my research instead of Gina, that's fine. The point is, I want the same person editing it." He turns to leave but pauses in the doorway and looks back at us over his shoulder. He sniffs loudly. "Why does it smell like buffalo wings in here?"

"I'm going to kill you," I say after Cooper leaves. "That was so embarrassing."

Luci laughs. "I really do think he likes you, and you two would look great together."

"I met Ethan."

"That's why you called me fourteen times this weekend?"

I nod. "I got stuck in the snow on the way home Thursday, and he gave me a ride."

"So Cooper led you to Ethan."

I hadn't thought of it like that, but in a way Luci's right. I should be the one thanking Cooper. When I finish telling Luci the rest of the Ethan story, she closes her eyes. "I just can't believe this is happening. You really met a man named Ethan."

I smile. "It's really happening. I finally met him."

Luci stands. "Now that deserves a hug."

Chapter 9

As I edit Cooper's report on cell phones, my own sits quietly next to my keyboard. Every few minutes, I sneak a look to see if the red light that indicates I have a message is blinking. It never is. Waiting for Ethan to call is harder than it was waiting to meet him.

Over the past few years, cell phones have transitioned to mini portable computers, and they're being used to do much more than just make calls, Cooper writes in the report. *They're GPS units, game consoles, Internet connections, cameras, camcorders, televisions, and even movie screens.*

I stop reading and glance at mine again. You forgot *torture device*, I think. Wherever I am, whatever I'm doing, it's there taunting me, a constant reminder that Ethan hasn't called and Neesha hasn't e-mailed.

I look across my desk toward Luci's. She's the poster child for ergonomics over there. Her head's positioned toward her computer, her spine is erect against the backrest, her shoulders relaxed and her hands perfectly aligned with her forearms as she types. "Do you think he'll call?" I blurt out.

Luci stops typing, glances at me, and then peers into the coffee mug on her desk. "Tea leaves say soon as put phone away, he call." She laughs. "Patience, Gina. It's only been a few days."

Five, to be exact. What is he waiting for? I always thought as soon as we met, we'd be inseparable. Sometimes, I imagined we'd get lost in conversation during our first day together, catching each other up on our lives. We'd be wrapped in a blanket in front of a roaring fire, and both of us would be surprised when a ray of sunshine streamed through a narrow opening in the curtains. Ethan would look at his watch. "Wow, it's seven in the morning," he'd say. "We've been talking all night." He'd kiss me and then he'd whisper, "I've been waiting my entire life to meet someone like you." And then, just like that, we'd be living together as man and wife.

My computer buzzes, indicating I have an e-mail. I turn my attention away from the phone and back to work. The e-mail is from Cooper. *"When can I expect my report?????"* I lift my hands off the keyboard toward my chest and clench them into tight fists. It's not that Cooper can't be bothered to type a greeting or sign his name on his e-mails that irritates me. It's the extra question marks. I imagine they mean, *Why don't I have it yet? What's taking you so damn long? What the heck do you do down there all day anyway?*

I take a deep breath and count to ten before responding, something I learned from my mother. *"**Hi, Cooper!** I have other priorities and haven't gotten very far with your report yet. I'll send it to you by the end of the day tomorrow or early Friday. **Hope you're having a good day, Gina.** "*

I can't help myself; I bold *Hi, Cooper* and *Hope you're having a good day.* I imagine Cooper noticing the difference in font. *I should try to make my messages friendly like Gina's,* he'll think. Yeah, right. More likely Cooper will be annoyed that I took time away from editing his report to type the unnecessary words.

His reply comes a minute later. *"**Thanks for the quick response, Gina**. I wish you were as speedy with my report. **Best, Cooper.**"*

His response causes me to laugh, and I happily go back to editing his report on mobile torture devices.

A light snow is falling on my drive home. The weatherman on the radio insists it won't accumulate, but when I get home the flakes are heavier and my driveway and walkway are coated with the white stuff. The motion lights do not snap on when I step out of my car, so I plod my way around to the back of the house and up the stairs in the dark. As I unlock the door, I hear ringing. I rip my hand off the key and on the pitch-black landing grope through my purse for my phone. My hand lands on it, and I wrench it out. I don't recognize the number and I take a deep breath before answering. As I'm saying hello, the phone slips out of my gloved hand and bounces halfway down the staircase. "Yikes!" I race down the five steps to where the phone has landed, but by the time I pick it up, no one is on the other end. "Call back, call back," I chant as I climb up the stairs again and enter my apartment.

Five minutes later I am sitting on the couch with the phone in my hand. I feel it vibrate before it rings and answer immediately.

"It's Ethan, the guy who helped you out during the storm," he announces, his voice softer and less steady than it was in person.

"Right, the guy driving the red pickup truck who helped me out on the highway."

"No, I was driving a bl—You're playing with me."

"Gotcha."

He laughs. "I was worried about you driving in the snow tonight."

Ethan was worried about me! "I'm an excellent driver."

My imitation of Dustin Hoffman must be pretty good because Ethan responds, "If you say so, Rain Man."

The line is silent for a moment. Then we both speak and stop speaking at the same time. "Go ahead," I say.

"I just wanted"—he clears his throat—"do you still want to get together?"

"Absolutely!" I scream it so loudly that I expect my downstairs neighbor to bang on the ceiling.

"How about Saturday night? We could go bowling and to dinner."

"Bowling?"

"Ya, bowling. When's the last time you went?"

I have no idea, but I try to sound definitive. "My twelfth birthday party."

"My twelfth was monumental. First game of Spin the Bottle," he pauses. "I made it to second base with Holly Pierce. I swear she was in a D cup before high school."

I imagine a young Ethan fumbling with the breasts of a voluptuous twelve-year-old, and I'm jealous. Ridiculous.

In the background I hear a man's voice calling Ethan's name. "Got to run," he says. "I'll pick you up at six on Saturday."

At lunch on Thursday, Luci takes me to the mall to pick out an outfit for my date with Ethan. She drags me into a store where a beefy man dressed in black wearing an earpiece guards the door. Inside two perfectly groomed saleswomen wearing fitted jackets, short skirts, and long boots look me up and down and immediately turn their attention to Luci.

"My friend has the most important date of her life Saturday," Luci explains. "She needs a casual outfit that makes her irresistible."

The two women look at me again. They may as well be looking at roadkill the way their mouths contort and their eyebrows furrow. Wishing I could stare back defiantly, I hang my head. "Let's go someplace else," I whisper.

"You get this, Marnie," the taller of the two says. "I've got inventory out back."

"Where are you going on the date?" Marnie asks without looking at me.

"Bowling," I answer.

"Excuse me?" Marnie says while the fleeing saleswoman cackles.

"We want to try on jeans and figure-flattering sweaters," Luci says.

"What size is she?" Marnie asks.

Luci folds her arms across her chest and glares at Marnie until she looks at me.

"Ten," I answer.

Luci suddenly grabs my waistband and pulls it away from my hips. "Whatever size you think you are, you're at least a size smaller. An entire other person can fit in here with you."

Great. Now Luci's on their side.

The saleswoman directs us to the fitting room while she collects outfits for me. Luci stretches out in a chair while we wait.

A few minutes later the saleswoman enters the dressing room with two styles of jeans in sizes eight and ten and a pile of medium-sized and large sweaters. I close the door to my stall and try on the size ten jeans and large sweater. I check myself out in the mirror. Perfect, I think. One and done. We can get out of here.

I open the door. Marnie frowns. Luci shakes her head. Next, I try on the same pants one size down. The jeans choke me around the waist. "Too small."

"Let's see," Luci demands.

I step into the hallway, and Luci and Marnie exchange a look.

Marnie moves her finger in a circular motion that I guess means turn around so I do. "Try on the other style in the smaller size," Luci says to me. Looking at Marnie she adds, "We need a size six in those."

"Put on the red sweater," Luci says. When I have it on, Marnie has returned with size six jeans, which she hands to Luci. Luci points to my sweater. "The next size down," she instructs Marnie.

Luci tries to hand me the size six pants, but I refuse to take them. "Those won't fit."

"We're not leaving until you try them." She flings the jeans over the door and plops back in the chair to show she means business.

I grab the jeans and return to the stall. I squirm and squeeze my way into them. I finally pry them over my hips, but can't button them. I open the door to show Luci. "See."

Marnie returns with a smaller sweater. Luci snatches it from her. "Does it come in blue?" she asks.

Marnie spins on her heel. Luci hands me the red sweater and tells me to put it on with the size eight jeans. When I have the outfit on, I look in the mirror. The sweater plunges at the neck, revealing cleavage I never knew I had.

I open the door to find Luci standing right there. "Wow! You look amazing. Turn around." I spin. Luci whistles. "Ethan's going to love that view at the bowling alley," she says.

We hear Marnie's footsteps approaching. Luci hurriedly gathers the neatly folded pile of clothes that don't fit and balls them all up. When Marnie reaches us, Luci exchanges the rumpled clothing for the blue sweater.

Marnie stares at Luci for a moment before retreating to the store floor. "Enough," I say. "You're being really hard on her."

"She needs to be reminded that she's a salesclerk selling clothes that other people design," Luci says. "She has no reason to be so snobby."

When Marnie returns I'm wearing the blue sweater. "Too drab," Luci says. "Does it come in a lighter blue?"

Marnie puts her hand on her hip. Her lips part ever so slightly, and the tip of her tongue rises to the roof of her mouth. Whatever it is she wants to say to Luci, she decides not to. Her tongue returns to the floor of her mouth, and her lips squeeze shut.

Almost fifteen minutes later, the other saleswoman returns with the lighter sweater. She hands it to me and disappears before Luci has a chance to ask for something else.

I end up buying that sweater, the red one, and the size eight jeans. Marnie rings up my purchase. "So, how much have you lost?" She finally looks at me.

"Excuse me?"

"Your clothes are so big. I assume you need a new wardrobe because you just lost a lot of weight."

Chapter 10

I leave the office at seven o'clock on Friday night. It's pathetic that I'd rather work late than go home to my empty apartment. Only one other car remains in the parking lot, Cooper's. I look up at his office. His window is lit up while the rest are all dark. As I start my car, Takeout Taxi pulls up next to the curb. I pass the entrance to the building and see the driver carrying a brown bag to the front door. Cooper is there to meet him. I don't know what gets into me, but I beep. Startled, Cooper looks in my direction. I wave. He smiles and waves back. I drive off feeling a pang of sadness for him eating alone at his desk on a Friday night, but I guess it's no worse than me eating alone in front of the television.

I suddenly realize how hungry I am, so I call Salvatore's, the pizza place around the corner from my apartment. When I arrive to pick up my food, Sal Senior, the restaurant owner, leans against the counter. Like always, he's wearing a black shirt and bright red tie. His salt-and-pepper hair is slicked back with grease in a style that he's probably been wearing since the 1950s. If anyone needs help from one of those makeover television programs, it's this guy. "Gina." He smiles at me and then turns his head over his shoulder and shouts in Italian to his son, Salvatore Jr., who goes by Tory, "Your girlfriend is here."

Tory, dressed in his usual tight jeans and black T-shirt accessorized by a thick gold ropelike chain and matching bracelet, prances to the register. "Your pizza will be a few minutes." His gray eyes scan me up and down, and he licks his lips as he speaks. I zip my ski jacket higher and hand him a twenty. He punches my order into the register and then looks up and smirks. "For someone who eats so much pizza, you sure look great. Do you work out a lot?"

Honest to God, I should have made grilled cheese at home. I retreat to a chair near the counter without answering. From where I'm sitting, I can hear Salvatore and Tory talking in Italian. I don't know why it's never occurred to them that I speak the language. Everyone always tells me I look Italian.

"Why don't you ask her out?" Salvatore asks.

"Someone as beautiful as her, she must have a boyfriend," Tory answers.

I'm wishing I weren't there and trying not to look at them. Out of the corner of my eye, I notice Salvatore swat Tory in the head. He's still speaking Italian. "What's the matter with you? Don't you think? She's here alone most weekend nights ordering a small pizza. There's no boyfriend."

I kick the floor with my boots and promise myself that I will never come to Salvatore's alone on the weekend again. Several minutes later, Tory calls my name. "So, umm," he says, leaning over the counter toward me, "I get off work at nine o'clock. Maybe I could take you for a proper dinner."

"I have a boyfriend," I blurt out. Tory pulls the pizza out of my reach. "His name is Ethan." He stares into my eyes. I can tell he's trying to figure out if I'm lying. The silence makes me uncomfortable so I keep talking. "I'll bring him here sometime."

This seems to satisfy Tory. He hands me the box. "I'd like to meet him. Make sure he's good enough for you."

I've just finished eating my pizza and am watching television when my cell phone rings. I was so sure no one would call me tonight that for once, the device is not nearby, and I have to go to the kitchen to retrieve it.

Ethan's name, which I happily programmed into the phone after he called on Wednesday, flashes across the screen. I swallow hard and pick up.

"Hey," he says. "There's something I have to tell you before our date."

My heart rate doubles, and I feel my chest getting hot. I pace back and forth in the kitchen, certain that he's going to tell me he has some kind of sexually transmitted disease.

"I'm married," he says.

I feel all the air whooshing out of my body, leaving me deflated. I would have preferred herpes. "I can't go out with you," I blurt out. Even as I'm saying it, though, I'm wondering if I can. I have to get off the phone before I change my mind. "Good-b—"

"Wait," he interrupts. "It's not as bad as it sounds."

I've seen enough bad movies to know how this works. "Let me guess," I say with as much sarcasm as I can muster. "Your wife's awful, but you're staying with her until the children are older."

"No." He makes a sound that's either a laugh or sob. "She asked for a divorce. We're separated," he whispers. "I moved out about a month ago."

I'm standing in the middle of the kitchen, and I sink to the floor. "I'm sorry. Really." I stop speaking. The line is silent for a few seconds. "You should call me again when the divorce is finalized."

"No, Gina, please." He makes the same weird noise again. This time I'm certain it's a sob. "The only time I've laughed or smiled in weeks was the time we were together."

I move from the kitchen floor to the couch. I lean over so my head is between my knees. I know it's not smart to go out with him, but this is Ethan, the guy I've been waiting for since age thirteen. The man I'm supposed to marry. I let out a deep breath.

"Jack told me not to tell you, but I want to do the right thing. Can't build a meaningful relationship without honesty," Ethan mumbles.

A meaningful relationship, one that leads to marriage. "Who's Jack?" I ask.

Ethan tells me Jack is a friend he grew up with who he's currently living with. He had to move from New Hampshire to Massachusetts because he had no one else to stay with.

I ask him how long he was married. He answers seventeen years. "I came home from work one night, and Leah, that's my wife, was waiting by the door with her suitcase. She said she didn't want to be married anymore. I never saw it coming."

I learn he met Leah the first day of high school and proposed on graduation day. Neither of them went to college. They don't have any children, but they do have a dog, a golden retriever named Brady that Leah kept. "I miss the dog more than I miss my wife," Ethan says.

We talk for nearly three hours. "I should let you go now," Ethan finally says. "Can I still see you tomorrow?"

I clutch the phone tightly. He's not married, I tell myself. He's separated. It's not like I'm breaking up a marriage; it's already broken. If he decides he wants to fix it, I'll encourage him to do so. I imagine myself teary-eyed as I tell him I'm happy he's working things out with Leah. I swallow hard, thinking about the devastation I would feel. Is it worth the risk? Of course it is. His name is Ethan.

"Looking forward to it," I say, hoping it sounds believable after my long pause.

Chapter 11

At five thirty on Saturday, I hear the crackling of snow and ice on the driveway. I look out the window and see Ethan's Jeep. He's a half hour early. I race to the bathroom and check myself out in the full-length mirror. I have to say, the outfit Luci picked out looks good on me. Who cares that the waistline of the jeans is going to cut off my circulation. I look great.

I come out of the bathroom expecting to hear the doorbell. Should I open the door before he rings the bell? No, that would make me look too eager. A minute or two passes, and Ethan still isn't at the door, so I peek out the window. He's sitting in his Jeep with his head resting on the steering wheel. Before I can figure out what he's doing, he lifts his head and the Jeep backs out of the driveway.

Remain calm, I tell myself. *He must be trying to kill time because he doesn't want to be so early. He probably assumes I'm not ready. That has to be it.* I sit on the couch and thumb through a magazine, *Brides* magazine to be exact. I've already read the entire thing. I bought it the day Ethan and I ate breakfast together. I was embarrassed bringing it to the register and carried it across the store with the cover pressed tightly to my chest, afraid all the people in the store would know the purchase was ridiculously premature. "Look at her left hand. There's no engagement ring," I imagined a happily married brunette whispering. "Engagement ring?" The husband laughed. "She hasn't even had a date with the guy." Despite my humiliation when buying the magazine, I'm glad I did. It gave me a great idea for the flowers in my wedding bouquet: cosmos.

Thirty-five minutes later, Ethan's still not back. Did he change his mind? Why would he come all this way and then leave? Maybe he got an emergency call. Maybe Leah called and said she doesn't want a divorce after all. He's driving up to New Hampshire right now to reunite with her.

I stuff the magazine in the trash, go to my bedroom, and lie on my bed. The ceiling fan above me spins. I watch the blades go 'round and 'round. I must have jinxed myself by purchasing that magazine. How could I have been so stupid? The doorbell rings, startling me from my thoughts. I jump off my bed and race to the front door. When I open it, Ethan extends a bouquet of flowers. "Sorry, I'm late. I would have been early but I forgot flowers."

He left to get flowers. Honest to God, I want to cry. Happy tears. They're beautiful flowers, too, a fragrant bouquet of pink roses, tulips, miniature carnations, and hot pink spray roses. Hmmm, what are those two back there, cosmos? Couldn't be, but they are. Another sure sign from Ajee, I know it.

"Thank you!" I hug him. His entire body stiffens and he pulls away quickly.

"We should really get going." He's looking at the floor. I glance down to see what has captured his interest. Nothing there but the tan linoleum tiles.

I put on my coat, and we make the long walk down the stairs and around the house to his Jeep in silence. We've been together for less than five minutes, and we've already run out of things to say to each other. Brilliant. Quick, think of something, anything. "Thanks again for the flowers." God help me. That's the best I can come up with.

"You're welcome." He opens the passenger door, and I step in. The discarded soda cans and candy wrappers that littered the interior the last time I was in the Jeep are gone. The dashboard and leather seats shine with a new coat of Armor All, and the scent of vanilla lingers in the air.

Ethan takes his time walking to his side of the car, but finally the driver's door opens and he climbs in behind the wheel. He puts the key in the ignition but doesn't turn it. He leans back in his seat and covers his face with his hands.

Oh no, he's going to tell me he doesn't want to go on this date after all. "Are you okay?" I ask.

He looks at me for the first time since my ill-advised hug. "Sorry.

I'm just nervous. Really nervous. I almost cancelled. I haven't been on a date with anyone but Leah since eighth grade."

I picture Ethan as a little boy riding his bike next to a freckled-face girl with pigtails. She's sort of fat. They pedal up to Friendly's, where they split the Reese's Pieces sundae. I think back to my first date just before the start of eighth grade, a few weeks after Ajee made her predictions. Joey Messina and I doubled with Josh Levine and Neesha to the movies. Joey's brother was the usher, and he let us sit in the balcony even though it was closed. Josh and Neesha sat in the last row, Joey and I in the first. I kept turning around to look at Neesha. The first few times, Josh had his arm around her; later they were kissing. I elbowed Joey. "Neesha's grandmother predicted Josh would kiss Neesha and look." He turned to face them and then looked back at me. "Do you want to make out, too?" He leaned toward me. I jolted backward in my seat. A guy should never ask a woman if she wants a kiss. He should just do it.

The truth was, though, I didn't want Joey kissing me. I wanted to meet and kiss Ethan. Josh Levine was kissing Neesha and that was a sure sign Ethan was on his way. And now, all these years later, here we are finally on our first date.

"I'm really nervous, too, if that makes you feel any better."

He smiles. "You're lying. Why would you be nervous? You've probably been on dates with tons of guys."

But this is my first date with my future husband, Ethan. I wonder if he would be more or less nervous if I actually said it out loud.

A smattering of cars are spread throughout the parking lot, and Ethan pulls into a space by the front door. He hops out of the driver's seat and races around the vehicle to the passenger side so he can open my door. He extends his hand for me to grab on to while I climb down. Although I'm perfectly capable of getting out of the car without his help, I find his gesture sweet. I like it even more that he continues to hold my hand as we walk into the bowling alley.

Inside, colored lights blink and eighties music blares from the speakers. The guy at the front desk has long, greasy dark hair tied back in a ponytail. His eyes linger on my chest, and I pull my sweater up higher. He leans toward me to hand me the shoes. All I can smell is smoke. "Lane seven," he says in a voice ravaged by cigarettes.

Fifteen to twenty teenagers are using lanes eight through twelve, and a gray-haired man and woman are bowling in the first aisle against the far left wall. Ethan and I sit on the bench next to each other to change our shoes. When he removes his left work boot, I notice his sock has a hole by the big toe, and that little imperfection makes me want to hug him. "So, should we wager?" Ethan asks as he laces up his bowling shoes.

"Loser buys dinner," I say.

"Nah, has to be more interesting than that."

I'm still bent over my shoes. I straighten up to look at him. His sweater is the same exact shade of blue as his eyes. It makes them sparkle. "What did you have in mind?"

He gives me that same confident grin from the diner. "A massage." The way he says the word leaves no doubt he expects a happy ending, and I feel myself blushing.

"You're on," I say.

He taps my knee before standing. As he walks to get a ball, I notice his jeans fit in a way that's going to make it really fun to watch him from behind all night. He picks up and puts down several balls before settling on one he likes. Then he steps into the lane, extends his hand with the ball in front of him, takes three quick steps forward, bends, and hurls it down the aisle. A crashing sound echoes through the room as the ball strikes the pins. All but one fall. He waits for that ball to come back and then rolls it down the lane again. It hits the lone standing pin. Ethan pumps his fist. "Can't wait for that massage." He winks as he returns to the bench.

I stand. "Maybe I'm a ringer." He laughs while I look at the balls in the tray and choose a bright orange one.

Behind me Ethan coughs. "You sure you want that one? I think it's a little heavy."

"I like big balls." Even before the words are out, I'm wishing I could reel them back in, because honestly, I didn't mean it that way. I try to act like my words were intentional by winking at Ethan. Only, I've never been able to wink, so both my eyes shut like I'm having some kind of blinking spasm. Oh God. I turn my back to Ethan, approach the foul line, and hurl my too-big ball down the alley. It starts off straight for the pins, but then veers to the right and ends up in the gutter. I turn to look at Ethan. All the color has drained from his face, and he's running his hand through his hair. "Just setting you up before I raise the stakes," I say.

He doesn't smile or say anything. Instead, he studies me like he might be tested on my appearance later. "You're left-handed." His tone is accusatory and then quieter, "Leah's left- handed."

The air between us suddenly feels a lot heavier. "Yeah, but I bet she can hit at least one of the pins."

He shakes his head and looks down. "Nah. She doesn't like bowling. She never comes with me." Something about what he says bothers me, and it's more than the fact that this is the second time he's brought up Leah in less than an hour.

He stands and steps into the lane with me. He picks up a bright blue ball. "This ball is a better fit for you. It's lighter." He hands me the ball. I cradle it in my right hand and insert the fingers on my left hand into the holes. He puts his hand over mine. I can feel his heat radiating from it as he adjusts my grip.

When he pulls his hand from mine, he tilts his head in the direction of the pins, indicating I should try again. So I step up to the foul line, heave the ball down the alley, and like before it veers off into the gutter.

"Let me show you." He holds the ball in front of him near his waist. "You want to start with your ball down here, in front of you, and then when you're ready to approach the line, raise it. Keep it up in front of you and let gravity help you pull it down. To throw it harder, hold it up by your face. To throw it slower, hold it near your chest." He then has me mimic his motion. "Think of it as one continuous movement." I imitate his moves. He shakes his head. "It needs to be more fluid." A few minutes later, he is confident I have mastered the movement and walks to the back of the lane.

I approach the foul line with the ball up near my chest, keeping my eye on the center arrow and roll the ball toward the pins. It stays straight the entire way and collides with the center pin, knocking it and all the others on their sides. I jump in excitement, and by the time I land, Ethan is right there with his arms around me. "You did it," he shouts. Then before I have time to think about what's happening, he kisses me.

I have been fantasizing about my first kiss with Ethan since Ajee told me about him. Sometimes the kiss took place on a beach with a soft red glow in the distance, just before the sun dropped from the sky and disappeared into the ocean. Sometimes it happened on a dance floor as we clung to each other in dim lights while Nat King

Cole crooned, "When I fall in love, it will be forever." No matter where the kiss happened, my knees always buckled and I swear I saw stars. Tonight, I see no stars and my knees don't buckle. I do hear what sounds like thunder in the distance as the bowling balls in the lanes next to us roar down the alley and crash into the pins.

My last first kiss is in a bowling alley. How about that! The thought causes me to laugh, and I abruptly pull away from Ethan.

He removes his hands from my waist and steps backward. "What's so funny?"

"Sorry. Nothing. Really."

"You were laughing about something."

"I've been imagining what our first kiss would be like for so long. I just never pictured it in a bowling alley, that's all."

He folds his arms across his chest. "You couldn't have been imagining it for too long. We've only known each other for a week."

I look down at my feet and try to figure out how I can talk my way out of this. Surely, I can't tell him about Ajee's prediction. "Well, I've been thinking about it since the diner." That's true. "I was kind of hoping you'd kiss me that day."

He smiles, and God love him, bad teeth and all, it's a big, open-mouthed smile. When we know each other better, I'll recommend a dentist. He steps toward me again. "Is that so?"

I nod. He gently touches my cheek. "You have no idea how bad I wanted to kiss you." And just like that his lips are on mine again. This time the kiss is not tentative. It's long and lingering with the promise of much more to come.

"Hey," one of the teenagers from lane nine yells. "Get a room."

Despite the kiss at the bowling alley and Ethan's flirtatious talk of massages, he walks me to my door and gives me a quick kiss on the lips.

I pull the keys from my purse and turn to unlock the door. "Do you want to come in?"

He doesn't respond so I turn to face him again. "I think I'll collect that massage another time." He looks down and kicks at the hardened snow on my landing with the toe of his boot. "That is, if you want to see me again?" He raises his head. His expression lacks all of his earlier confidence.

"Can't wait," I answer.

Chapter 12

Trouble is brewing at work on Monday. I can tell by the way Jamie and Luci are huddled over a spreadsheet when I arrive just before nine o'clock. Jamie is wearing a white button-down shirt and tie instead of his usual golf shirt, and Luci looks fabulous in a pin-striped skirt and matching jacket. "What's going on?" I ask.

Neither one of them looks away from the spreadsheet they're studying. "We've been summoned by the 9:07," Jamie answers.

The 9:07 is a meeting of TechVisions's executive team that occurs every Monday at seven past nine. Apparently most of the company's vice presidents can't get to work on time. Occasionally Jamie and Luci are requested to attend this meeting to review our department's statistics. Sadly, the data has nothing to do with how many errors Luci and I find. Instead it measures how long it takes us to edit each report.

"How do the numbers look?" I ask as I hang my ski jacket on the back of the door over Luci's long wool coat.

"They look like we could use a few more editors," Luci says.

Jamie pats her shoulder. "Not going to happen."

"Maybe if I can dazzle them with my brilliance it will." Luci retrieves a clip from her purse, gathers her long auburn hair, and arranges it into a twisted bun. She then opens her desk drawer and removes a pair of glasses. The lenses have no prescription. "I look smart glasses, hair up?" She says this in her fake Chinese accent while she fingers the diamond cross pendant around her neck that reveals her true Irish-Catholic heritage.

"Don't start," Jamie warns, but he's smiling. He may be the only one in the company who still gets a kick out of Luci's impersonations.

Jamie's BlackBerry buzzes, and he and Luci hustle out of our office.

Great. Now I'm going to have to wait at least another hour before telling her about my date with Ethan. I called several times yesterday and left a few messages, but she never got back to me. What fun is a first date if you can't rehash it with your best friend? I fire up my computer. Before checking my work messages, I log in to my personal e-mail, hoping for a message from Neesha. Instead there is an e-mail from my mother.

Mrs. Bonnano's son Anthony is coming to visit in early April. He's a chiropractor and more importantly single. You should come down. Dad and I will buy your ticket.

That's her entire message. Honest to God.

Should I tell her about Ethan? No, it's too soon. I hit Reply and write a two-word response in all caps: *NO THANKS!*

I imagine the warm day in May when my parents return to Westham. I'll visit them with Ethan in tow. I can see the look of shock on my mother's face as she shakes his hand. "Did she say your name is Ethan?" she'll ask, not able to believe it. Then she'll glance out the living room window toward the Patels' old house and feel sorry she ever doubted Ajee.

I close my Yahoo! account and open my work e-mail. Twenty-two unread messages. Welcome to the workweek. I click on a message from Jamie. Gail Germain, Luci's and my least favorite analyst, submitted a report last Tuesday, and neither Luci nor I have started it. Jamie's message tells me I must do it today. I sigh loudly, wondering how Luci always manages to avoid the worst assignments. I open Gail's thirty-page document on cloud computing in the health-care industry and read the first sentence. *"A recent survey of major health care organizations in Western Europe, Techvision reveals that IT budget allocation for cloud computing is generally not a priority for Western European healthcare providers."* When an analyst can't even get the name of our company right, I have very little faith the rest of the information in their report is correct. I reread the sentence, turn on redlining, and change the sentence to what I think it should say: *A recent TechVisions survey of major health-care organizations in*

*Western Europe reveals that IT budget allocation for cloud comput-
ing is not a priority.*

An hour later I am only on page four, and each sentence I have
read so far is marked up heavily. Gail Germain should not be allowed
to write. I decide I need a caffeine IV to get me through this report
and head to the café for the next best thing, a cup of coffee.

I am just returning when Luci storms into the office. "They think
we're taking too long editing." She picks up the stack of reports in
our in-box and flips through them. "Twenty reports by twenty different analysts," she says. "It's so obvious that we're understaffed, but
instead of hiring more editors, they want us to come up with a plan of
how we're going to speed things up."

"How about we sign up the analysts for writing classes?" I suggest.

Luci plops down on the corner of my desk and helps herself to a
sip of my coffee. "Well, the executives decided there needs to be a
committee to brainstorm for solutions and you are on that committee."

"No!"

She picks a piece of lint off her sleeve. "It's a committee of two.
You and Cooper Allen." She winks. "I was going to volunteer but he
asked for you." She looks me directly in the eye when she says this,
and she keeps her face straight. Luci is a very good liar.

"Being on a committee will take time away from editing, and our
numbers will get even worse."

Luci shrugs and stands. As she retreats to her desk I receive a
meeting invite from Cooper. I groan as I read it. "Well, I guess I don't
have to worry about the committee taking time away from editing because Cooper wants to meet at five thirty tonight."

"Did you expect anything else?" Luci asks. She takes a sip of coffee, and I realize that she hijacked my cup. "You and Cooper alone
after hours. I like it."

I glare at her as she pulls four packets of Sweet'N Low from her
drawer and dumps them into my coffee. Why is she joking about
Cooper and not even asking about my date with Ethan? I begrudg-
ingly accept Cooper's meeting invite and go back to editing Gail's report.

A few minutes later, Peter from the mailroom bounds into our office carrying a vase of pink roses. He's so big that he completely fills
the space separating my area from Luci's. At the sight of Peter with

flowers, Luci stacks the papers spread over the middle of her desk into a neat pile to clear space. "Hey, Corrigan." Peter always calls Luci by her maiden name. "Relax. These are for Gina."

"Really?" I'm as surprised as Luci.

Peter sets the vase on the corner of my desk where Luci usually sits. She leaps up from her chair and takes two quick steps across the room. "I am so sorry. I forgot all about your date. It must have gone well."

I ignore her because I am opening the card that came with the flowers. I read it silently and smile. "Well?" Luci asks. Before I can answer, she swipes the card out of my hand and reads out loud. "*Thanks for a great time Saturday night. Looking forward to getting to know you better. Ethan.*"

"A great time. We know what that means," Peter says.

Luci hands me the card. "So you slept with him."

"Of course not. It was only the first date."

Luci laughs at the outrage in my voice.

Peter slips his thumbs into his empty belt loops and yanks up his jeans. "It's good to know some women still have morals." He looks pointedly at Luci, and this time they both laugh.

After Peter leaves, I recount my first date with Ethan. "He didn't want to come in?" she repeats, making me feel worse about it. I imagine no guy has ever left Luci at the door.

"I think maybe it had something to do with Leah," I say. It's the only thing I can come up with.

Luci was looking at her monitor, but now she turns her head so that she's looking at me. "Who's Leah?"

"Ethan's wife. Ethan's ex-wife, well, his soon-to-be ex-wife," I stutter.

This grabs Luci's attention, and she's back sitting on the corner of my desk before I get all the words out. "He's married? You never told me that."

"He's divorced," I say and then quickly correct. "Soon-to-be divorced."

Luci picks up the flowers and smells them. "Oh Gina, you can't start a serious relationship with a man in the middle of a divorce."

"It's one date. Hardly a serious relationship."

"Come on, Gina."

I lean back in my chair. Part of me knows Luci is right.

She stands. "I don't like this at all," she says. "Be careful."

By 5:10 Luci has left for the day and I am alone in the office still editing Gail's report. I hear someone clear their throat and jump in my seat. I look up. Cooper Allen is standing in front of my desk dressed like he's about to commit a crime in a black pea coat, heavy black gloves, and a black ski hat. "I didn't mean to startle you," he says.

"You look like you're about to rob a bank or something," I say, willing my heart to stop beating so fast. Cooper studies me without speaking. "Because you're dressed all in black," I clarify.

He holds my gaze. "I'm going to get dinner, not to rob a bank. I was wondering if I can get you anything?"

He continues staring directly in my eyes. I squirm in my seat and look down. "No thanks."

"What did you have for lunch?"

I look up. His arms are folded across his chest, and his eyes are scanning my desk. "A salad."

"Then you must be starving." The truth is, I am hungry, but how weird is it that Mr. Senior Vice President Cooper Allen is offering to fetch my dinner? "What do you like on your pizza?" he asks.

"Peppers, please."

He returns thirty minutes later carrying a large pizza box with a bag resting on top of it. He moves my flowers to Luci's desk and places the pizza in their old spot. He then reaches into the bag and pulls out paper plates and napkins. Next he hands me an Arizona iced tea with ginseng, my favorite. "How did you know I like this?"

He points to my recycling bin, which is filled with empty bottles. He takes off his coat, hat, and gloves and throws them on Luci's desk, almost knocking over the vase.

While I open the pizza box, he wheels her chair around her desk and positions it so that we're sitting across from each other at my desk. For a moment we both just look at the pizza, breathing in the scent of melting mozzarella and tomato sauce.

"Please," Cooper says, gesturing with his hand toward the pizza.

I take a piece. A string of cheese stretches from the box to my plate. I try to break it with my fork but don't succeed. Cooper lifts his hands and breaks the string of cheese with a karate chop. *"En garde,"* he shouts.

His movement and scream are so unexpected that I giggle. He laughs, too. It's the first time I have ever heard him laugh. Unlike his speech, which is usually slow and deliberate, his laughter is an unrestrained boisterous roar. It makes me realize that Cooper Allen has an entire other life away from TechVisions.

"People say *en garde* when they're sword fighting—not doing martial arts," I say.

"You want to edit my speech now, too," Cooper says, but he's smiling, and the dimples that appear in his cheeks transform his entire face.

For the next three hours, I explain the editing process to Cooper in excruciating detail while he furiously pecks at the keyboard of his phone. Every now and then, he interrupts me by raising his hand like a police officer stopping traffic and asks for more details. I swear my voice is hoarse from talking so much.

Just before nine, the phone that he is typing into sings. I know the voice is Frank Sinatra, but I don't recognize the song. Cooper apologizes, spins in his chair so that his back is to me, and takes the call. He listens for a minute or two and then says, "I'll call you later." A few seconds later, his voice is more urgent. "Monique, I said . . . Monique, I'm still at the office. I'll call you later."

Figures Cooper has a girlfriend with an exotic name. Monique. I bet she's very fancy.

He rotates the seat of the chair so that he's facing me again. "Sorry, I didn't realize it was so late. We should schedule another meeting." He scrolls through his phone to look at his calendar, and we plan to meet at three o'clock on Friday.

Cooper and I walk to the parking lot together. Biting cold air blasts us as soon as we step out of the building. I zip up my jacket higher and quicken my steps. Cooper keeps pace. He is silent until we reach my car. "As soon as I get home, I'm going to make a huge mug of hot cocoa," he says, rubbing his gloved hands together.

I open my door. "With whipped cream?"

"Fluff," he says.

"That sounds delicious." I slide into my car. "Good night."

"Drive safe," Cooper says.

"Safely," I correct as he pushes my door shut.

He fakes a look of exasperation as I drive away.

Mr. Senior Vice President of Mobile Devices, TechVisions's golden boy, drinks hot chocolate with Marshmallow Fluff. Who would have ever thought?

Chapter 13

I lean against Ethan's chest. He wraps his long muscular legs around my waist. His arms circle my torso, and he pulls me back even closer toward him. He moves his head forward and rests his chin on my shoulder so that the sides of our faces touch. His stubble scratches my cheek. I don't know if it's because of his proximity or because I'm cold, but I shiver.

"Relax," he whispers. "There's nothing to be afraid of."

Standing behind us, a college-aged boy with a runny nose gives our tube a push, and soon we are careening down a snow-covered hill. "Woohoo!" Ethan shouts as the sled accelerates. It veers to the right and climbs halfway up the icy wall separating our lane from the one next to it before centering itself again. A large bump looms a few feet in front of us. Ethan must see it, too, because he squeezes his thighs, trying to hold me in place. We hit the bump. The tube soars into the air and lands with a *thump*. Miraculously, we manage to hang on and continue the ride to the bottom of the hill.

Ethan untangles himself from me, stands, and pulls me to my feet. "You all right?" he asks.

I reach down for the tube. "Again," I yell, racing off to the rope tow that will drag us back to the top of the hill.

Ethan catches up to me and pulls me into an embrace. "You're fearless. I love it." The entire way up the hill, all I'm thinking is *I love it*. Just one word away from the sentence I've been dreaming about him saying to me since middle school.

When we get to the top, Ethan picks a lane at the end that is called the Speed Bump. He climbs into the back of the tube and stretches his legs out over the front. The only way for me to fit in there with him is to sit on his lap, so I do. It's impossible not to notice that he is rock-solid under his ski pants. He positions his arms around my waist and rests his gloved hands on my outer thighs. As we wait for the attendant to push us, Ethan slides his fingers back and forth on my inner thigh. He presses his cold, wet mouth against my exposed earlobe. "I think when we're done with this, I'll be ready to collect on last week's bet."

He's so hard to figure out. When we're out in a crowd, he acts like he can't wait to be alone with me, but when it's only the two of us at my place, he can't wait to get out of there. Just an hour ago when he picked me up, he gave me a chaste kiss on the lips. "Do you want to sit down, have something to eat or drink?" I asked.

He tucked his hands into his coat pockets. "I think we should go. Don't want to run out of daylight." It was just a little after one.

Now he leans closer, his breath hot against the icy cold side of my face. "If you do a good job, I might even return the favor." His fingers slide higher. All the way through my ski bib and jeans, I can feel my skin tingling. Ever since he touched me at the diner, I have been craving more. I finally understand the meaning of crazy with desire.

"Ready?" the attendant asks.

Ethan's fingers stop moving. The sled takes off at a breakneck speed. Beneath me, Ethan's hips rise and fall over each bump as I shriek with excitement. At the steepest part of the hill we hit a bump and lose control. Ethan and I are thrown overboard while the tube soars high into the air. I land facedown in a pile of snow while Ethan ends up on his backside. "You hurt?" he asks, rushing to my side.

"I'm fine."

"We don't have to do this anymore," he says helping me to my feet.

"Of course we do."

"No," he says. "You've been a good sport long enough." He walks toward an attendant to return our tube.

I quickly make a few snowballs and toss them at his butt, but my aim is so bad that two connect with the back of his head. "What the—" He turns around just as another snowball whizzes by his shoulder. "What are you doing?"

"We can't let a hill beat us. Don't you dare return that tube." I'm already armed with another snowball, and I cock my arm.

He drops the tube and holds up his arms. "I surrender."

Ninety minutes and twelve runs later, I can no longer feel my toes or fingers. Ethan's lips are blue and the tip of his nose is bright red. "Had enough?" he asks.

I nod, and we head inside the ski lodge, where we strip ourselves of our hats, gloves, ski pants, and jackets. I settle into a seat by the fire while Ethan goes to the bar to order us hot chocolates with butter-scotch schnapps. A few minutes later, he makes his way across the crowded floor balancing two steaming hot beverages and a bowl of popcorn.

"Thank you," he says, sliding a mug topped with whipped cream in front of me. "I've been wanting to do that for so long, but Leah would never go." He pulls his cup closer and blows on it.

I try to imagine Leah, but all I can see is a big ball of boringness loafing on the couch.

"What is Leah like?" I ask, suddenly desperate to get a clear image of her.

Ethan sips his drink. "She's . . . I don't know." He shrugs. "Hey, let's not talk about Leah." He leans across the table and reaches for my hand. "I'd much rather hear about you."

We return to my apartment at six thirty. Ethan holds my hand tightly and leads me around the walkway in the dark. When we get to the top of the stairs, he takes the keys from me and unlocks the door. I enter, and he follows closely behind. I turn on the light in the kitchen, and we remove our jackets and gloves. I take a few steps toward the living room, expecting Ethan to follow. Instead he grabs my arm and spins me toward him. He eases me against the wall between the living room and the kitchen and kisses me. He keeps his hands on my shoulders, pinning me in place with my arms around his waist. We stand like this for a few minutes. He uses his tongue to separate my lips. Inside my mouth, his tongue gently explores while his hands begin to travel down my body. Slowly, he begins to thrust his tongue in and out of my mouth, and soon he is moving his hips against me in the same rhythm. I mimic his every motion.

It's crazy: We're both fully dressed, yet every inch of my body is buzzing with energy. I don't remember ever feeling this way before.

We remain lost like this for several minutes. He grabs the bottom of my sweater and yanks it over my head. I unzip his sweatshirt, and he shrugs out of it while unsnapping my jeans. "Let's move to the bedroom, babe." He begins to walk, but I remain rooted against the wall, not sure I want things to move so quickly. "Please, babe."

He takes my hand in his and gently pulls me. We make it halfway down the hallway when Ethan's phone rings. It's not a normal ringtone. It's a woman voice saying, "Pick up, honey. Pick up."

Honey? I pull my hand from his. He freezes and then slowly turns so he is facing me. His phone continues squealing, "Pick up, honey. Pick up."

"Leah," he says. The ringing finally stops. "I didn't change the ringtone."

"Why not?"

He stiffens his shoulders and slowly exhales. "I just didn't think of it. She never calls." As if to prove him a liar, the phone starts speaking again. Ethan pulls it from his pocket. "Must be important," he says while retreating to the kitchen.

I remain standing in the hallway. "This isn't a good time," I hear him say. Then, "What happened? Leah?" A few seconds later. "Calm down, babe. He's going to be fine."

Babe. Why is the soon-to-be ex-wife "babe"? I thought *I* was "babe." My stomach contorts and I rush into the bathroom. I come out a few minutes later to find him sitting at the kitchen table staring at his lap. I slip back into my sweater and position myself in the seat across from him. Ethan looks up at me. "Brady's missing," he says.

"The dog?"

He nods. "She left him in the backyard while she was out. Came home, the gate was open. Brady's gone." He rubs the stubble on his chin. "Not sure what she expects me to do. Takes over three hours to get there." He glances at his watch.

"Has this happened before?"

He shakes his head. "But she can't latch the gate. I always have to do it." He stands and grabs his jacket. "Gotta go."

"Are you driving there?"

"I'm gonna make some calls. Get some friends in the area to search." He embraces me quickly and rushes out the door.

As I turn the lock, I wonder if Leah's inability to work a latch will open the door for a reconciliation.

Chapter 14

The sound of sleet pelting the roof wakes me early Monday. I check my phone for messages from Ethan, but there are none. He drove to New Hampshire yesterday morning to look for Brady, but when we spoke at bedtime, the dog was still missing. Ethan promised to text if anything changed. All night, I tossed and turned, wondering where he was sleeping. Now I type him a quick message: *Any luck?* Thirty minutes later, I'm showered and dressed for work, but Ethan still hasn't responded.

Outside, my car is encapsulated in layers of ice. I struggle to get the key in the sleet-covered lock. I finally manage, but the door won't open because it, too, is frozen. I brace my boot on the side of the car and pull with all my might. The door doesn't budge. I try again. I hear a loud *snap* and see the ice cracking apart. The door springs open, throwing me backward. The side of my face smacks against the frozen ground. I cry out and remain lying on the hard, cold ground. After a few seconds, I struggle to my feet. In the car, I look in the visor mirror. A big red welt appears just below my left eye. Excellent start to the week.

Twenty minutes later, after chipping the sleet off my front and back windshields, I back out of my driveway. Still no word from Ethan. As I turn off my street, a sander going the other directions blasts my car. The salt and pebbles ping against my door. The side of the road I am driving on hasn't been treated yet, and my car slips and slides at every corner. Finally, I make it to the highway, where I merge into an endless line of brake lights. I glance at my silent phone on the pas-

senger seat every few minutes as the car inches forward. From behind, sirens approach. A few seconds later, a police car, fire truck,
and ambulance pass in the breakdown lane. The traffic comes to a
dead stop. I settle back into my seat. The DJ reads a list of school
cancellations, and I change the station, pressing buttons until I land
on a Kelly Clarkson song. I sing along. The driver in front of me
flicks cigarette ashes out his window. The song ends, and now the DJ
on this station starts to announce school closings.

Several songs later, the traffic still isn't moving but my phone finally
rings. "He was at a neighbor's a few streets over," Ethan announces. "He
didn't have his tags. She didn't know who he belonged to."

"Why wasn't he wearing his tags?"

"Leah, man. Took his collar off." He sighs. "Who knows why?"
The driver behind me blasts his horn. "What's that?" Ethan asks.

I tell him about my morning and the welt on my face. "Oh babe,
I'm sorry." I wince at his words, remembering how he called Leah
the same thing, and again wonder where he spent last night. Would it
make me sound overly jealous if I ask him? "How about I take you to
dinner tonight to make up for your rough morning?" he asks.

By lunchtime, the sleet has turned to a hard downpour. Because
it's so nasty, the cafeteria is more crowded than usual. Luci and I
stand in line for the salad bar. A few feet in front of us, a skinny guy
from accounting sneezes, spraying the cover protecting the lettuce
and other ingredients. Luci and I exchange a look, return our plastic
containers to the stack where we got them, and head for the deli.

Cooper and Gail Germain are the last two in line. We step in behind them. Gail is bending Cooper's ear, and neither notices us. "It
took them over a week," she says. "And almost every word was
rewritten. Unnecessary edits."

Luci elbows me.

"I'm sure they had their reasons," Cooper says.

Gail folds her arms across her chest. "It wasn't any better. Just a
week late."

I fight the urge to kick her. "I'm sure they enhanced it," Cooper
says. "Gina and Luci do a good job."

Luci clears her throat. Gail and Cooper both turn. I wave. Luci
places her hands on her hips. "We didn't just enhance it. We made it

readable." She looks directly at Gail. "You should take a remedial grammar class."

Gail starts to respond, but Cooper interrupts. "Gina, what happened to your face?" He steps toward me. Then, most unexpectedly, he raises his hand and touches my bruise. All the sound from the café disappears. He gently rubs the injury with the tips of his fingers. My legs feel wobbly. Why is Cooper Allen touching me? I rest my hand on Luci's shoulder to keep my balance while stepping backward out of his reach.

His ears redden. "Looks like it hurts," he says.

"It does," I answer, but I can't look at him.

"Did you ice it?"

I nod, still looking at the ground. I hear the guy behind the deli counter yell, "Next!" Gail says Cooper's name, and a second later he's ordering a roast beef sandwich.

I finally look up. Luci's studying me with her head cocked. "What?" I ask.

"I think you know," she says.

I get home at six o'clock to find Ethan's Jeep in my driveway. It's angled so his headlights illuminate the area under the broken motion light. A ladder leans against the house, and he stands near the top removing the old bulb and screwing in a new one. I smile, thinking this is exactly something my imaginary Ethan would have done. As I make my way across the driveway and up the stairs to the landing, I notice the ground I'm walking on is covered with a blue pebble-like substance. An almost empty bottle of Ice Melt rests on the hood of Ethan's car.

He climbs down the ladder and embraces me on the walkway. "Hey, you." He rubs my bruise with his thumb. "Poor baby," he says as he kisses it. I hold him tightly, not wanting to let go, ever. "What do you say we head out to eat?" he asks as he pulls away from me to collapse his ladder. "I'm starving."

As we drive to the restaurant, he tells me about the search for Brady and the joy he felt when he saw him. "I took him on a really long walk this morning. It was hard to say good-bye." The light in front of us turns yellow, and Ethan steps on the gas. I clutch the handle on the door. "I miss 'em so much," he mumbles.

"Wait, what?" I ask, not sure if he said *him* or *them*. He glances at me, but says nothing. "Who do you miss?" I ask, trying to make my voice as neutral as possible.

"Brady," he says quickly. "I miss Brady." Now he's right on the bumper of the small car in front of us.

"Where did you stay last night?" The words are out before I even know I'm going to ask the question.

He jerks the steering wheel, moving into the left lane, and zooms past the car in front of us. "In the guest room, Gina," he answers with a tone that makes me feel as if I've been reprimanded. We drive in silence for the rest of the way to the restaurant. Ethan pulls in to the parking lot and kills the ignition. As I unfasten my seat belt, he places his hand just above my knee and squeezes. "Hey," he says. "I told Leah about you."

"What did you say?"

He leans toward me and pulls me into his arms. "Told her I met a great girl." He pushes a strand of hair behind my ear and kisses me. It's the kind of kiss that makes me want to skip dinner and head back to my apartment. I swear he knows it, too, because when he pulls away, he gives me that cocky smile. "I have to eat," he says. "I haven't had anything all day." I climb out of the Jeep wondering if he can read my thoughts or if I actually spoke them out loud.

Mariachi music plays in the lobby as we enter and another party waits to be seated. Ethan and I pull off our gloves and unzip our coats. I realize I'm still wearing my work access badge around my neck and lift it over my head. Ethan takes it from me and studies it silently. "Wow," he finally says. "You look . . ." He abruptly stops speaking and hands me back the badge.

"I look what?"

"Never mind," he says.

I study the photo. I can tell by how frizzy my hair is that it was raining the day the picture was taken. The photographer zoomed in so close on my face that you can almost count the pores on my nose. "What an ugly picture."

Ethan shakes his head. "No, Gina. You're beautiful." He kisses me on the cheek. "You could never look ugly." His words sound sincere, but something about his expression looks haunted.

The hostess is ready to seat us and leads us to a booth against the back wall, next to a family with three small children. A toddler in a booster seat points at my face. "Boo-boo," he says.

"Yes, boo-boo." I smile.

"Don't point, Aidan," his mother says and lowers the boy's small hand back to the table.

I slide into the booth opposite Ethan and study his face as he reads the menu. Our kids will probably have brown eyes like me. I hope they get his straight, shiny hair and the cleft in his chin. Ethan looks up at me and smiles. Please let them have my teeth.

"I can't even remember the last time I had Mexican," he says. "Leah hates it." Just like that, the image of Ethan and my children vanishes. I must frown because Ethan closes his menu. "Shit." He says it so loudly that the mother at the next table gives us a dirty look. "Jack warned me not to talk about Leah. Sorry."

"That's okay," I lie as the busboy arrives with chips and salsa.

Ethan reaches for a chip and soaks it in the dip, which leaves a trail across the table as he lifts the chip to his mouth. "So, tell me about other advice from Jack," I say as Ethan chews.

He swallows. "I can't give those secrets away." He winks.

The waitress arrives to take our order. She's a blond, fair-skinned girl of about nineteen or twenty. Her name tag says Rosalita, but I'd bet anything her name's Britney or Taylor or something like that. She reads the specials from a notepad. "Chicken in a chocolate mole sauce," she says, pronouncing it like a bump on the skin or the animal.

"Mo-lay," I correct.

She writes something in her notebook and turns to Ethan. "And for you?"

"No," I say. "I don't want the mole. I was just—Never mind. I'll have chicken fajitas."

She scribbles something and turns back to Ethan. He orders shrimp fajitas and jumbo strawberry margaritas for each of us.

"Tell me about Jack," I say when she leaves.

Ethan smiles. "Jack's the man. Always has my back. He was the best man at my . . ." He shakes his head. "Sorry."

The waitress returns with our drinks. The glasses are filled so high that the contents overflow and drip onto the table. I take a large sip to make room in the cup. All I can taste is tequila. For a few minutes, we sip in silence.

"Has Jack ever been married?" I ask, not sure why I'm so curious about this guy.

"No way," Ethan says. "He's had, like, two girlfriends his whole life. Leah set him up with both of them." He removes the straw from his drink and takes a huge gulp. "Do you have any friends you can introduce him to?"

The only single friend I have is Luci, and I don't want her breaking this guy's heart. "None that would be a match."

"How can you say that when you haven't even met him?" Ethan asks. From across the restaurant I hear the sizzling of vegetables on a hot plate approaching. "My friends aren't good enough for yours?"

I think he's kidding, but I'm not really sure. "I only have one single friend," I say. "She's still recovering from her divorce."

He slumps in his seat but doesn't say anything.

The waitress arrives and places the sizzling fajita vegetables in front of Ethan. Behind her, the busboy deposits a plate with chicken mole and brown rice in front of me. "I ordered the chicken fajitas," I say.

Rosalita consults with her notepad. "Says here chicken mole."

"Mo-lay," the busboy and I correct.

"Right, that's what I gave you," our waitress says.

I exhale. "Never mind. I'll eat this."

"So," Ethan says after they leave. "Come over Saturday. You can meet Jack. I'll cook you dinner, and if it goes well, breakfast, too."

I laugh. "Did you really just use that cheesy line on me?" I really am horrified.

"Pretty bad, huh?" Ethan hangs his head.

"Terrible."

"Cut me some slack," he says, assembling his fajita. "I'm brand spanking new to this dating thing."

Chapter 15

Eight fifteen in the morning has become my favorite part of the day. That's what time Ethan calls. Usually I'm merging off the highway and onto the long, curvy single lane road that winds around the reservoir to my office park. Typically Ethan is in line at the drive-through at Dunkin' Donuts. He gets a box of munchkins and four medium coffees for him and the three other guys on his construction crew. This week they are renovating a kitchen on the south shore.

"The lady says she's going to cook us all a gourmet dinner when it's done," he says. "She's pretty cool." He mumbles something that sounds like *"keep the change."* "She gave me a recipe for chicken potpie. I'm going to make it for you tomorrow night."

"Looking forward to it," I say.

"I got her recipe for Belgian waffles, too," he says. "Maybe I'll make them for breakfast. Think you'll still be around?" He has trouble finishing the sentence because he's laughing so hard.

"You are the king of bad lines," I say.

"And you're my queen."

"What's on for the weekend?" Luci asks when I get to the office. She is sitting at her desk eating a blueberry muffin. I notice there's one waiting for me on my desk, as well.

I hang up my coat and position myself behind my desk before answering. "Ethan's cooking me dinner at his place." I break off a piece of muffin.

"Cooking you dinner," she says with a wink.

Even though it's my best friend I'm talking to, I feel myself blushing and suddenly realize how nervous I am about tomorrow.

"Do you want to go to the mall at lunch?" Luci asks. "We could go to Victoria's Secret. I'll help you pick out something for tomorrow night."

"Thanks. I'm all set."

"You can't wear your granny underpants," Luci says, her expression deadly serious. Once while we were shopping, I picked up a three-pack of Jockey briefs, and Luci has never let me hear the end of it. Apparently she only wears thongs or lacy underwear. "I'm serious. Do you have any sexy lingerie?"

I actually do. A red lacy teddy. I've worn it once. The day I tried it on. I blush as I remember thinking that if I bought it, I might get lucky. It was after I took a visualization lunchtime lecture at work. HR insists we attend crap like that once a quarter.

Luci continues to stare at me. In a very quiet voice she asks, "This isn't going to be your first time, is it?"

I glare at her. "Very funny."

"Then why are you acting so weird?"

"Because it's been a while, and Ethan sounds so confident. What if I disappoint him?"

Luci stretches out her legs so that her feet are resting on the wall behind my desk. "In this area, men are rarely disappointed. They also tend to overpromise and underdeliver." She reaches for my arm and squeezes it. "You'll be fine. Relax." Then she gives me her Luci devilish grin. "Are there any questions I can help you with?"

My mother never talked to me about sex. Neesha was the only friend I ever discussed it with, but we were young and inexperienced. Our conversations were mostly about when our first time would be. Neesha planned to wait until college, while I planned to wait until Ethan. When I told Neesha this, she said, "I don't think you should wait until then."

"Why not?" I wasn't allowed to have my own phone, but the one in the kitchen had an extra-long cord. I stretched it down the hall and into my room.

"You should do it lots of times before you meet him so you're good at it," Neesha answered.

Before I could respond, there was a knock on my bedroom door. Without waiting for a response, my mother burst into my room. I was lying on the floor next to the door, and it banged against my head. "Ouch!" I screamed. "I'm on the phone."

"You're going to rip the receiver right out of the wall stretching the cord like that," my mother yelled.

My father was steps behind her. "Who are you talking to? That better not be long-distance to Texas again or you'll be paying the bill."

On the other end of the line, Neesha giggled. "I miss Dominick and Angie." Since moving to Texas, she'd taken to calling my parents by their first names.

"I have to go."

Now her words bounce around inside my head: *"You should do it lots of times before you meet him so you're good at it."* While I didn't wait for Ethan, I didn't exactly follow Neesha's advice, either. I am thirty-six years old and have slept with a grand total of two men: Nick Brisas, who was my boyfriend sophomore and junior years at BC, and Ray Palermo, who I dated in my early thirties.

"How many men have you slept with?" I ask Luci.

"I don't know," she says. "But at least four this month."

I study her face to see if she is teasing. I don't think she is. "The month isn't even half over."

Luci stands and shrugs. "Making up for lost time I guess." Her voice has that tinge of hurt it always has when she's talking about anything that vaguely relates to Kip.

For the next few hours, Luci and I work on the stack of documents in our in-box. She is editing one of Gail's reports and occasionally reads a nonsensical sentence out loud. "What do you think she means?" she asks, exasperated.

I look at her and shrug, glad to be working on one of Cooper's reports. He is actually a decent writer, and I am flying through it. I finish it just before lunch and e-mail it back to him. "Great report," I write.

Within minutes of me hitting the Send button, my office phone rings. "Hey, I have some bad news." It's Ethan.

"What's wrong?"

"Leah called," he sneers. "She told me she packed all my stuff into boxes. She's going out of town this weekend, and she said if they're still there when she gets back, she's going to take them to the dump." He is talking three times faster than usual and finally pauses for a breath. "I have to drive to New Hampshire tomorrow to get them. Sorry, but there's no way I'll be able to get there and back in time to cook for you."

"Why do you still have stuff at Leah's?" I ask.

"Jesus, you sound like her."

I flinch. He has never spoken to me in such a harsh tone before. I feel Luci staring at me across our desks and spin my chair so that I'm facing the wall behind me.

"I'm sorry, Gina. I shouldn't have said that. It's just that it's still my house, too, and Leah refuses to acknowledge that." He pauses. "We fought about Brady. That's why she's doing this."

"Well, do what you need to do. We'll have dinner another time."

"I'm sorry," he says again. "Thanks for understanding."

By the time I hang up and spin around, Luci is back on the corner of my desk. "What's going on?"

"Leah's threatening to throw away all of Ethan's stuff so he has to go to New Hampshire tomorrow and get it. He won't be back in time to cook me dinner." I work hard to make my voice sound like it's no big deal.

"He still has stuff there? How long have they been separated?"

I shrug. "A month or so."

Luci sighs. "Gina, walk away. Really, he has no business starting a new relationship right now."

"It's fine."

Luci stands. "No, it's not." She reaches into her purse for her wallet. "Let's go to lunch."

As I get up, my phone rings again. "Hey," Ethan says. "You don't think I still have my stuff at Leah's because I want to move back there?"

"Do you?"

"Of course not. I just haven't had time to drive up there and get it. That's all."

"Well, get it all this weekend and be done with it."

"I have an idea," Ethan says. His voice has the same playful tone from this morning's call. "Why don't you come with me? It's a long ride. I'd love the company. And, I could, umm, take you for dinner and breakfast up there."

"You want me to go to New Hampshire with you?"

"We'll get a hotel room and spend the weekend. I'll show you the White Mountains. It'll be fun."

Luci taps me on the shoulder. I didn't even notice her walk over here. She violently shakes her head. I spin my chair away from her, but she turns it back. Ethan is saying something about waterfalls and how beautiful the White Mountains are. I watch Luci pick up a pen and write the words *"Don't go!"* on my desk blotter.

She's probably right. I shouldn't go. On the other hand, I am thirty-six years old and single. I've spent the past twenty-two years waiting for a man named Ethan, and now here he is, asking me to go away for the weekend. "I'd love to go with you."

Luci stands straight up with her hands on her hips and stomps out of the room. When Ethan and I finish our conversation, I catch up with her at the elevator. Peter from the mailroom is also there. He's dressed in a large red T-shirt with gold letters that say I'LL NEVER TELL.

"What does that mean?" I ask as Luci pushes the button for the second floor.

"I'll never tell," Peter answers. Luci turns to look at him. They both laugh.

"I guess I walked into that."

"Yeah, seems like you don't know what you're walking into today," Luci says.

Peter raises his eyebrows at me, but I ignore him. "Hey, ladies, it's Friday. A bunch of us are heading to Last Chance after work. Want to join us?"

The doors slide open. "I'll think about it," Luci says.

I step out of the elevator and almost collide with Cooper. He's carrying a plate with four chocolate chip cookies and a small carton of chocolate milk. "Is that your lunch?" I ask.

"The lines for real food are too long. I don't have time to wait, which reminds me, I have to push our three o'clock this afternoon to four thirty, okay?" he says as he boards the lift.

"Jesus, Cooper," Luci answers. "Four thirty on a Friday. Are you asking her to a meeting or on a date?"

Cooper's cheeks flush, but the elevator doors close before anyone says anything else.

* * *

Back in our office, Luci and I sit across from each other at our desks eating our salads. "It's a really bad idea for you to go to the house Ethan shared with his wife." She points her fork at me. "Really bad idea."

"It's not a big deal. We're stopping by for a few minutes to pick up some boxes. Leah won't even be there."

"You don't get it, Gina." She wipes her mouth with a napkin. "My divorce was the worst time of my life." She balls the napkin up and tosses it into the garbage can. "I know you don't want to hear this, but a guy going through a divorce has no business dating. He needs to process why his marriage failed and then get over it. Stay away from him. Give him time."

"He's the one who pursued me."

"He's reeling, Gina, and he's just looking for a warm body to hold on to."

"So he doesn't really like me, is that what you're saying?"

She leans back in her chair. "I'm saying he has no idea what he's doing right now. I had such a hard time getting over my divorce. I'm not even sure I'm over it now." She pauses and studies her nails. "I did so many stupid things that I wish I could take back."

"Like what?"

She stands and walks to the corner of my desk. "Promise not to tell anyone?"

"Yes."

She looks down. "I slept with Peter." She looks up and into my eyes. I laugh and wait for her to smile. She doesn't. "I'm serious."

There's not even a hint of amusement on her face. "Peter, from the mailroom?" She nods. "Shut up. You didn't."

She nods. "I did."

"Where did you do it, the mailroom?"

"Actually . . ." She smiles and taps my desk.

"Gross!" I pull open my bottom drawer, take out my Clorox Wipes, and scrub the spot she just pointed at.

Back in her chair, Luci laughs. "I'm kidding. About your desk, not about Peter." I study her face and see no hints that she's joking or lying. "Do you remember that night we played darts with him at Last Chance?"

I feel my stomach turning as I remember Peter, all two hundred fifty pounds of him, in his black and gold Bruins shirt, and his sweaty, ruddy face, making a bull's-eye and then grabbing Luci and kissing her on the lips. "Yes."

"Well, I had too much to drink so he gave me a ride home. It just happened."

I remember wanting to leave but Luci insisting she wasn't ready. "Don't worry. I'll be sure she gets home safely," Peter had said while stroking his goatee.

"Did you know he was drafted by the Blue Jays for pitching but blew out his elbow before making it to the majors?" Luci asks.

I picture his sad hazel eyes and big body. Then I see him younger, smiling and muscular, dressed in a baseball uniform. He stands on the pitcher's mound, leans in for the sign from the catcher, goes into the windup, and screams in pain as he releases the ball. Just like that, his dream is over. I want to run to the mailroom and give him a big hug. "That's awful," I say. Then, I can't help it, a vision of him now with his huge stomach hanging over his naked waist appears in my head. His sausage-like fingers fumble with the buttons on the red cashmere sweater Luci was wearing that night. I toss the rest of my salad in the trash and leave for the restroom.

When I arrive at Cooper's office at four thirty, he's on the phone. "They grossly miscalculated in Australia," he says. "The Aussie four-G network isn't robust enough for their product." He squints so that his dark eyes are barely slits. I notice small lines around the corners of his eyes. They make him look sexy. Oh God, what is wrong with me? I look around his office. In addition to his desk and two guest chairs, there's a table and a couch in here. The bookshelf next to the door displays various awards that he's won at TechVisions. There's one picture of him with his arm around a disturbingly beautiful dark-haired woman. Must be Monique, his glamorous girlfriend. She looks extremely familiar. Maybe she used to work here. Maybe that's how they met. Cooper looks at me and with his hand mimics someone talking too much. I smile and he smiles back. His teeth are straight and white. I think of Ethan's yellowish teeth with the gaps between them and their varying lengths. Maybe I should find out who Cooper's dentist is and recommend him?

Cooper must have hung up the phone because when I look at him again, he's studying me with his hand on his hip and a half smile. "Well?" he asks.

"Did you have braces as a kid?" I blurt out.

He cocks his head and squints. "I asked you how late you can stay, and yes, my father was an orthodontist."

"I can stay until five thirty, and I'm sorry about your father."

Cooper points to the guest chair, so I sink into it. "You're sorry that he was an orthodontist?"

"No, I'm sorry he passed."

Confusion washes over his face. "Why do you think he died?"

"You said he was an orthodontist."

Cooper shakes his head and opens a notebook on his desk. "He's retired, not dead."

We have all this great technology and still no way to edit the spoken word. I feel my chest and neck getting splotchy. I look up at Cooper. We both laugh when we make eye contact. The laugh starts small but suddenly explodes into uncontrollable snorting. Just when it's about to end, we make eye contact again, and it picks up steam and keeps going. Tears stream down Cooper's face, and I'm hunched over, holding my stomach when it finally does end.

"Anyway," Cooper says, "where were we with this project?"

"I'm supposed to tell you about the types of mistakes we find."

It's almost 7 p.m. when Cooper and I finish categorizing the types of errors Luci and I find when editing. He looks at his watch. "Whoops, it's well after five thirty."

I shut my notebook and stand. "I should really get going."

He stands, too. "Sorry I kept you so late." He shoves his hands in his pockets and shifts his weight from leg to leg. "Do you have a big date with Mr. Flowers tonight?"

Mr. Flowers? Then I remember he saw the roses Ethan sent to work. "I, no. I'm going to meet Luci and some people at Last Chance. It's karaoke night."

"Do you do karaoke?" he asks.

"Depends on how many drinks I've had."

He laughs. "I'd like to see that sometime."

I walk to his door. When I get there, I turn to face him again. He is standing in the same exact position watching me. "Do you want to come?"

He sways from side to side. "I'd like to, but I have"—he pauses and looks down—"a thing at eight o'clock."

A "thing" probably means a date with Monique. I step out of his office and am in the hallway when he calls after me. "Gina, another time?"

"Yes," I say. "I'll check your calendar and schedule the next meeting."

He studies me with the same squinty look he had when I first got here. "I was talking about—" He stops suddenly. "Never mind."

I ride the elevator back to my floor wondering if Cooper Allen just asked me on a date. No, he couldn't have. He's dating Monique.

Chapter 16

I am just getting home from the gym on Saturday morning and still in my sweaty clothes when Ethan arrives. Since our first date, he has been consistently early. "You're not supposed to be here for another forty-five minutes," I say.

He pulls me into a tight embrace. "I couldn't wait to see you." He starts to kiss me, but I squirm away, thinking about how much I must smell. After all, I just spent the past hour on the elliptical.

"I'm going to take a shower. Make yourself at home." His eyes twinkle, and he looks like he wants to say something but refrains.

Twenty minutes later, I'm showered and dressed. Ethan is sitting at the kitchen table sipping coffee from a Styrofoam cup and reading the paper. I notice another cup of coffee and two plates set up on the table. There is a lemon pastry on each plate. This is so close to my fantasy that my heart begins to race, and I feel light-headed.

"Are you all right?" Ethan asks when he sees me staring at the table.

"I'm perfect." I feel like I'm dreaming. Any moment now the alarm is going to sound. Ethan continues to watch me, so I sit at the table and take a sip of my coffee and stare at the pastry. Would it be rude to tell him that I don't like lemon? Yes, it would. I pick up the pastry and slowly bring it to my mouth. I bite off the smallest piece and immediately reach for my coffee. I must have made the sour face I make when I eat anything with lemon.

"You don't like it?" Ethan asks.

"I love it." Just to prove I'm telling the truth, I bite off a larger piece. *Yuck, it's gross. So sour.* Ethan watches me closely. *Keep chewing; don't spit it out.* I force the pastry to the back of my mouth and then down my throat and immediately gulp a large swallow of coffee to wash it away. "Yummy," I say. Like I would ever really use that word.

Ethan smiles. "Lemon is my favorite," he says. Great. Why didn't I just confess that I don't like it? Now I'm going to have to pretend to like it for the rest of my life. Idiot.

We finish eating breakfast—well, most of my pastry is still left—and head down to Ethan's Jeep. He insists on carrying my overnight bag and opens the Jeep door for me. Chivalrous, just like I always imagined he would be. Before he pulls out of my driveway, he leans over and kisses me. Luckily he tastes like coffee and not lemon.

The sky above is bright blue, and the streets below are wet with melting snow. The windows of the Jeep are halfway down so that at a red light, we can hear water flowing into the sewers, washing away the season's doldrums.

Ethan switches on the radio, and twangy music fills the car. I turn the channel to a top-forty station. Adele is singing about setting fire to the rain.

"What does that even mean?" Ethan asks.

I shrug. "Don't know, but she sure sounds good singing it. She has a beautiful voice."

"She's fat, isn't she?" Ethan asks.

I glare at him. "What does that have to do with her singing?"

"It has everything to do with her appeal as a star."

"I bet if she were a guy, you wouldn't comment on her weight."

He laughs. "Yeah, if she were a guy I probably wouldn't be checking out her body, that's true." When the song ends, he turns the radio back to his country station. Some guy is singing about being good at drinking beer.

"Really, this is what you listen to?" I ask. He switches off the radio. "I guess we don't agree on music," I say.

"I'm sure we can find something we both like." He thinks for a minute. "Do you like eighties music?"

"Sure."

He sings a few lines from Bon Jovi's "Livin' on a Prayer." Though I only know this because I recognize the words. He sings it with a twang. "You sing something, and I'll see if I recognize it," he suggests.

I think and settle on a Cyndi Lauper song. I sing in key so it only takes Ethan a few lines to name the tune. "Time After Time," he shouts. "You sounded great." He smiles. "You have a beautiful voice and a beautiful body." I feel myself blushing. He reaches for my leg and caresses my thigh, sending chills up and down my spine. "I can't wait to see more of it tonight." His voice sounds velvety.

I know I should say something flirty back, but I just sit there embarrassed, trying to think of an appropriate response. "Me too," I finally say. He takes my hand into his and squeezes it.

We drive in silence for a few minutes. Then he starts singing again. The words coming from his mouth sound like Billy Joel's "Only the Good Die Young," but the tune is more Garth Brooks's "Friends in Low Places."

We continue playing our version of *Name That Tune* for several miles. Our game ends when I stump Ethan on Foreigner's "Waiting for a Girl Like You." It's not a fair victory because I substitute boy for girl. It's the only line I know, so I keep repeating it: first like it's an opera; then I do a disco version, followed by Motown, and finally I perform it with a twang before Ethan invokes the Mercy Rule, which I instituted miles ago to get him to stop singing "Born in the U.S.A."

After being on the highway for an hour and a half, we turned off onto a two-lane road, which we have been on for almost ninety minutes now. There's a lot more snow up here than at home, but unlike ours, it's still mostly white, not sullied by car exhaust and road salt.

A half hour later, Ethan turns off the main road onto a small, winding street that appears to be carved through a mountain. I marvel at the beauty of the area. "You have to see it in summer," he says. "I'll bring you back so we can hike to some of my favorite waterfalls." He tells me about the area, but I'm not listening. Instead, I'm imagining him dropping to one knee and proposing at one of those waterfalls, a ray of light bouncing off the pear-shaped diamond as he slips it on my finger.

We pass a sign for Glory, and Ethan takes a few turns. Finally, he pulls into a long driveway flanked by six-foot snowbanks on each side. Although Ethan told me nothing about what the house looked like, I envisioned it as a small Cape. Wrong. It's an exquisite log cabin with two levels of porches, the front side of the house donning more windows than logs. A tall fence, also made from logs, stands to the right enclosing the backyard. "Look behind you," Ethan instructs when we get out of the Jeep.

I turn. The view I have is like an award-winning panoramic photograph of mountain peaks, only it's real. Incredible. The Ethan I imagined lived in a house with lots of windows that faced an ocean. Sometimes he lived in a high-rise in the heart of the city. Never did he live in a big house made of logs nestled into a mountainside. No wonder he sings with a twang.

We make our way across a stone walkway that leads to the front door. It hits me then that I am approaching the house Ethan lived in with his wife. While I was sitting around year after year waiting for him, he was living a whole other life with someone else. It's just not fair. He should have been looking for me.

"What the . . ." Ethan suddenly shouts. His stride becomes quicker as he heads toward a pile of boxes on the left side of the porch. He peeks inside one and immediately flips it shut. "Jesus Christ, she didn't pack up my stuff. She crammed it into boxes and dragged them out here for anyone to walk off with." He kicks the stack. A box from the top tumbles off, banging loudly on the porch.

I stand frozen at the bottom of the steps not knowing what to do. Ethan exhales loudly and turns to face me. "She could have left the stuff inside," he says. I nod in agreement, wondering why she put all his belongings out here. Ethan runs his hands through his hair. "Sorry, I just wasn't expecting this. I'll show you around before we load the Jeep."

He reaches into his pocket for his keys. A feeling of doom overtakes me. Why would Leah go to the trouble of piling the boxes outside if he can get into the house? "It's okay, Ethan. I don't really want to see the inside. Let's just go."

He jiggles his key lightly in the lock and then abruptly pulls it out. "Must be the wrong one," he says over his shoulder. He reaches into his pocket for another key chain.

Oh boy, she changed the locks. "Really, I don't want to see the house."

He tries two more keys with the same results, his jiggling of the key getting increasingly aggressive. I take a step backward on the walkway, thinking how awful it must feel to be locked out of your own house.

Ethan goes back to the first key. "I know this is the right one." He fiddles with the key for a few seconds and then yanks the key chain from the lock and fires it into the snowy bushes. "She changed the locks. She changed the damn locks." He kicks the door and then rests his head against it. "It's still my house," he whispers. "It's still my house."

I often have the most inappropriate response to stressful times: laughter. I fight hard to swallow the sound before it escapes, revealing me for the awkward thirty-something I am. Slowly, I walk up the stairs. When I reach him, I rub his back. He shakes my hand off his shoulder and rips his cell phone out of his pocket. Without even looking at me, he storms down the stairs, bumping me hard, and stomps toward the fence leading to the backyard. I watch him fumble with the latch while regretting my decision to come here. I should have listened to Luci. Damn. The gate swings open, and Ethan disappears behind it.

A few minutes later, I hear him yelling, "I still pay half the mortgage." His voice echoes around the house. "He gave it to us. Not to you."

I shouldn't be standing here listening to this. I grab a box from the porch and take it to the Jeep. I carry over another one. "I'm not talking about it anymore, Leah. The lawyers can figure it out." His voice breaks with emotion. Then, much louder, "I said I'm not talking about it anymore." A few seconds later, "I'm hanging up now." He's quiet for a minute, and then in a chilling voice, "You're going to be so sorry, Leah."

The yard is silent except for the sound of melting snow dripping off the roof and onto the stairway. I have loaded three of five boxes when Ethan appears at the fence, a golden retriever with a blue Patriots bandanna around its neck next to him. I slowly approach the gate. The dog jumps up on me and licks my face. "Easy, buddy," Ethan says, grabbing the dog by its collar. "Gina, this is Brady. Brady, Gina." The dog barks at me, and I grab Ethan's arm, pulling him in front of me.

Ethan laughs. "Are you afraid of him?" *Afraid* is not the right word. I am terrified. "He won't hurt you. I promise." Ethan lifts Brady's paw and places it in my hand. "Nice to meet you, Gina," he grumbles. Despite his joke, his clenched jaw and fist reveal that he is still furious.

Cautiously, I pet the dog. He looks up at me with warm, friendly eyes. *There's nothing to be afraid of,* he seems to be saying. I pet him for a few minutes, and then Ethan kneels in the snow and hugs him. "I miss you so much, buddy," he whispers into the dog's neck with more tenderness than he has ever spoken with to me. He continues hugging Brady. I feel like they should be alone so I walk toward the house.

When I get to the porch, I hear Ethan saying good-bye. A moment later, he is next to me. We grab the remaining boxes and load them into the Jeep. Ethan stares at the house for a few moments before climbing into the driver's seat. He puts the key in the ignition and throws the car into Reverse without saying a word.

"Are you all right?" I ask as he backs out of the driveway.

He slams on the brakes, puts the car in Park, and opens his door. "I'll be right back."

He disappears behind the house again. I wonder what he's doing back there and think about Luci saying how her divorce was the worst time of her life, how she did things she regretted. A few minutes later, the gate swings open and Brady comes bounding out with Ethan trailing him. Ethan opens the Jeep's back door, and Brady leaps in. Ethan shuts the back door and climbs back into the driver's seat.

"What's going on?" I ask.

"What do you think?" Ethan snaps as he backs out of the driveway at breakneck speed.

"You're stealing Brady?"

His usual beautiful blue eyes are icy. "He's my dog. I'm not stealing him, Lee—" He stops to exhale.

"Did you tell Leah that you're taking him?"

"Drop it, Gina. He's my dog. I should have never left him here." Ethan steps on the brake at the stop sign at the end of his street. A car comes around the corner. The driver slows when she sees Ethan. She waves. He glares at her and then peels out onto the next street.

"Who was that?" I ask.

"Leah's tramp of a friend, Karen. She's probably going to check on Brady."

"What's going to happen when she finds out he's not there? You'd better tell Leah you took him."

Ethan takes a look at Brady in the rearview. "No way."

"Ethan . . ."

He pounds the steering wheel with his fist. "She gets the house, she gets our friends. I get the dog."

I jump at the sound of his fist hitting the steering wheel. "I just don't want you to get in trouble."

"How am I going to get in trouble for taking my own dog? Just drop it."

"Is Jack going to be okay with you bringing home a dog?"

He pounds the steering wheel with his fist again. "Jesus, you're relentless. Let me worry about that."

We're more than three hours away from home. I fold my arms across my chest, lean back in my seat, and stare out the window. Maybe this is how Ethan was with Leah all the time. Maybe that's why she wants a divorce.

We drive without speaking, Brady's panting the only sound in the car. When we reach the main road, Ethan turns into a grocery store parking lot. He stops the Jeep and leans into the backseat to pet Brady's head. "Are you thirsty, boy?" He looks over at me. "Do you mind staying here with him? I'll be right back."

Brady's standing in the back between the driver and passenger seats. He nuzzles my arm with his head. I pet him silently, no longer afraid of the poor dog who's about to be embroiled in a custody battle. A police car pulls into the parking lot. The cruiser turns up the aisle where we are parked. I imagine Leah's friend Karen calling the police when she discovered Brady missing. I crouch lower in my seat. The police car slows as it approaches the Jeep and then stops in front of it. Brady barks, and I tell him to be quiet. I feel my heart pounding through my jacket. I look to the store, but there is no sign of Ethan.

A car parked a few spaces in front of us backs into the aisle. The police car pulls into the empty spot, and the driver gets out and walks into the store. I curse my overactive imagination.

A few minutes later, Ethan returns with a leash, dog bowl, dog food, and water. He also has a bag of chips and two sodas. He puts the bowl on the backseat and fills it with water. Brady immediately laps it up, and Ethan fills it again. The police officer comes out of the store. Ethan watches him and hurriedly climbs into the driver's seat.

He throws a bag of chips at me and puts the sodas in the cup holders. "Change of plans. We're not staying or stopping for lunch. I need to get Brady out of here." He glances at the cruiser. I swear his hands tremble as he starts the Jeep. We drive to the exit, the officer right behind us. Ethan turns right onto the road and checks his rearview mirror. The cruiser is still there. Ethan sits erect in the driver's seat with his hands locked in the ten and two positions on the steering wheel. We both appear to be holding our breath as we sneak glances into the mirror. *Hi, Mom and Dad, can you help? I'm in jail for stealing a dog. But, Mom, I did it with a man named Ethan. I finally met him.*

Three miles up the road, the blue flashing lights come on. "Damn," Ethan mutters as he pulls the Jeep to the side of the road. Will Luci pay my bail? The police car races by us. I let out a deep breath. Ethan wipes his forehead and cracks open his soda before pulling back out onto the road. "I thought maybe Karen reported Brady stolen," he says, and he laughs. I don't say anything. I just turn the radio on, tune it to a pop station, and sit back in my seat.

An hour later, Ethan's cell phone resting in the console between us rings. I see the caller ID says "Leah," though the ringtone is different from when she called last time. Ethan turns down the radio and smirks as he says hello.

A high-pitched scream comes from the cell phone. The only word I can make out is "Brady." Ethan's tone is nasty as he responds, "He's here with me." More words from Leah. I'm not certain, but I'm pretty sure she calls him a bastard. Ethan interrupts her, "You're irresponsible. I can't trust you with him. You've already proven how untrustworthy you are." Then, "You really want to go there?" He sounds incredulous. "You left him alone. He didn't even have water." More silence. "The lawyers will figure it out." Ethan disconnects the call and punches the steering wheel again. I jump in my seat. Brady barks.

Ethan reaches behind him into the backseat. "You're okay now, pal. You're with me." Brady keeps barking, and Ethan pulls to the side of the road. He puts Brady on a leash and walks him into the woods. Again, his cell phone blasts and Leah's name flashes across the screen. If I pick it up, I wonder what Leah would tell me about Ethan. Would she warn me to be careful? Tell me he has a terrible temper and a violent streak? His outbursts today are mild compared to what she's put up with for years? Or is this just him being pushed to his limit and at his absolute worst?

When Ethan returns to the Jeep, he notices the missed call and turns off his phone. He looks over at me. "I couldn't leave him there, Gina. She doesn't care about him. She goes out of town for the weekend and leaves him alone. She has a friend check on him once a day, and she thinks that's okay. He's better off with me. He really is. I love him." His voice breaks as he finishes speaking. I reach over to hug him.

He holds me tightly. "I'm sorry about today," he whispers. "This isn't how I thought it would go."

This is him at his worst, I decide, and I can help him through it.

Chapter 17

"The only reason he took the dog was to get back at his wife." Luci points her pen at me as she speaks.

I am powering on my computer. When the start-up tone ends, I respond, "He loves the dog and was worried about him."

Luci stares at me while clicking her pen. She has the same expression she often has when she's explaining to an Ivy League analyst the difference between *it's* and *its*. "Listen to me carefully, Gina." She stops clicking and again uses the pen as a pointer. "He took the dog as a way to get back at his wife. That was his only motivation."

"You don't even know him." I give her the angriest look I have, but she's not even looking at me anymore.

Her eyes are glued to her computer monitor while her fingers sprint across her keyboard. "I don't have to know him. I know that crazy in love often turns to plain crazy when it's unrequited, and kidnapping your wife's dog with your new girlfriend qualifies as crazy." She looks up across her desk at me, and her voice softens. "Sorry, but I can't stress this enough. You really shouldn't be dating him right now."

"Knock it off."

Luci flinches. She and I stare at each other across our desks. After several seconds she looks down at her keyboard and begins typing. How about that? I finally beat Luci Chin at a staring contest.

For the next hour, the only sounds are the clicking of Luci's and my fingernails on the keyboards and muffled voices from the mailroom next door. I occasionally steal glances at Luci, but she is concentrating very hard on whatever it is she's working on and doesn't notice, or maybe she's ignoring me? It's hard to tell. After almost ninety minutes of neither of us saying anything, which might be a record, Luci lets out a startled yell, "Oh my God." I look up. "Come here." She excitedly beckons me to her desk.

I roll in my chair to her side of the office and look at her monitor. I gasp when I see what's on her screen, an Internet dating site. "Are you doing online dating?"

She glares up at me. "I was looking for men named Ethan for you." She turns back to the screen and points to a thumbnail image. "But look who I found instead."

"Whom," I correct, leaning toward her computer and peering at the photo of a short man with short dark hair. It looks like Cooper Allen. Luci clicks on the photo. It triples in size. It's definitely Cooper. He's dressed in shorts and a T-shirt that has a number pinned to it. A sign that says 10K FOR KAYLEIGH hangs in the background. Cooper's user name, MobileMan, appears next to the photo, and below that is his age, thirty-seven. He's only a year older than I am? Impossible. I had him pegged at forty-five at the youngest.

Luci clicks on Cooper's user name, and more details appear. She points to his height, which is listed at five-ten. "Liar," she says. She's right. I'm five-four, and Cooper is only a little bit taller than I am. Luci, who is five-seven, towers over him, although she usually wears heels.

Luci reads Cooper's profile out loud:

"About Me: I have a stable career and am goal-oriented." She laughs. "Yeah, at TechVisions. Big whoop.

"I'm intelligent and can carry on meaningful conversations, but I can also be playful. There's nothing I enjoy more than a good laugh— well almost nothing."

Luci scrunches her nose. "Gross!"

"I like to play as hard as I work and when I'm not in the office you'll find me on my sailboat, mountain bike or cheering on one of the local sports teams. My darkest secret is that I love karaoke. Seriously. I've been told I do a mean Frank Sinatra.

"Cooper does it his way," Luci sings off-key.

"I could go on and on, but I think it's better if we meet so that you can make your own conclusions.

"About My Match: The woman I'm looking for has a down-to-earth attitude, high moral character, and easygoing personality. She

likes to laugh, even at herself. She can spell and has good command of the English language." Luci elbows me. *"She does not watch* Jersey Shore *or* The Bachelor. *She's attractive but is not obsessive about her looks. She loves to eat but keeps herself in shape. She doesn't get frazzled by setbacks and is prepared for life's little emergencies. She's looking to meet a great guy who wants a committed relationship.*

"Wow!" Luci screams, pointing to the About My Match section. "He may as well have said her name is Gina Rossi."

"Thank you," I say. "I am down-to-earth, easygoing, and intelligent, but I do watch *The Bachelor*, so I'm out."

Luci uses the cursor to highlight some of the text: *likes to laugh, even at herself; can spell and has good command of the English language; loves to eat but keeps herself in shape.* "Even if he doesn't realize it, he's describing you."

"Why is Cooper on a dating site? He has a girlfriend."

Luci shakes her head. "He definitely doesn't have a girlfriend."

"Monique," I say. "There's even a picture of her in his office."

"I've never noticed it." She clicks on the photo section. There is one other picture, Cooper sitting on a tan carpet with a girl who might be five and a boy who appears to be a little older. The Candy Land game board is spread out in front of them.

"How sweet is that?" I ask, and I swear to God, my eyes tear up.

Luckily, Luci doesn't notice. "Cooper Allen playing Candy Land. It's making my head hurt," she says.

She abruptly fumbles for the mouse and clicks off the page. I hear footsteps and then Jamie's voice. "What's making your head hurt?"

"The data in this report. Gina's helping me figure it out. I think we've got it now."

"You guys have to work faster," Jamie says. "The analysts are complaining about turnaround time."

"You spilled something." Luci points to a small brown spot on Jamie's white shirt.

I roll back to my desk and reach into the bottom drawer. "I have a detergent stick that will get that right out."

Jamie takes the stick from me. "You keep that in your desk?"

I nod while Luci says, "That's Gina. Prepared for life's little emergencies."

"Gina," Jamie says. "How are things going with Cooper?"

I feel my chest tighten. I look at Luci. She raises her eyebrows. "Umm, what do you mean?"

"Haven't you two been brainstorming ideas for improving turnaround time?" Jamie runs the detergent stick over the stain on his shirt.

"Oh, that." The tightness disappears. "We don't have a plan yet, but we're working on it. It's hard to find time to meet with Cooper's schedule."

Jamie hands back the stain remover. "You and Cooper have to get together and get to it."

Luci giggles. Jamie looks at her. "I was just saying the same thing."

Chapter 18

Brady's first week at Jack's has not gone well. On Monday, while Ethan and Jack were at work, he peed all over the living room rug. Tuesday night, Jack left a steak on the table while he went to the garage to get a beer; when he returned to the kitchen, he found the plate shattered on the floor and Brady in the corner gnawing what was left of the meat. "He's only allowed in my room and the garage now," Ethan says and then yawns.

I take a deep breath. "Maybe he'd be better off at Leah's?"

"No way." We are talking on the phone so I can't see Ethan's face, but I imagine he scowls when he says this. "It will get better. I hired a dog walker to take him out during the day while I'm at work. She starts tomorrow."

I immediately imagine a dowdy, middle-aged woman dressed in a long skirt and flannel shirt matted with dog hair. "What's her name?"

"Amber."

Definitely not a middle-aged woman, then. Probably a high-school or college girl. "How old is she?"

He sighs. "I don't know, Gina. Twenty-something, I guess." In the background I hear Brady bark. "Settle down, buddy." Ethan's tone is much gentler than the one he just had with me. "What I do know is that Brady liked Amber and Amber liked Brady. Right, buddy?" Brady barks again.

"Did Brady like me?" The question pops out of my mouth before I realize what I'm saying. I immediately regret asking it because it makes me sound so needy. On the other hand, it's Thursday, and I haven't seen Ethan since Saturday so I'm feeling a bit insecure.

Ethan laughs. "Oh yeah. He told me he really wants to see you again. In fact, he suggested I cook for you on Saturday night."

"I knew I liked that dog."

It's there waiting in my in-box when I wake up Friday morning, sandwiched between spam from Ann Taylor and CareerBuilder, an e-mail from Neesha. My hand trembles as I click on her name. The first thing I notice is that her message is lengthy. This makes me smile, remembering how much she loved to talk.

> *Gina Rossi!!*
>
> *How wonderful to hear from you. I too have thought of you so many times through the years, wondering how in the world we ever lost touch. For crying out loud, we were BFFs before anyone knew what BFFs were!*
>
> *Thank you for the kind words about Ajee. She would have loved that you referred to her as enchanting, but my husband, Ashley, and I had a good laugh over that. She was one of a kind, and we all miss her terribly.*
>
> *In typical Ajee fashion, she made a ludicrous dying request that I promised to honor. Ready for this? She made me swear that I would spread her ashes in the yard of our old house on Towering Heights Lane. I have no idea how I'm going to be able to do this. I was going to ask the people who live in the house now for permission, but Ashley doesn't think that's a good idea because they will think it's creepy. He thinks I should just sneak into their backyard and do it. Can you imagine if they catch me? Sorry to bother you, I'm just fertilizing your backyard with my grandmother's remains.*
>
> *Of course, I've considered not honoring her request, but Ashley says I have to. A promise is a promise after all, and Ajee said she'd haunt me if I didn't comply. Knowing her, she'd find a way to pull that off.*
>
> *So, I plan to come to Westham in the spring and spread Ajee's ashes in the yard of 18 Towering Heights Lane. Hope-*

fully, you will be my coconspirator? I will be in touch with the exact dates of my visit. I can't wait to see you and catch up.

I have two children. My son is Ashley Junior, we call him AJ. He's four, and his sister Jayda just turned eight. They are precious! I've attached a photo of them with Ashley so you can see everyone.

Looking forward to catching up!

Love, Neesha

PS: You will see Ashley looks nothing like Josh Levine, but he does look a bit like Johnny Depp, yes?

I read the message again. As I do, I can clearly hear Neesha's fourteen-year-old voice in my head. I picture Ajee in her sari, and I wonder why in the world she would want to spend eternity on Towering Heights Lane.

I reread the part about Neesha's family. She named her daughter after her mother. I close my eyes. A memory of Neesha's mom flashes through my mind. She was wearing tan shorts, a green tank top, and flip-flops, her long black hair was tied in a loose ponytail, and she held a fork like it was a microphone, dancing around the Patels' porch singing "I Will Survive." She bowed when she finished. Neesha and I were sitting under the umbrella at the patio table on the other side of the porch. We clapped and yelled, "Again, again."

"Please, no." Dr. Patel laughed as he said this. He was sitting with us under the umbrella, and he got up to flip the burgers on the grill, stopping to kiss Neesha's mom as he walked by. Neesha and I were probably five at the time, which would have made Mrs. Patel thirty-three. She'd die less than two years later from breast cancer at an age younger than I am today. A shiver runs up and down my spine as I click on the attachment to look at the picture of Neesha's husband and kids.

The first thing I notice is a little girl, with long black hair, uneven bangs, and a gap-toothed smile. I swear I'm looking at Neesha when she was eight. Next to the girl is a handsome, dark-haired man with his arm around her shoulders. He does look like Johnny Depp. The man's other arm is around a small boy, who has his eyes. They are all sitting on a bench, palm trees in the background. I imagine Neesha standing in front of the bench, taking the picture. Well, good for her. She deserves this beautiful family.

I know that forwarding the picture to my mother will probably result in another invite to Florida to meet Mrs. Bonnano's son or in a lecture about how I've ruined my life, but I can't help myself. My mother will be thrilled to see a picture of Neesha's daughter and learn that her name is Jayda. My mom and Mrs. Patel were best friends. Through the years my mother often remarked how much she missed Neesha's mother. In fact, sometimes I think part of my mother's annoyance with Ajee was that Ajee's presence was a constant reminder that Neesha's mother was never coming back.

A few seconds after I send the message to my mother, she responds: *"Neesha's children are beautiful. Jayda would be so proud."* Her next line is coated in sarcasm. *"So, Neesha's returning to Towering Heights Lane. Maybe you'll meet Ethan soon."*

Chapter 19

My GPS leads me off the highway and onto a long, winding back road. "Turn right on Maple Avenue," the male voice instructs. He has an Australian accent. I named him Jonah and imagine he is over six feet tall with bulging biceps and six-pack abs. He has a healthy tan, sun-streaked sandy brown hair, gorgeous blue eyes like Ethan's, and unlike Ethan, a toothpaste-ad killer smile. Even though Jonah's good-looking enough to be a movie star, he's really smart. He's Australia's top architect. When he's not working, he loves to ride the waves. Someday I'm going Down Under, and he's going to give me surfing lessons. We'll have a torrid affair. He'll fall in love and beg me not to leave, but of course, I'll have to.

I told Luci about this fantasy once. She turned sideways in the passenger seat and pushed her Maui Jims off her eyes and back into her hair. Her green eyes studying me, squinting. "Gina, we're signing you up for online dating, stat." Of course, I refused. I still can't believe Cooper is using an online dating site. The whole idea of posting a profile with a picture and contact information for any weirdo to see is just too creepy. I'd probably end up living my last days on a mattress in a basement, handcuffed to a pipe while some three-hundred-pound sociopath who hasn't bathed since George Bush left the White House has his way with me.

"Turn left on Marsh Street," Jonah instructs. "In point seven miles, turn right on Seaside Avenue." I pass a general store, the parking lot empty now. I imagine coming here with Ethan in the summer. We'll have to fight for a parking space and wait in line to buy our sandwiches, ice-cold drinks, and other provisions for a long, relaxing day at the shore. I see myself putting our items down on the counter in front of the register, while on my left hand a shiny pear-shaped diamond sparkles.

"Approaching right turn." I flip on my blinker and turn onto the narrow street where Ethan lives with Jack. I pass a row of small Capes, most of them gray. "You have reached your destination," Jonah says.

I park next to a black Ford Fusion and study Jack's house for a moment. The only things distinguishing it from the homes around it are the painted yellow clapboard and the pole proudly flying a Boston Celtics flag at the end of the gravel driveway. I get out of the car and head toward the front door, feeling the stones crunch under my boots. In the distance, I hear the sound of waves crashing. This place couldn't be any more different from the mountainside log cabin Ethan shared with Leah.

I reach the front door and ring the bell. I hear barking from the garage. "Quiet, Brady," a male voice snarls. The door swings open. A basketball-player-tall man with bright red hair stands on the other side. He does a double take and his mouth gapes open when he sees me. I wonder if I have something smeared on my face or if my hair has frizzed so much it now looks like a Brillo Pad. That happens sometimes no matter how long I spend straightening it. The man says nothing, just stands there looking at me like maybe he's never seen a female before. "You must be Jack," I finally say through the storm door separating us.

He blinks twice and nods. "And you must be Gina." He pushes the door open and steps to the side for me to enter. "Ethan's in the kitchen." He points upstairs. "Take your shoes off before heading up."

He stands watching me with his arms folded across his chest as I balance myself on the railing and pull off my boots. He's giving me the heebie-jeebies the way he's studying me so intently. *What are you looking at?* I scream inside my head. When I finish taking off my boots, he gestures with his arm for me to climb the stairs first. Is it ridiculous that I'm a little afraid to turn my back on him? We get to the top of the stairs. It smells delicious up here, like chicken potpie. Jack takes my coat and disappears to a closet down the hall.

Ethan emerges from the kitchen, smiling. "You made it." He gathers me in his arms, kisses me hello, and hugs me tightly. His scent, a combination of sawdust and pine, is already familiar. Jack returns, wearing a jacket himself now. Good, he's leaving. Only, he doesn't. He stands there watching Ethan and me embrace, so I pull away.

Ethan follows my gaze to Jack. "Have a good night."

Jack doesn't answer, just stands there shaking his head.

"What gives?" Ethan asks.

"You're something else, man," Jack says.

"What did I do now? Don't tell me you're still pissed about Brady?" Before Jack answers, a buzzer sounds. Ethan shrugs and heads back to the kitchen.

I start to follow him, but Jack grabs my arm, his hand tightly wrapped around my elbow, his fingernails digging into my sweater. He tilts his head toward the living room. "Come with me. I want to show you something before I take off."

Something about the way he says it conjures up memories of my parents sitting me down to talk in the days after Matthew Colby disappeared. "Don't ever go anywhere with a stranger," my father warned.

Jack must sense my hesitation. He loosens his grip on my elbow. "It will just take a second." He guides me toward the couch and tells me to sit. When I do, he walks across the room to a built-in bookcase, pulls a stack of photos off one of the shelves, and flips through them. He finds the one he wants and heads back toward me.

He sits down next to me and hands me a picture of Ethan on a motorcycle with a woman standing next to him holding a helmet. I take a deep breath while I study the photograph. Ethan's looking at the woman with a huge grin, seemingly unaware that the picture is being taken. She, on the other hand, seems oblivious that Ethan is there. She's looking directly into the camera with an impatient expression. She has long dark hair, big brown eyes, and an olive complexion. I can't stop staring at her. Jack leans forward so that he can see my face. "Leah?" I ask, my voice shaky.

"So you see the resemblance."

"She's a good-looking woman." I force myself to laugh, but I'm remembering when Ethan and I first met, how he did the same double take Jack did. Is this why he's dating me, because I look like his soon-to-be ex-wife?

"When I first opened the door, I thought you were Leah coming to reclaim Brady," Jack says.

"Why did you show me this?"

He cracks his knuckles and leans back on the couch. "Ethan's a good guy. He's like a brother to me, but this thing with Leah. It's got him all messed up."

Ethan enters the room, dish towel in hand. He makes a sweeping gesture with it. "Dinner is ser—" He stops speaking when he notices the photo in my hand. He crosses the room in two giant steps and peers down at the picture. "Oh man, why did you drag that out?"

"The resemblance is uncanny," Jack answers. "I wanted Gina to see."

"You're out of your mind." He takes the picture from me. I swear he caresses the image of Leah with his index finger. "They look nothing alike."

"Come on, man."

"I don't see it," Ethan snaps. Maybe it wasn't a caress. Maybe he was trying to erase her.

"You're full of it," Jack says.

"We have the same coloring," I say. It's an attempt to stop the hostility from escalating, because even if Ethan doesn't see it, his soon-to-be ex-wife could be my twin, the sister I always wanted. How could he not see it?

"Whatever." Ethan tosses the photo on the coffee table. "Let's go before dinner gets cold." He heads back into the kitchen without waiting for me.

I stand. Jack gets up, too. "Hey," he says, "Leah really screwed him over. He's still fragile." He pauses, pulls his keys from his coat pocket. "Just be careful."

I walk into the kitchen wondering what I'm supposed to be careful of.

At dinner, Ethan is the perfect host. He instructs me to sit, pours me a glass of white wine, and serves me a bowl filled with chicken potpie with a buttery, golden-brown, flaky crust and a steaming hot filling of creamy potatoes, large chunks of chicken, and soft carrots. He leans across the table toward me, waiting for me to take a bite. "So, what do you think?" His face is serious, and his fingers drum the table as he waits for me to respond.

"It's delicious." The drumming stops, and he smiles, practically breaking my heart. No one has ever wanted my approval so badly before.

He hands me a piece of corn bread. "Try this. Tell me what you taste."

I bite into the spongy yellow bread. My throat burns as I swallow. "Jalapeño."

"My secret ingredient." He winks. I can't help myself. I lean across the table and kiss him.

By the time the meal is over, we've killed off half the pie, the pan of bread, the entire bottle of wine, and most of another.

"Where did you learn to cook?" I ask.

He laughs. "It was a matter of survival. Leah's idea of cooking is slapping peanut butter and jelly on burnt toast."

After his reaction in the living room, I've been careful not to mention her or the picture, but since he brought her up, I figure she's fair game now. "So, do you really not see a resemblance between me and Leah?"

"A lot of women have long dark hair and brown eyes, Gina." He picks up his plate and takes it to the sink. I do the same.

"It's more than that," I say as he rinses his plate.

He yanks on the handle of the faucet to shut the water off. "Believe me, Gina, you're nothing alike." I can't tell if it's a good thing, the way he says it. We work in silence. When the kitchen is clean, he wraps his arms around me. "Sorry. Leah's hundreds of miles away, and she's still screwing up my life. Believe me, you're nothing alike. You're so much prettier than she is." He kisses me softly, and my body responds the same way it always does. It's not unusual for men to be attracted to a certain type of woman, I think, as I kiss him back. Ethan's type is dark hair, brown eyes, and olive skin. No different from me liking men with blue eyes and dark hair. He's backed me against the counter, and his kisses are rougher now. He whispers again as his fingers glide down my body unfastening buttons, "And so much sexier." I feel the counter's hard edge cutting into my back as Ethan's body presses into mine. By the time he lifts me and carries me into his room, I've forgotten all about the picture of Leah.

Chapter 20

The host at the Italian restaurant uses short, clipped sentences when explaining that after an hour, she gave our table away because she assumed we weren't coming. We can clearly see two empty tables, but she insists we will have to wait at least thirty minutes before being seated. Ethan and I decide to have a drink at the bar, which has more unoccupied than occupied stools.

It's my fault we're late. Well, really, it's because of the effect Ethan has on me. Ever since that weekend he cooked me dinner. It's like he's shaken loose years of repressed longings and cracked the foundation of my self-restraint. Now each time I see him, a tsunami of uncontrollable desire rushes over me. We've spent the night together a dozen times since then, and each time is better than the last. I can tell he enjoys the power he has over me because he prolongs the foreplay until I'm pleading, arching my back so high a double-decker bus could drive underneath.

When he came to pick me up tonight, he gave me that suggestive smile before kissing me hello. That's all it took. I was reaching for the button fly of his Levi's. He pushed my hand away, laughing. "Slow down, Speed Racer. We've got dinner reservations." But as he said it, he was sliding one hand under my skirt while pushing me against the refrigerator with the other.

Now, seated at the bar with drinks in front of us, he uses his index finger to trace small circles on my thigh, each inching higher than the last. He leans toward me so that his breath is hot on my ear. "Do you think you can make it through dinner?" His voice is low, intimate.

"Can you?"

"We could just go back to your place." Before he even gets all the words out, I'm off the bar stool putting on my coat. "You're so easy, Rossi." He drains the last of his beer from his mug and stands.

I brush the back of my hand near his inner thigh and can feel that he wants out of here as much as I do. "And you're not?"

As we make our way to the door, the hostess calls Ethan's name. He looks at me. I shrug. I will show him I have self-restraint. I will show myself I have self-restraint. "We came all this way."

"So unfair," he says.

"I'll make it up to you later." I try to give a suggestive smile, but I'm sure it just comes off as goofy.

He pouts as the hostess leads us to our seats. It's the worse of the two tables that have been empty since we arrived, so close to the table next to it that Ethan and I both feel compelled to greet the elderly couple sitting there. They are each eating big bowls of pasta, and all I can smell is garlic.

The hostess leaves us with menus and a wine list. "Do you want to share a bottle?" I ask.

Ethan shrugs.

"You're not going to pout all through dinner?"

"I might," he says.

"I'll make it up to you later tonight, and then again even later. And then again in the morning."

This elicits a smile from him. "Let's get some Chianti."

I don't have to look at the menu to know I will get the chicken parmigiana. It's pretty much what I always get at Italian restaurants. Ethan figures that I am the expert on all things Italian and decides he will get the chicken parm as well.

A waiter stops by with bread. Ethan orders our wine and our dinners. I like it that he orders for me. I excuse myself to go to the restroom. As I get up, Ethan grabs my wrist and whispers, "You can make it up to me now. I'm right behind you." He gives me that same suggestive smile he gave me when he came to pick me up tonight.

I wind my way to the back of the restaurant wondering if he's serious. Part of me hopes that he is; the other part disgusted that I have this hope. The restroom, a single room with a toilet and sink, is in a hallway by a back door. We could pull it off here, I think, as I enter and lock the door behind me. I take my time in the room, even touching up my makeup. Finally, there is a knock on the door. My heart stops. He can't really think I would do it here?

"Are you almost done in there?" It's a woman's voice. I should be relieved, but all I feel is disappointed.

I push open the door. It's the old lady from the table next to us. "It's all yours."

What's happening to me? Was I really just considering having sex in a public restroom? It's like I have morphed into a teenage boy. Earlier today, I was sitting next to Cooper Allen in a meeting. His leg accidentally brushed against mine under the table and that got me wondering what kind of lover Cooper would be.

He's methodical with his analysis, examining every single possibility before making a recommendation. I imagined him applying the same methodology when exploring his partner's body, determined to find every spot that mattered. Unlike the other analysts at TechVisions, Cooper never loses his temper. He always has to be in control. That probably means he prefers giving to receiving. Then, of course, Cooper is the company's golden boy, the stereotypical overachiever. This got me thinking Cooper wouldn't be satisfied unless his partner had multiple orgasms. And then I couldn't help but imagine me as that partner, and that made me snap out of it. Fantasizing about TechVisions's top revenue generator. Lord, help me.

Back at the table, Ethan sips wine while talking to the old man next to him. I take my seat, and the man shifts his gaze to me. "You have to be Italian."

I tell him that I am, and he asks me if I speak the language. I answer him in Italian.

"It's rare for people of your generation to speak it. How did you learn?" His speech is much faster than it was in English, and it takes me a moment to form the words to answer. Finally, I tell him that when my grandparents were alive, they would only speak to me in their native tongue.

He compliments me on my mastery of the language.

Ethan waves his hand in front of my face. "What are you two talking about?"

The man laughs. "I told her she is very beautiful and you are lucky to have her."

Ethan grins and reaches for my hand. "I know."

The woman returns to the table, and the man turns his attention to her.

"I was just about to join you," Ethan says, "but she got up." He tilts his head in the direction of the old woman. I can't believe it. He's serious. He thought I would do it in a public restroom. He thinks I'm that kind of girl.

The waiter arrives with our food. "Let me feed you a bit of mine, and then you can feed me a bite of yours," Ethan says.

"But we ordered the same thing."

"So." He cuts a piece of chicken. His eyes lock with mine as he slides his fork into my mouth. I chew, and he continues to stare. Maybe this is supposed to be sexy? I laugh. He laughs, too. "My turn." I feed him.

A few minutes later the waiter approaches the table next to us with a piece of tiramisu that the couple shares. The man hands the woman a small gift-wrapped package. I watch her open the box and extract a pair of pearl earrings. "It's our forty-eighth anniversary," the woman says to us.

I salute her with my wineglass. "Congratulations."

I look at the man. "We're very lucky. It's rare for marriages to last so long these days," he says.

Ethan snickers and refills his wineglass. He doesn't notice my glass is empty, so after he puts down the bottle, I pick it up.

"How long have you been married?" the woman asks.

I tell her that we're not married, but Ethan speaks at the same exact time and says, "Seventeen years."

I look at him. He immediately looks down. "Sorry," he mumbles.

The woman and man both look at us with raised eyebrows. "I'm married. She's not," Ethan finally says. His words may as well be a kick to my stomach the way they leave me gasping for my breath. The old couple exchanges a glance. I can tell they have it all wrong.

"He's getting a divorce."

The couple, who was looking at me so kindly before, is now looking at me like they walked in on Ethan and me in the restroom. The woman shakes her head. I look to Ethan for help, but he's busy trying to twirl the fettuccini around his fork and lost in his own thoughts.

"No, really. He was in—"

The man cuts me off. "It's none of our business." He signals to the waiter for the check.

The wife studies me for a moment. "*Sfasciafamiglie. Vergognati*," she mumbles.

The man tries to shush her, but she keeps talking. Frantically, he says, "She speaks Italian." The woman abruptly stops speaking, but it's too late. I heard the names she called me. They pay the check in silence and hurriedly put on their coats.

Ethan, still busy trying to figure out how to twirl the pasta around his fork, finally looks up. "I'm so sorry, Gina. It just slipped out. I wasn't thinking."

"That woman just called me a homewrecker."

He glances toward the door the couple just walked through. "I didn't hear her say that."

"She said it in Italian."

"It makes no sense that she would say that. Are you sure you understood her?" He twirls more fettuccini around his fork.

"Yes, I'm sure. She said it because you told her you were married."

The fettuccini uncoils, and he drops his fork.

"Do you still consider yourself married?"

Ethan picks up his napkin and twists it. "I don't know. I guess technically I am until the divorce is finalized." He shrugs.

Oh God, I am that kind of girl. I'm sleeping with a married man. "I shouldn't be dating you. I should be encouraging you to work things out with Leah."

He laughs. "Leah doesn't want to work things out."

"Do you?"

He hesitates. "There's no chance for that." He picks up his fork, and this time instead of twirling the pasta, he cuts it with a knife.

I've barely touched my meal, but I can't take another bite. I push my plate away. Ethan watches me. "Come on, don't let what that woman said ruin your dinner. It's not even true."

I want to tell him it's not the woman who has ruined dinner, but him. Instead, I say nothing.

Chapter 21

My cell phone buzzes on my desk. It's a text from Ethan. The second one he's sent today. I ignored the first. It came at seven thirty this morning and read, *"How long r u going 2 b mad?"* This one simply says, *"Well?"* He called six times yesterday; twice he left messages. His first was carefree: "Hey, why don't you drive down here tonight? I miss you." Four hours later, when I still hadn't returned his call, he tried again: "I can spend the night at your place, but Brady has to come. Is that okay?"

Brady can come, but you can't. That's how I wanted to reply, so instead I said nothing. I can't forget the way that old woman looked at me with disgust when she found out Ethan was married. I can still see the despair on his face and the hurt in his voice when we were talking about whether he wanted to work things out with Leah.

My office phone rings. I can tell by the ringtone that it's an outside call, so I let it go to voice mail. Luci has been in meetings all morning, but she's back at her desk now. She stands and retrieves her coat from the back of the door and then tosses me mine. "We're going to an early lunch so you can tell me what's going on with Ethan."

"What do you mean?" I slip my arms into my coat's sleeves. Luci is digging through her purse for her keys, but she looks up long enough to give me a nasty look that says, *Duh!*

As we cut through the parking lot to Luci's car, we pass Cooper walking toward the building. He has a laptop bag flung over one shoulder and a briefcase over the other. "Gina, I need to talk to you," he says.

Luci answers for me. "Now's not a good time, Coop. We're going to lunch." She walks by him, but I stop.

"It's Cooper, Luci. Not Coop."

She waves her hand to dismiss him. "It's a dumb name." Luci is at her car now, and she opens the driver's side door.

Cooper yells after her, "Yeah, well, Luci Chin is a dumb name for an Irish girl." I laugh. Cooper glances at me, and he laughs, as well. Luci gives us the finger, which causes us both to laugh harder. Soon, we are hunched over holding our stomachs and gasping for breath. Cooper pulls himself together first. "Are you going to get dim sum?" he asks, causing the laughter to start again.

Luci beeps and beckons for me to move it. "I'll call you when we get back from lunch," I say to Cooper.

"Seriously, where are you going?"

"Umm, I think Last Chance."

"Would you mind bringing me back a turkey club with sweet potato fries?" He unzips his briefcase and reaches inside it for his wallet. "Ask them to make the bacon extra crispy." Luci beeps again.

"I got it." I walk away before Cooper pulls out his money. When I get to Luci's car, I sneak a glance back at him. He's standing in the spot I left him looking at me. I wave, and he waves back.

When I slide into the car, Luci turns the radio off. "What was so funny?"

I shrug. "I guess your name."

She turns sideways. "Even if the two of you don't realize it, there's something going on between you."

"He has a girlfriend," I say.

"Interesting that you didn't say you have a boyfriend." She backs out of the parking space and heads for the row Cooper is now walking down. "He has a nice ass," she says. She beeps and blows him a kiss while I check out his butt. She's right.

Luci told the waitress she did not want fries with her chicken sandwich so now she's helping herself to mine. She picks up the ketchup, and I have to knock her arm away from my plate.

"I never heard of someone not liking ketchup before," she says.

She squirts some onto her plate and moves a handful of fries from my dish to hers. "So, what did Ethan say to the couple at the restaurant that got you so mad?"

I've already told her exactly what he said, but she was distracted by a middle-aged and elderly woman being seated at the next table. The older woman was hunched over the walker she was using, and the younger woman kept asking, "Mom, are you all right?" When the older woman finally made it to her chair she said, "I'm ninety-two years old. I'm as good as I can be."

"God, don't let me live to be ninety," Luci whispered.

"Why?" I asked. "That woman is fine. She's enjoying a lunch out with her daughter."

Luci glared at me and changed the subject back to Ethan. So now I repeat that the couple asked how long we'd been married and he answered seventeen years.

"Seventeen years! How old is he?"

"He's thirty-seven."

Luci counts on her fingers.

"Twenty," I say before she figures it out. "He got married when he was twenty."

"That's nuts." She takes the remaining fries from my plate.

"I don't know, after seeing the picture of Leah and then . . ."

"Leah, the ex-wife." Luci is talking with her mouth open, and I can see the red mush from the mixture of french fries and ketchup. "You didn't tell me you saw a picture of her. Where was it? I hope it wasn't on his nightstand because that would be bad. Really bad."

I stir the ice in my cup with my straw. "It was in a stack of pictures in the living room. His roommate showed it to me." The waitress stops by our table to ask if we'd like anything else. I order Cooper's turkey club to go.

"Who's that for?" Luci asks as the waitress walks away. Then she corrects herself before I can. "For whom is that?"

"Cooper."

She raises her eyebrows.

"Leah looks a lot like me."

"Looks like you how?"

"If you looked at her picture quickly, you'd think it was me."

Luci leans back in her chair. "That's creepy."

I nod and look down.

"Gina, Ethan was married for seventeen years. He isn't even divorced yet. He has no business dating. Believe me when I tell you he has no idea what he's doing right now."

I pull my glass closer and take a long pull on my straw. "Why did you and Kip get divorced?"

Luci studies me for a moment without saying anything. She looks over at the old woman and her daughter and then slowly turns back to me. "Kip wasn't sure if he wanted kids, and we agreed to wait another year or so before making a final decision." She picks up her napkin from her lap and wipes her mouth. "I got scared my window of opportunity was closing so I went off the pill without telling him. I got pregnant a lot faster than I thought I would. I really thought he'd be excited, but when I told him, he flipped out."

"What? When were you pregnant?"

She shakes her head. "I miscarried the day after I told him. How's that for bad timing?"

"Luci, I'm so sorry. I had no idea." I am a failure as a friend. How could I not notice that something so monumental was going on?

She swipes the area under her eye with her index finger. "He said he could never trust me again, and that was that."

The waitress comes with Cooper's meal and the bill. I hand her my credit card.

"It took me a long time to get over my divorce, Gina. Hell, I'm not even sure I'm over it now, and I wasn't married half as long as Ethan." She stands and walks off toward the restrooms. She returns a few minutes later as I'm signing the receipt. "I hope you're going to make Cooper pay for his meal," she says. "He makes at least double, probably triple what we do."

Cooper's door is shut when I get to his office so I knock and peek through the long window next to it. He motions for me to come in and stands as I enter.

"How much do I owe you?" he asks, reaching for the briefcase on the corner of his desk.

"My treat."

He has already pulled out his wallet. "Well, thank you." He swallows hard and slides the wallet back into his briefcase. "I'll take you out sometime."

"It's not necessary."

He squeezes his hands together. "Right."

"What was it that you wanted to talk to me about?"

He sits and points to the guest chair. "We haven't come up with any recommendations for speeding up editing, and I'm starting to hear about it."

"You've cancelled our last three meetings." It comes out sounding defensive.

"I know it's my fault." The amount of eye contact he is suddenly making with me is really uncomfortable. I look down. "The problem is, I'm usually straight out during the day." He pauses to clear his throat. "Do you have any time after work one night?"

The last thing I want to do is work overtime, but this is Mr. TechVisions I'm talking to. He'd never understand that. "I guess so."

Cooper laughs. "Don't sound so enthusiastic."

I shrug.

"How about tomorrow night?"

"I guess we should get it over with."

He laughs again. "I'll be at a client site, but I'll call you to figure out where to meet. It will be fun." I stare blankly at him. "You'll see."

When I get home from work, Ethan's Jeep is parked in my space. I pull in behind him and brace myself for an argument. I slowly get out of my car. I look inside his vehicle and see that it's empty. I walk around to the back of the house to get to my apartment, and he's sitting on the wooden staircase. He's looking down at a spot on his jeans; one hand is tucked inside the pocket of his brown leather jacket and the other clutches a single red rose. My heart softens just a little. He must hear my shoes clicking on the flagstone walkway because he looks up. Our eyes meet. He smiles, stands, and descends the stairway to meet me at the bottom. He doesn't say anything. He just wraps his arms around me and nestles his head onto my shoulder. "I'm sorry, Gina," he whispers after several seconds. "I don't want to work things out with Leah. I want to make things work with you, and I never should have told that couple I was married." I hold him just as tightly, needing to believe him and wishing Ajee had warned me it would be this hard. "Sometimes I'm going to say and do stupid things," he continues, "but that doesn't mean that I don't love you."

I stiffen and pull away from him. "What did you just say?"

He hands me the rose, puts his hands on my shoulders, and looks directly in my eyes. "I love you."

I've been fantasizing about a man named Ethan saying those words to me ever since Ajee made her prediction. In all my fantasies,

I always say, "I love you more." Here in the actual moment, though, I can't bring myself to say those words because they wouldn't be true, not yet anyway. Instead, I say nothing and just stand there grinning like a fool.

It doesn't surprise me at all that the morning after Ethan tells me he loves me, I hear from Neesha again. It's another sign from Ajee indicating her third predictions are about to come true.

Hello old friend!
I've scheduled my trip to Westham. I'll be there next Wednesday, April 17. I want to let you know that I sent Ajee's ashes ahead to your address. I don't trust the airlines with them. Thank you for suggesting I stay with you during my visit. I hope you meant it, because I'm going to take you up on it. It will give us more time to catch up.
Can't wait to see you,
Neesha

Chapter 22

Jesus, Mary, and Joseph. What have I gotten myself into? Cooper Allen is standing on my landing with an overnight bag. What exactly does he think is going to happen on this work date? It's not even like I'm cooking for him. We're walking to Salvatore's to brainstorm ways to speed up the editing process. On second thought, maybe this will take all night, or several nights.

I push open the screen door. He steps inside and immediately loosens his tie. "I've got to get out of this monkey suit," he groans. "Where can I change?"

He's already removed his suit jacket, and now he's unbuttoning his shirt. I spy his dark chest hair. Damn, it's incredibly sexy. "Not here!" I point to the bathroom. He rushes by me like he has Montezuma's revenge.

I pace my kitchen floor trying hard not to think of him stripping down in my bathroom. A few minutes later he reappears wearing wind pants, a Dartmouth College hooded sweatshirt, and sneakers. His transformation from uptight executive to frat boy is more pronounced than Clark Kent's change into Superman. There's a masculine ruggedness about him when he's dressed like this. I can't stop staring. "What?" he says.

My mouth gapes open. Clearly I can't tell him what I'm thinking, so instead I say, "I feel overdressed now. I should change." I'm still wearing the same outfit I wore to work: a black skirt that rests just above my knees, a red V-neck sweater, and high black boots.

"Don't change. You look great." His voice has the same authoritative tone it does at work, but I notice his ear tips are bright red.

"Luci picked out this outfit," I blurt out. Almost thirty-seven years old, and I still haven't learned how to accept a compliment. Good Lord.

Cooper takes a few steps into the living room and slowly rotates his head as his eyes scan my apartment. "This isn't how I imagined your place." He shoves his hands into the pockets of his wind pants.

My stomach muscles contract. Cooper has spent time imagining my place? "What did you think it would be like?"

He squints. I imagine he's trying to bring up an image in his head. "I figured you'd be in the suburbs, a town house or a condo." He eyes my bare white walls and tan leather couch. "Bright colors, lots of artwork. Big throw pillows. Just a lot more homey."

I suddenly see my sterile living space through his eyes. I'm embarrassed. I never made an effort to decorate the place because from the time I moved in more than a decade ago, I always believed I was just days away from meeting Ethan and moving into his spacious domicile. It never occurred to me that Ethan would be homeless, relying on the kindness of an old friend for a place to sleep each night.

"Where do you live?" I ask.

"Westham."

"No, you don't." I feel the muscles in my stomach squeeze tighter.

"It's actually a nice town," he says defensively.

"I grew up there. My parents still live there."

"You're kidding. What street?"

"Towering Heights Lane."

He lifts his hand mimicking an airplane taking off. "When I'm feeling ambitious, it's on my jogging route. I'm on Birmingham Circle."

My face flushes. "That's where my first boyfriend lived. Two Birmingham Circle. He broke up with me days before the prom because I wouldn't sleep with him." Oh. My. God. I can't believe I just told Cooper Allen I wouldn't put out in high school.

Cooper looks down at the floor, and then his eyes float back to mine. "He sounds like a jerk." There's a beat of silence, but then he continues, "I asked Mary Jane Lucas to my prom. She said she wanted to go with someone taller so I didn't go." He shrugs.

As Cooper and I approach Salvatore's, two women rush by and enter the restaurant. Although we are right behind them, they don't bother to hold open the door, and it slams on Cooper's face. Clayton is full of rude people just like them.

Inside, three or four people wait at the takeout counter, but only a handful of booths are occupied. Sal Senior leads the two rude women to a table next to a crying baby and then comes back to seat us. "Gina!" He takes both my hands in his and kisses me on each cheek. When he pulls away, he inches closer to Cooper. "Who is this?"

"This is my friend Cooper." The two men shake hands while I realize I have elevated Cooper from coworker to friend.

"Cooper?" Sal mutters. "Is that your first or last name?" He doesn't wait for an answer. "She's our favorite customer. You better treat her right."

I expect Cooper to tell Sal that we're just colleagues, here to finish a project. Instead, he straightens himself and answers solemnly, "Of course, sir."

Sal reaches down to pat him on the shoulder and leads us to a quiet booth in the back. As we pass the table with the two women who rushed in front of us, Cooper whispers, "Karma's a bitch." They are glaring at the baby in the high chair, who is screaming even louder now.

Sal leaves us with menus and makes his way to the noisy infant. He leans down and says something to the mother, who smiles and nods in response. Next thing I know, Sal has removed the baby from the high chair and is holding him over his shoulder, pacing back and forth. The wailing stops.

Watching Sal with the baby makes me miss my parents. I imagine my dad trying to get an infant to stop screaming and then immediately replace the mental image of my dad with my mother. I feel my heart squeeze. Please let Ajee be right about Ethan so Mom and Dad can be grandparents.

"What's good?" Cooper asks. I turn my attention to him. He's watching me over his menu.

"All I ever get is pizza, but I'm sure everything is delicious."

"I love Italian food," he says.

"You should stop by my parents' sometime," I say. "My mom would love to cook for you."

"Next time I run up that hill," Cooper says.

For some reason, I can picture it: Cooper at the kitchen table with me and my parents. He's sitting in the chair we used to refer to as

Neesha's. "What's your handicap?" my dad asks while my mother scoops more manicotti onto his plate. "*Mangia! Mangia!*" she says.

Sal has returned to our table. "Ready to order?"

"I need another minute," Cooper answers. "In the meantime, we'll take a bottle of Chianti."

Alcohol? Now I really feel like we're on a date. "We have lots of work to do. We shouldn't drink."

"We need to get creative." Cooper shrugs. "I thought it might help."

A few minutes later, Tory brings the wine to our table. His black T-shirt shows off his shiny giant biceps. Wait, why are his muscles shiny? Did he lube up before coming to work?

"So this is why you won't go out with me?" He looks Cooper up and down while maneuvering the corkscrew. Cooper's studying me with that squinty look of his. Probably waiting for me to correct Tory. "When you get tired of him, you let me know." Tory winks and fills our wineglasses without giving either of us a taste first.

After Tory leaves, Cooper continues to stare at me. I've never met someone so comfortable making so much eye contact without saying a word. He picks up his wine. "Cheers," he finally says.

I tap mine against his and take a large sip. Cooper continues to stare. I put my wine down and open my menu again. Cooper drops his head to his menu, as well.

Sal meanders to our table. "What's it gonna be?" He's looking at me. Cooper answers, "Gina will have a pizza with peppers." He stops. "Right?" I stare at him and nod.

"Big surprise," Sal says.

"I'll have the broccoli, chicken, and ziti," Cooper finishes. Sal raises an eyebrow at me. Maybe he's thinking real men don't eat that. That's what I'm thinking, anyway. "On second thought," Cooper says, "I'll have the chicken parm."

"Much better," Sal says while I nod in agreement.

"So I'm that predictable?" I ask after Sal leaves.

"I analyzed the situation," Cooper explains. "First, I looked at the market indicators, which include your earlier admission that you always get pizza here and the fact that the first time we ate together, you asked for peppers. Based on those market indicators, I confidently forecast what I thought would be the result, a pizza with peppers." He grins.

"You really are a nerd." I smile as I say it.

Cooper reaches for the wine bottle and fills my glass almost to the top. He doesn't pour more for himself. Is he trying to get me drunk? "Tell me about growing up in Westham," Cooper says. "Sisters? Brothers?"

Definitely a first date question. I take a large sip of wine before answering. I tell him all about Ajee and her fortune-telling business and how Neesha and I used to spy. I don't mention that Ajee predicted I would marry a man named Ethan. "Neesha's coming next week to spread Ajee's remains at her old home. She sent the ashes ahead," I say. "They should arrive any day." I take another huge sip of wine. "I'm sort of creeped out by the idea."

"I don't blame you," Cooper says. He refills our glasses as Sal brings the food.

During dinner, Cooper helps think of ways we can spread Ajee's ashes without the Murphys knowing. We don't come up with anything good until I tell him the Murphys are moving. "Make an appointment to see the house. I'm sure the owners will leave, and you can spread the ashes before, after, or maybe even during the Realtor's tour."

His plan is perfect. It could even lead to Neesha making an offer on the house. If the table wasn't between us, I swear I'd hug him.

After Tory clears our plates, Sal brings us a complimentary piece of tiramisu. Cooper and I both pick up our forks. He grins. "Ready, set, go!" Our utensils plunge into the spongy pastry, and we race to see who can eat the most. In less than a minute, we've eaten all but one bite. I scoop it up, but Cooper knocks it off my fork with his. He laughs as he tries to spear it. I bang his fork away, pull the dish toward me, and conquer the last piece. "That's cheating." I don't know how he manages to say it because we're both laughing so hard.

Tory reappears. "Guess we should have given you two pieces." He collects the plate. Cooper smiles at me. "Love a girl who loves dessert," he says.

The description of his ideal mate from the online dating profile pops into my head: *She loves to eat but keeps herself in shape.* "I'm going to have to do an extra twenty minutes on the treadmill tomorrow."

We get back to my apartment shortly after nine. Cooper comes inside because he has to get his bag.

"We didn't get any work done," I say.

"We'll have to do this again then." He leans toward me. I think he's going to kiss me. Instead, he hugs me quickly. "See you tomorrow."

I watch him walk down the stairs, and all I'm thinking is, *Cooper Allen just hugged me.* I really wish it had been a kiss. Before the thought is even finished, I give myself a mental slap for betraying Ethan, even if the betrayal is only in my mind.

I left my phone at home during dinner. I check it now and see that I have two missed calls from Ethan. I call him back, and he answers before the first ring even finishes. "Where you been, girl?"

"I had dinner with a friend from work."

"Ah," he says. "Luci?"

"Yes." The lie isn't even a decision. It comes out before I have time to think about it.

"I want to meet her," Ethan says. "Maybe we can set her up with Jack. He's still so uptight about Brady. He needs to get laid. Even Amber said the same thing."

"Why would the dog walker complain about Jack?"

"Because he's a pain in the ass about Brady." He pauses. "So, what do you say? Will you arrange a night out with Luci?"

"I'll try." Now I am deliberately lying. Luci and Jack are not a good idea, and I don't want her anywhere near Ethan.

Chapter 23

The package is waiting on the steps the next day when I get home from work. I know it is from Neesha immediately. I recognize her handwriting on the label. It was always incredibly messy, and I see that it hasn't improved. If I didn't know better, I'd think her daughter or son addressed the package. My name slants upward in big, loopy letters, my street address slants downward, and the town and state are slanting both up and down, with an uneven amount of space between each letter.

I bend to pick up the box. I'm surprised by how light it is. Inside my apartment, I place the package on my table, thinking about what's inside. Ajee's ashes. I close my eyes and picture Ajee, her salt-and-pepper hair and those big dark eyes that saw things no one else could. I wonder if she foresaw how her own life would end. Saw her remains in an urn traveling halfway across the country. If she could see her own future, did she try to do things to change it?

If she had told me that Ethan would be going through a divorce when I met him, would I have waited? Certainly I would never be dating a man who was technically still married if Ajee hadn't told me I was supposed to marry him. In this way, knowing my fate is making my fate possible. This doesn't sit well with me.

I think about leaving the package as is until Neesha arrives next week, but I have second thoughts. It seems wrong to treat Ajee that way. Before I can decide what to do, my doorbell rings. Luci is supposed to pick me up at six thirty to go to the movies. Today at work, she won tickets to a screening by being the hundredth caller to a radio station. She tried calling at ten, noon, two, and finally won at four. In all, she must have called that radio station over a thousand times. If Cooper knew, he would remove the phones from our office to improve editing turnaround time. There would be no need to brainstorm ideas.

I open the door. A cold blast of wind practically rips it from the hinges. Luci's standing there in a long wool coat, hat, and gloves. It's the first week of April, and out of principle, I've already packed my winter clothes away for the season. "I was bored," she says as she comes inside. I take her coat, and she wanders to the living room. "Sometimes don't you just wish there were someone here to greet you when you got home?" She plops herself down on the couch. I study her. Her usually bright green eyes look dull, like they're covered with a coat of dust.

I sit down next to her. "What's going on?"

"Kip, he . . ." She leaps to her feet. "I need a glass of wine." She heads directly to my wine rack on the corner of the kitchen counter and pulls out a bottle of pinot noir she gave me for Christmas. "You don't mind if I open this?" She pulls the corkscrew from a kitchen drawer as she asks.

I get two glasses while she opens the wine. She pours us each a generous amount. "Here's to being single." As she clinks her glass against mine, she notices the package on the table. "Did you get a gift?"

"No, it's Ajee's ashes."

"What?" she asks.

I sigh because I've already told her a few times that Neesha is coming here next week to spread her grandmother's remains. I tell her again while she drains her wineglass.

"Get me scissors. Let's open up the package," she instructs.

I go to my desk and return with scissors. I start to cut open the box, but I'm hesitant. I can't believe that all that's left of Ajee fits in this small box. My phone rings. I stop what I'm doing to answer it, glad for the interruption. It's Ethan. I go into the other room to talk to him. When I return, the box is open, and a cylinder-shaped object wrapped in multiple layers of Bubble Wrap rests next to my glass of wine on the table. "You do the honors," Luci says.

I finish my wine before picking up the container. Under all the protective wrapping is a beautiful turquoise brass urn. I set it on the table and take a step backward.

Luci laughs. "She's not going to come to life and pop out of there." She taps her knuckles against the urn, and they make a clanging sound. "This is beautiful." She points to a gold trim circling the urn just under the cover. "Look at the details."

I step closer and notice the trim is actually individual gold roses strung together. "Ajee loved roses," I say. "She planted a rosebush in the Patels' yard as soon as she moved in."

Luci places her fingers on the lid of the urn, and I quickly reach for it. "What are you doing?"

"Maybe if I open it, she'll come out like a genie and we'll each get to make three wishes."

I remove the urn from her reach. "What would you wish for?"

"Easy. An endless supply of wishes, money, and hot lovers." She carries our glasses to the sink to wash them while I struggle to recork the wine bottle.

When we return from the movie, Ethan's Jeep is parked behind my car. He steps onto the driveway and waves when we pull in. I had no idea he was coming over, and I'm excited that he's here.

"Is that Ethan?" Luci asks. "Did you know he was coming?"

I shake my head as Ethan opens the passenger door of Luci's car. "You sounded freaked out by the ashes," he says. "I didn't want you to be alone with them."

"Wow," I say. "It was really thoughtful of you to drive up."

"Please," Luci mutters. "He just wants some action."

Ethan leans into the car and looks at her. "Nothing wrong with that, is there?" He smiles.

Luci extends her hand. "Luci Corrigan Chin." I give her a startled look. She never uses her maiden name.

"You two sure have been spending a lot of time together," Ethan says.

"What do you mean?" Luci asks.

Oh no. "Thanks for tonight, Luci." I lightly push Ethan so that I can get out of the car. He doesn't budge.

"Pizza last night. The movie tonight."

Luci rolls her tongue across her upper lip. "Pizza last night," she repeats slowly. She pokes my forearm. "That's some story that went with that pizza, too. Right, Gina?"

I glare at her. "What story?" Ethan asks.

"Oh," Luci says. "I had my heart set on Thai. Gina had to talk me into having pizza. In fact, she owes me big for agreeing to the pizza. Right, Gina?"

I glare at her again. "Right, Luci." I push Ethan away with more force. He finally moves back so that I can get out of the car. When I step on the driveway, he pulls me into his arms and kisses me on the lips; his tongue darts inside my mouth while his hands run up and down my body. Although I'm embarrassed he's groping me like this in front of Luci, my body responds the way it always does to his touch, and I can't wait to get upstairs. His hands land on my butt, and he pulls me closer.

"Take it upstairs," Luci yells.

Ethan pulls away from me and leans back into Luci's car. I can't even look at her I'm so embarrassed. "I was thinking you, me, Gina, and my buddy Jack could all go out one night," Ethan says.

"Just so happens I'm free tomorrow," Luci answers.

The office smells like hot sauce when I arrive on Friday. Luci's sitting at her desk eating her eggs. "We have so much to talk about that I don't even know where to start," she says. I hang up my coat—a light spring jacket even though there were flurries on the drive in today—and sit down. "Ethan is not what I was expecting." She takes her breakfast to my desk and plants herself on the corner.

"What were you expecting?"

She puts a forkful of eggs into her mouth. She chews and swallows before speaking again. "Someone more refined. Someone a little bit shy about shoving his tongue down your throat and feeling you up in front of others." She stops and pushes the eggs around on her plate with her fork. I feel my face burning with shame. "Someone who's been to the dentist in the past decade, for Pete's sake."

"That's not nice." I can't say it with much conviction. Ethan's teeth are horrible.

"Look," Luci says, "I can see what his appeal would be. He's sort of sexy. At least until he opens his mouth. I think a fling with him is harmless, even good for you. But, Gina, he's not the guy for you long-term."

I shake my head. "No one has ever affected me like he does." I blush as I say it.

"There's a big difference between love and lust," she says. "After a while, the sex will get old."

I turn to face my monitor. Luci stays where she is, eating her eggs. "Who did you have dinner with Wednesday night?" Her breakfast is gone, and she tosses the plate into my garbage can.

"It's not what you think."

"I don't think anything. I just want to know who you had dinner with."

"Cooper and I need to get the project done. He has no time during the day."

"So you and Cooper worked at dinner." Luci uses air quotes around the word *worked*.

"Yes." There's no way I'm going to tell her we didn't get any TechVisions business done.

Luci stands. "Then why did you tell Ethan you had dinner with me?"

"I told him I was with a friend from work. He assumed it was you. I didn't correct him."

Luci walks to her desk while I'm speaking. She sits before responding. "Ask yourself why you didn't correct him."

Chapter 24

Jack sticks out in the crowded bar because he's several inches taller than everyone and because his hair is bright red. He's standing beside a table talking to Ethan, who is slouching in the booth looking at his watch. We are seventy-five minutes late because I couldn't figure out what to wear. I finally settled on jeans, but we stopped along the way so Luci could pick out a new top for me. It's a silver tank top with sparkling red glitter. I'm wearing a red button-down sweater open over it.

I point out Ethan and Jack to Luci. She stares at Jack and makes a face like she just found out Santa Claus isn't real. "You didn't tell me he's a ginger."

I tousle her own red locks. "I didn't tell you anything about Jack. You're the one who agreed to meet him." All day, I've been worried about this get-together. I don't know what I'm afraid of. I just know it's not a good idea.

Luci pushes her way through the mob. I follow in the path she clears. A guy who doesn't look like he's old enough to be here drinking, yet holds a fresh beverage in his hand, grabs her arm. "What's the rush?" he asks.

Luci eyes the dark liquid in the tall glass. "What are you drinking?"

"Long Island Iced Tea."

Luci shakes her arm free. "Can I try?"

He hands her the drink. For a minute I'm afraid she's going to douse him with it. Instead she takes a large sip. "Delicious." She slowly licks her lips and leans toward the guy's ear. "Mind if I keep it?" I've never heard her voice so low.

"Ahh, no. Of course not." He smiles.

"Thanks." She quickly turns away from him and continues pushing her way through the crowd.

He looks at me. I shrug.

When we reach the table, Ethan stands while Jack sits. "Finally," Ethan says, leaning in to hug me. He smells like whiskey. "Jack here was just about to leave."

"You're over an hour late," Jack whines.

Luci eyes him. "I'm Luci, and I promise you, I'm well worth the wait."

Jack's face turns the color of his hair as Luci slides into the booth next to him.

Ethan takes my hand. "Let's get you a drink," he says, pulling me toward the bar. I don't want to leave Luci alone with Jack. I'm afraid she'll interrogate him about Ethan. That's it. Luci's going to find things out about Ethan tonight that I don't want to know.

I look back at our table. Jack's and Luci's heads are bent toward each other. He's listening to something she's saying. His face is very serious, without even a hint of a smile. *Please don't let there be a long line at the bar.*

Ethan squeezes my hand. "Looks like they're getting along."

"For now." Luci will be nice to Jack just long enough to get the information she wants. What that information is, I don't know yet.

Four televisions at the bar are all tuned to a hockey game, and each TV has a deep crowd stationed in front of it. "Bruins winning?" Ethan asks a big bald guy.

"No score yet," he answers.

Ethan watches the game while we work our way to the front of the line. I look back at our table again, but I can't see over the crowd behind me. Fifteen minutes later, we return to the booth with a pitcher of beer and two Long Island Iced Teas. "Just in time," Luci says, sliding her empty glass to the edge of the table and pulling a fresh drink toward her.

"What were you guys talking about?" I ask.

Luci sucks on her straw for a minute. "Amber," she says.

"The dog walker?"

"Yup," Luci says. "She seems to have taken a particular liking to Brady."

"Can't blame her," Ethan says, staring at Jack. He stretches his arm across the back of the booth so that his hand rests just above my shoulder. "Her time with him is about to be cut in half, though. Leah and I agreed on joint custody today."

I break out into a coughing fit as my sip goes down the wrong way. When I compose myself, I turn to Ethan. "You spoke with Leah?"

"We've agreed to make the divorce less contentious," he says. "Sharing Brady is the first step."

The barroom suddenly breaks out in applause. For a minute I think everyone is happy about Ethan and Leah getting along, but no, the Bruins have scored a goal. "You're so going to owe me," Ethan says to Jack.

Jack glances at the television. "That's okay. Me betting against a Boston team is a sure way to guarantee they'll win."

Luci laughs.

"How's this custody thing going to work?" I ask. "You and Leah live, like, four hours apart."

"Closer to three. We're meeting in the middle. Sunday's the first drop-off."

"Where are you meeting?"

Luci leans across the table, closer to me.

"A burger joint in Portsmouth that allows dogs." Ethan shrugs. "Leah picked the place."

"You're having lunch together?"

Luci grabs my wrist. "Gina, let's go to the ladies' room."

"How often will these switches take place? Are you going to have a date every time?"

"It's not a date."

Luci stands. "Ethan, get up so Gina can get out of the booth." When he doesn't respond, Luci more forcefully adds, "Now."

Ethan snaps to his feet. I bump his shoulder as I move past him.

He sits down again, and as we start to walk away I hear him say, "Women, man."

Luci puts her arm around my shoulder. "Are you okay?"

"I'm fine."

When we get to the restroom, she studies herself in the mirror.

"Does our health insurance cover Botox?" She glides the tip of her finger across faint creases at the corners of each eye. "He's not ready for a serious relationship, Gina." She places each hand at the outside edge of each eyebrow and pulls her skin toward her temples. "You never want to be the one who comes after the wife."

"He's having lunch with Leah," I say. "I really have no reason to be mad. If I were a good person, I'd be encouraging him to work things out."

"You are a good person, and he's not going to work things out with her."

I enter a stall, pull down my jeans, and crouch over the toilet seat. On the wall to the right is a red heart around the words *Megan Loves Luke*. Next to the heart in black writing is the message *Luke Loves Crystal*. Under that someone else has written *Love Sucks*.

I hear the clicking of heels, and then Luci's pointy black shoes appear outside the stall. "Divorce is tough," she mumbles. "It can do a number on you."

If I had a pen with me right now, I'd be tempted to write *Ethan Loves Leah*. I give up trying to go to the bathroom. My bladder gets paralyzed when I know other people can hear. I stand, pull up my jeans, and flush. I swing open the bathroom door, and Luci steps backward just before it hits her.

She enters the stall. I go to the sink to wash my hands. "I just don't want you to get hurt, Gina," Luci says over the sound of her pee stream hitting the water in the toilet bowl. "Keep it casual."

It's just awkward talking to someone who is going to the bathroom. "I'll see you back at the table."

I pause in the hallway outside the restroom to collect myself. I think of Ajee and remember her insisting, "You must wait. You must wait for Ethan." Why didn't he wait for me? Why did he love Leah first?

I head out of the hallway back to our table. Ethan stands as soon as he sees me. Before he lets me sit, he wraps me into a tight hug. "Gina, Leah and I are over. I promise. But she was such a huge part of my life for so long. I want our split to be amicable."

"I know." I'm thinking I will go back to the restroom with a marker and write: *Gina Hates Leah!*

Luci returns and announces that she is hungry, so she and Jack head to the bar to order food. A few minutes later Jack returns by himself. He pouts as he sits. I glance to my left and see Luci perched on a stool. A bartender leans over the bar toward her, laughing at something she just said. She makes it look so easy.

"Striking out?" Ethan asks.

"She told me she doesn't do redheads." Jack laughs. "She's something else. I think I'm in love."

"She didn't really say that," Ethan says, looking at me.

Jack and I both nod. "She did." I didn't hear it, but I can certainly imagine it.

A few minutes later Luci returns with potato skins and mozzarella sticks. "What's wrong with redheads?" Ethan asks.

Luci laughs. "Hey, there can't be a ginger more beautiful than this one." She points to herself. Jack laughs and drapes his arm around her. Luci lets it stay there for about three seconds. "So," she says as she shakes his arm off, "how long have you known Ethan?"

"We met in sixth grade," Jack says. "Some kids were picking on him on the basketball court, and I stepped in to stop them."

"My hero," Ethan says. "He's saved my ass countless times." The two clank glasses as I imagine a distraught Ethan showing up on Jack's doorstep after Leah kicked him out.

"So, Jack, did you like Leah?" I don't even know where the question came from. Ethan turns to look at me. Luci kicks me.

Jack swallows his beer. "Yeah, Leah was cool." He takes another gulp.

"She's still cool," Ethan says. When Jack, Luci, and I all stare at him, he adds, "He made it sound like she died."

Luci uses her fork to place a mozzarella stick on her plate. She cuts it into small bites. Jack reaches for the plate and picks one up with his hands. He stuffs the entire thing into his mouth. I know later tonight Luci will whisper to me about his atrocious table manners.

Ethan follows Jack's lead, picks up a potato skin, and downs it in two huge bites. "Did they not have silverware in the town where you two grew up?" Luci snaps.

"No silverware and no indoor plumbing. In fact, we lived in caves," Jack answers. He turns ninety degrees so that he is facing Luci. "How about you, princess, was it only silver spoons in the kingdom you lived in?"

"No, we had forks and knives, and we learned how to use them," Luci answers, but she's not even looking at him. She's staring at the bartender. He has a blond mustache and goatee. "I love facial hair," she says.

Jack touches his clean-shaven cheek while looking down at the table. "How do you and Gina know each other?"

Luci looks at her watch before responding. "We work together." She sighs and looks at her watch again.

This time Jack sees her do it. "We boring you?" he asks.

Luci nods. "Yeah, kind of."

Ethan laughs. He raises his glass and tips it toward Luci. "I like you," he says.

She glances at me and then back at Ethan. "Then do me a favor," she says slowly. "Don't hurt my friend."

Ethan puts his arm around my shoulder and pulls me toward him. "Never," he promises.

Chapter 25

Brady's barking wakes us early on Sunday. He's standing on Ethan's side of the bed with his two front paws on the mattress. Ethan rolls toward him and pats his head. "Someone's excited to see Mommy today." He jumps out of bed with more energy than he usually has and takes Brady outside while I lie there wondering if he was talking about himself or the dog.

Ever since he told me that he and Leah decided to make the divorce less contentious and share custody of Brady, I've noticed an extra bounce in his step. Is he hoping less contentious will lead to amicable and then to a reconciliation?

No point in lying here worrying about it. I get up and go to the window. My downstairs neighbor, dressed in a blue terry-cloth bathrobe, is pointing at Brady and saying something to Ethan, who is listening with his arms folded across his chest. When my neighbor is done speaking, he stomps across the lawn back to the walkway. A few seconds later, I hear the door downstairs slam. Crap. I'm not allowed to have pets in my apartment, and I'm pretty sure that's what the discussion was all about.

When Ethan comes back inside, he confirms my suspicion. "The barking woke him up. Says he's going to call the landlord if he sees Brady here again." I expect Ethan to be pissed, but he laughs and shrugs. Does he not care because he's planning to reconcile with Leah today? Should I be encouraging him to work things out with her? She is his wife, after all. I glance at the urn on the coffee table, wishing I could dump out the contents and put Ajee back together and make her tell me what I'm supposed to do.

Twenty minutes later, Ethan is singing in the shower. I don't recognize the song, but it's upbeat and hopeful and it depresses me. When he emerges from the bathroom, he's dressed in pleated gray Dockers and my favorite button-down shirt. It's bright blue and makes his eyes pop. I imagine that when Leah sees him in that shirt and is reminded of the tender way Ethan treats Brady, she'll realize she's made a big mistake.

"Do you want company for the ride?" I blurt out.

"Probably not a good idea," he says after a long pause. "I don't want to rub it in her face that I'm, you know, with someone."

I try to keep my expression neutral, but I'm sure my disappointment shows, because Ethan pulls me into his arms. "I'll come back."

It takes me a second to realize he's talking about today, not answering my unspoken question.

Ethan thought he'd be back by three. It is now four, and I haven't heard from him. In my mind, Leah ran into his arms when she saw him at the restaurant. "I made a big mistake. Forgive me," she pleaded. Ethan kissed her, and then the two of them and Brady drove off to their home in Glory to live happily ever after.

I spend the next several minutes imagining how Ethan will break the news to me. In the very worst scenario, he shows up at my doorstep with his arm around Leah. "Stay away from my husband," she says. Then she shoves me as Ethan looks on, laughing. In another version, he sends Jack to tell me. "I tried to warn you, but you wouldn't listen." His eyes scan my apartment. "Any chance Luci's here?"

More likely, Ethan will send a text: *"Great news, Leah's giving me another chance."* I decide I will be happy for him. *"True love prevails,"* I will write back. This last thought bounces around in my mind like a pinball. Something about it rings true. Ethan does love Leah. I will never be his first choice. I will be the one he settled for because Leah does not love him back.

To distract myself I check my e-mail. I have one message from my mother: *"Mrs. Bonnano's son arrived yesterday. He is very pleasant and has a nice sense of humor. I wish you would come down next weekend to meet him. Love, Mom. P.S. The old women down here are having a terrible time remembering his name and he answers to al-most anything. He probably wouldn't mind if you called him Ethan."*

I can imagine her laughing as she typed that last part. She proba-bly thought it was so funny that she read it out loud to my father. Then I see her laughter ending abruptly and hear her inhale. "She's going to end up alone because of that meddling old woman."

I should write and tell her that I finally met Ethan, but how can I do that when at this very moment he might be reconciling with his estranged wife? *"Dear Mom, pleasant and nice sense of humor are code words for overweight and receding hairline. Love you, Gina."*

Two minutes later, I receive her response. *"You're almost forty, Gina. Not too many men your age still have their hair or muscles. Miss you, Mom."*

What does she know? Ethan has both, and for that matter, so does Cooper. Oh God, it would serve me right if Ethan reconciles with Leah today after I lied to him about having dinner with Cooper.

By six thirty, I give up waiting for Ethan and make myself a grilled cheese sandwich and french fries. I just finish eating when he slumps through the door. His pained expression and slouched shoul-ders leave no doubt that it was not the happy reunion I've been envi-sioning all day. Still, I am not relieved. I get up to hug him. "What's wrong?" I ask, hoping he will tell me it was hard leaving Brady with Leah.

He rests his head on my shoulder. "She brought a friend." His voice cracks. "Ron." I pull away to see his face. Is it my imagination or are his eyes filling with tears? "Prick drives a Beemer," he says. "Spread towels on the backseat so Brady wouldn't soil the leather. What the hell did she bring him for?"

I don't know what's worse, if the happy scenes I imagined be-tween Ethan and Leah came to fruition or seeing him so upset that she's moving on. I really wish he hadn't come back today. Seeing him like this makes it impossible to deny that Jack and Luci are right. Ethan is not over Leah.

I turn my back to him and return to the couch. The urn on the cof-fee table mocks me. "You will help him get over her, Bella," I imag-ine Ajee saying.

Ethan follows me to the couch. "You're upset Leah's moving on. You're not over her." My voice is barely a whisper.

He doesn't look at me. "It was just weird to see her with someone else." He runs his hands through his hair. "This guy has some dough. His car. His watch. She was always on me because I don't make enough." He slides closer. He doesn't just look at me, he caresses my face. His fingertips trace my lips. As always, his touch causes an electric current to ripple through me. I feel myself leaning toward him. It's unfair the way my body betrays me.

"You should have come with me," he says, pinning me down.

"Why?"

"Because I missed you, babe." His hands are rough as they slide down my body.

His words and touch both feel like a lie. I push him off me.

"What's wrong?" he asks.

"It's just . . ." I stop because I don't know what's wrong other than it just feels wrong.

Chapter 26

A crowd of wary passengers waits in the baggage area. I scan their faces looking for Neesha. A dark-haired woman leaning against a pole catches my attention. I change positions so I can see her face. Definitely not Neesha. The woman opens her mouth wide to yawn. Great, now I have to yawn, too. Unlike her, though, I cover my mouth with my hand. I go back to searching the people lined up to retrieve their suitcases. A man pushes his way closer to the carousel. He doesn't bother to say "excuse me" to the waiting passengers he bumps along his way. His sense of entitlement infuriates me. *"Who do you think you are?"* I want to shout.

A college-aged girl squeals with excitement and runs toward the sliding glass doors, where she jumps into the arms of a boy her age entering the building. He picks her up and twirls her around. Observing their actions reminds me why I love arrivals. On the other hand, departures depress me, even when I'm traveling to someplace fun. I hate watching people say good-bye. The way they hug, clinging to each other like they might not ever see one another again. The last look over the shoulder as the passenger disappears through the security gate. I'll take arrivals over departures anytime.

A buzzer sounds, followed by a *plunk, plunk* noise that indicates the suitcases are now on the conveyor belt. I study all the dark-haired women, but there is no sign of Neesha. I check my cell phone but I have no new messages. Passengers drag their luggage off the carousel and toward the exit. A few minutes later the crowd has dispersed. One lone hard-shell red suitcase remains going 'round and 'round. I pull the suitcase off the belt and look at the identification tag. I recognize Neesha's messy scrawl before I read her name.

I roll the suitcase to a nearby bench and sit. Down the hall a buzzer sounds as another conveyor belt rolls into action. The exit doors open, and a dark-haired woman holding a cell phone steps inside. She looks at me. I stand, and then we are both running toward each other. "Neesha," I scream at the same exact time she yells, "Gina Rossi!" We jump up and down as we hug each other. We pull apart and study one other. There is no sign of my lanky fourteen-year-old friend with the long dark ponytail and mischievous close-mouthed grin. In her place is a beautiful, tall, curvy woman with long hair that curls around her face and a big toothy smile. She slides her cell phone into the pocket of her mint-green overcoat. "I couldn't get a signal in here so I had to step outside to call Ashley and the kids. Jayda is really upset that I'm gone. It's the first time I've ever left her, so I had to calm her down. Sorry it took so long."

Neesha tousles my hair. "What happened to the curls?"

I laugh. "I spend forty-five minutes each morning ironing them out."

"And at the same time I'm probably torturing my hair with the curling iron." She links her arm through mine, and we head toward the exit. "We always want what we don't have."

"You look great," I say as she takes her suitcase from me. "I see so much of your mother in you."

Neesha pauses. "You remember her?"

"Of course."

Neesha's eyes well up. "It's so great to see you, Gina. It really is."

Neesha and I are sitting on my couch scrolling through a photo album on her smartphone. Any awkwardness created by all the years of no contact melted away on the drive out of the airport. "This is my favorite," Neesha says. She hands me the phone. There is a picture of her children, Jayda and AJ, holding hands with Ajee. Ajee's hair, which was salt-and-pepper when she lived across the street, is completely gray, and there are more wrinkles at the corners of her mouth and around her dark eyes. "She was a pain in the ass, but I miss her," Neesha says.

The urn with Ajee's remains is on the coffee table in front of us. Neesha picks it up. "Jayda's teacher called Ashley and me in for a meeting," Neesha says. "Apparently Jayda was predicting gloom and doom for her classmates that she doesn't like. She convinced one little boy his parents were going to sell him." Neesha returns the urn to the table. "Turns out Ajee told Jayda that she, too, has the gift. Of course, Jayda doesn't understand. She thinks that means anything she says will come true."

"So, Jayda has the gift?"

Neesha crosses her legs under her on the couch. "You always were Ajee's biggest believer."

I sit up straighter. "What do you mean?"

"You never doubted anything she said."

"There was no reason to doubt her. The things she said always came true."

Neesha unfolds her legs and puts her feet back on the floor. "It's always the things she didn't say that bothered me." She reaches for the urn again, and I have a feeling she's thinking about the lump in her mother's breast that went undetected for so long.

"I think she did the best she could."

Neesha closes her eyes. "She always liked you. In fact, I think that's one of the reasons she wanted her ashes spread in Westham, so that we'd reunite."

"Why do you say that?"

Neesha hands me the urn. "She made me promise to spread her ashes at the house on Towering Heights Lane, and then she told me that while I was here I had to find you. She wanted me to tell you that he was close by, nearer than you think. She mumbled something about how history and furniture were making it harder than it should be." She shrugs. "Ashley and I were convinced she was hallucinating near the end."

"I met him," I say. "Soon after I saw Ajee's obituary." My mouth goes dry with the admission.

"You met Ethan." Neesha slaps her palm on her knee. "I wasn't even sure you'd still remember her prediction."

I tell her about how Ethan stopped to help me in a snowstorm and how we've been dating ever since.

"So Ash and I will be coming back to Boston for a wedding soon, then." She touches my hand as she says it.

"I hope so."

"Well, I want to meet him. I need to see this guy my grandmother saw so many years ago."

Chapter 27

Luci, Neesha, and I are meeting Ethan and Jack for drinks at a Chinese restaurant. Luci picked the place. She is already sipping on a Scorpion Bowl when Neesha and I arrive. I see her sizing up Neesha as we make our way to the booth. I imagine at some point in the evening Luci will lean over to me and point at Neesha's orange sweater. "Why's she dressed like a pumpkin?" she'll ask.

Luci stands when Neesha and I reach the table. She hugs me quickly. "I like your outfit, Gina." Last week at lunch we went shopping, and she picked out the cranberry blouse and brown trousers that I am wearing tonight. Luci extends her hand to Neesha. "Luci Corrigan Chin," she says. Neesha shakes Luci's hand and introduces herself. "Your sweater is an interesting color," Luci says.

Neesha points to Luci's cleavage. "Those aren't real, are they?"

I swallow hard, but both Neesha and Luci laugh.

A few minutes later, Ethan and Jack arrive. Jack's face sports the beginning of a goatee, and I wonder if that's because Luci told him she prefers men with facial hair the first time they met. He slides into the booth next to her and stretches his arm out against the backrest. Luci pointedly looks over her shoulder and edges closer to the wall. Ethan kisses me and then reaches across my body to introduce himself to Neesha. "You two look alike," he says, pointing at Neesha and then me.

Jack leans forward toward Ethan. "You're something else, man. You see a resemblance between Gina and her Indian friend, but you don't think she looks anything like Leah, who just happens to be Caucasian like Gina."

Neesha's sipping from the Scorpion Bowl and takes her lips off the straw. "Who's Leah?"

Luci pulls the drink toward her. "Leah is Ethan's ex-wife."

"There's no ex yet," Jack corrects. "Leah is still Ethan's wife."

I glare at Jack. Ethan takes my hand.

The waitress stops at our table. She is Chinese and has long black hair. Jack tilts his head toward her. "Let me guess, you think she looks like Gina, too."

"No," Ethan says. "I think she looks like Luci." We all laugh.

Luci drains the rest of the Scorpion Bowl. "We'll need another of these, please." Ethan and Jack both order beers.

Luci asks Neesha what I was like as a kid. The next hour or so passes without incident as Neesha and I reveal stories from our childhood. "My archnemesis, Patty Ryan, saw Gina and I looking at crib notes during a vocabulary test," Neesha explains.

"Saw Gina and me," Luci corrects.

"We're with the grammar police," Jack warns.

"Saw us looking at crib notes," Neesha continues. "And she told the teacher, Mr. Moran, right?" Neesha looks at me. I nod. "Gina was scared her mother was going to ground her for life. Meanwhile, she doesn't get punished, and I end up with no TV or phone privileges for two weeks."

I laugh, remembering when Mr. Moran called my house to talk to my parents. My father answered the phone. After he hung up, he playfully smacked me in the head, "Next time be smart enough not to get caught," he said, but he never told my mother.

"You didn't get punished for cheating, though," I remind Neesha. "You got in trouble for doubting Ajee's gift." The night before the test, Neesha and I locked ourselves in her bedroom to prepare crib sheets, tiny pieces of papers with the definitions, which we taped to the inside of our jean jackets. When I was going home, Ajee walked me to the front door so she could watch me cross the street like she did every night. This time, though, before she pushed open the screen door, she turned to Neesha and me. "Girls, if you cheat on your vocabulary test tomorrow, you will be caught."

The next day at the bus stop, I asked Neesha if she was going to use her crib notes. "Of course," she responded.

"But Ajee said we'd get caught."

Neesha rolled her eyes. "Ajee doesn't know everything, Gina. She just thinks she does."

When Mr. Moran called the Patels' house that afternoon, Ajee hung up the phone and turned to Neesha and me. "Stupid girls," she hissed. "I told you that you would be caught."

"You couldn't have possibly known that," Neesha answered. "You do not have a psychic gift."

Ajee gasped, sent me home, and grounded Neesha for two weeks.

"She hated it that I doubted her gift," Neesha says. "I guess it wasn't until she helped the police find Matthew Colby that I started to consider that maybe she was psychic."

Ethan tilts the mug in his hand so that the beer sloshes from side to side. "Your grandmother was psychic?"

Neesha leans over me to get closer to Ethan. "How can you not know that?" she asks. "My grandmother was the one who predicted Gina would marry a man named Ethan."

Oh crap. I can't believe she just said that. The noise in the room dims. The lights get brighter. Ethan's mug freezes in his hand on the way from the table to his mouth. Jack stops shredding his napkin. Luci leans back and rubs her palms together. My face heats up, and my neck gets splotchy. "Speaking of Patty Ryan," I say, "she's the Realtor selling your old house."

"Whoa," Jack whispers.

"Hold on," Ethan says.

"You didn't tell him." Neesha figures it out.

Ethan returns his glass to the table. "Her grandmother told you that you'd marry a man named Ethan?" His tone suggests he'd be more likely to believe that Bigfoot just entered the restaurant.

I nod.

"When was this?"

"I was thirteen."

The mug is back in his hand, and he finishes his beer in one large swallow. "That's nuts."

A look passes between Jack and Ethan. "How many other Ethans have you dated?" Jack asks.

I shift in my seat. "None."

Ethan leans over me for a clear view of Neesha. "How often was your grandmother right?"

"Almost always," Neesha answers.

"Give me some examples," Ethan demands.

Neesha runs through a litany of Ajee's accurate predictions. Jack listens with a skeptical expression, every so often interjecting, "Bullshit!" Ethan sits quietly. I can't tell what he's thinking.

"I know it sounds crazy," Neesha says. "But her predictions came true too many times. She definitely had some kind of gift."

Luci turns to Ethan. "So, you ready to exchange vows again?"

The muscles in his face tighten. He stands. "Gotta take a leak."

We're all quiet as he walks away. Jack stops slouching and sits up straight. "Listen, Gina," he begins. I want to block my ears or start screaming. "Don't get your hopes up. Ethan's still working through his first marriage. It's way too soon for him to be thinking of another."

"What is your problem?" I pull the Scorpion Bowl closer.

"I like you. I don't want to see you hurt," Jack continues. "I love Ethan like a brother, but he's not himself these days."

"What does that mean?"

Jack sighs.

The drink is almost empty. I make a slurping sound as I suck on my straw. Luci pulls the bowl away. "It means that Ethan isn't ready for a serious relationship," she says.

Out of the corner of my eye, I see Ethan making his way across the room. He's typing into his phone, and then he slides it into his pocket. When he reaches our table, he leans against the edge. "I'm kind of beat," he announces. "What do you say we call it a night?"

Jack flags down the waitress. When she arrives, he hands her his credit card without looking at the bill. Luci opens her purse, but Jack stops her before she can pull out her wallet. "Tonight's on me," he says.

As Jack settles the bill, Ethan walks me, Neesha, and Luci to the door. He holds my hand on the way. When we reach the exit, Luci and Neesha rush to the parking lot while Ethan and I pause in the doorway.

I expect him to say something about Ajee's prediction. Instead, he embraces me without saying a thing. I cling to him until he pulls away. "Good night." He holds open the door, and I walk through it. When I reach Neesha and Luci talking by my car, I look over my shoulder to wave good-bye, but he is already gone.

Chapter 28

For most of the drive to Westham, Neesha has been talking non-stop. As soon as I turn on to Towering Heights Lane, though, she stops speaking. As we make our way up the hill, she studies each side of the road. When I pull into my parents' driveway, she races out of the car to the edge of the street and stands with her hands on her hips, staring at her old home. We are here on a reconnaissance mission today because Neesha wants to find the perfect spot for Ajee's remains.

Neesha's eyes fill with tears as she studies the house she lived in until she was fourteen. We both stand silently looking at the house. I wonder if Neesha's thinking about her mother. It was a warm April day much like today when the ambulance took her away for the last time. "It looked better green," she finally says. One of the first things the Murphys did when they moved in was paint the house white.

"What happened to the maple?" She points to the barren spot near the left side of the house where the leafy tree used to stand.

"It fell during a storm junior year. Tore a hole through the roof."

"My mom loved that tree," Neesha says. "We used to collect the bright red leaves every fall and press them between wax paper."

An image of Mrs. Patel, Neesha, and me gathering leaves under the tree pops into my head. The sky above was bright blue, and the air had that crispness it only has in fall. Sanjit appeared from the back of the house and tossed acorns at Neesha and me when he thought Mrs. Patel wasn't looking. Then suddenly she had the garden hose in her hand, and she was spraying water in her son's direction. "Apologize or I'll soak you," she threatened. Stunned, Sanjit muttered, "Sorry," and slinked away toward the backyard.

The Murphys never use their garage. Today neither car is in the driveway so I tell Neesha we can explore their yard. Hesitantly, she crosses the street, and I follow. She immediately heads to the rosebush on the right side of the house. "This is it," she says quietly. We hear a car. Both of our heads turn to the street, but it's not the Murphys. "Let's get out of here," she says.

We head back to my house, and I enter my parents' code on the keypad outside the garage. Neesha and I squeeze around my mother's car and up the stairs to the door that leads inside. I open it and step into the family room, but Neesha freezes in the doorway. "It's like a wormhole to my childhood," she says as she enters. She walks through the family room to the kitchen, and I follow. She runs her hand across the counter. "I think of your mom every time I make macaroni," she says.

On Sundays, Neesha and I helped my mother prepare an afternoon meal. More often than not, it was homemade pasta. I'd get bored rolling out the dough, but Neesha never grew tired of it. She and my mom would stand side by side at the kitchen counter laughing while taking turns cranking the handle of the pasta maker. I'd retreat to the couch in the living room, where I'd read a book while my dad slept in his recliner with the TV tuned to a sporting event. If I dared to change the channel, he'd start awake. "I'm watching that."

"Gina," my mom would call from the kitchen. "You need to learn how to do this."

"Does she still refuse to buy boxed spaghetti and jarred sauce?" Neesha asks.

"Of course!"

Neesha pulls a chair away from the table, the seat we used to refer to as hers, and plops down in it. "I miss it here," she says. For a moment I think she's talking about my parents' kitchen. "I've always hated Texas. Ajee hated it, too. That's another reason she wanted her ashes spread here."

I sit in the chair next to her. "You loved Texas. That's why you didn't want to go to school here."

Neesha fingers the collar of her fuchsia sweater. "Gina, I didn't get into BC."

I freeze. "What?"

"I didn't get accepted," she says.

My eyes go to the phone on the wall. It's the exact phone I was on when Neesha told me she'd decided not to go to Boston College. I take a deep breath and exhale slowly. "You told me you wanted to stay in Texas with your high school friends."

She looks down at the table. "I was embarrassed."

"I don't understand. We were best friends. We told each other everything."

"I was really mad you got accepted and I didn't." She spins her chair so she is facing me. "I hated you for it."

"You hated me?" My voice cracks.

"I guess I was jealous." Neesha spins away from me, puts her elbows on the table, and buries her face in her hands. "You were living the life I wanted, in a house in Westham, with a mother who took care of you and a father who adored you. Then you got accepted to the school that more than anything I wanted to go to. I was stuck in Texas with a father who was never home and a grandmother who . . ." Neesha stops, looks up at the ceiling, and then turns to face me again. "Ajee didn't save any little boys there, Gina. Most people just thought she was crazy, and Sanjit and I were known as the crazy woman's grandchildren."

"You didn't get into BC," I repeat. "You lied to me."

"Sorry." She says it so quietly that I'm not even certain she said it.

"You knew how upset I was that you chose your Texas friends over me. I wrote you letters about it, and you just kept on letting me think that." My voice and body shake with rage.

"I'm not proud of what I did. After, I was too ashamed to tell you so I avoided you."

For almost twenty years I've been mad at her because she didn't go to BC with me like she promised. It never occurred to me that she didn't get accepted. I'm suddenly very hot. I take off my jacket and put it on the back of the chair. I roll up my sleeves and look at Neesha. She attempts a laugh. "Are you about to challenge me to fight?" she asks.

I really would like to slap her. "Why did you lie to me?"

"Why does it matter now?" she snaps.

"Why? Because we didn't talk for almost twenty years. And things in my life weren't as great as you think. All my friends got married and had children, and I was sitting around waiting for a guy named Ethan, and you're the only one who could possibly understand why, and I couldn't even talk to you about it."

I grab my keys from the table and race outside. I look over at Neesha's old house. The girl I thought was my best friend had hated me. I climb into my car and drive away, intending to go around the block. I end up on Cooper's street. I slow down as I pass his house. A minivan is parked in his driveway. A minivan? Is he dating a soccer mom? Damn. His front door swings open, and a dark-haired woman steps outside. My heart races. What if Cooper sees me stalking him? I press my foot on the gas and navigate back to my parents'. Neesha is sitting outside on the stairs. I park on the street but don't get out of the car. She slowly rises and cuts across the lawn. She climbs into the passenger seat. "The woman came home and saw me sitting here." She points to the Murphys'. Mrs. Murphy's car is now in the driveway. "She watched me for a moment and then raced inside."

As she speaks, I drive down the hill and head back to my apartment. Neesha turns the radio on. A few minutes later, my cell phone rings, cutting off the music. "There's a Hispanic woman sitting on our front steps." My mother's panic-stricken voice blasts out of the stereo speakers.

I glance at Neesha. We both laugh.

"Gina, why are you laughing? I think we're being robbed. I just called the police."

"Mom, I just left your house. It's not being robbed."

"Well, who is the Hispanic girl on the stairs?"

"It was an Indian woman."

My mother sighs. "I don't understand."

I shake my head and look at Neesha. "Hi, Mrs. Rossi," Neesha shouts into the speaker. "It's Neesha Patel. I'm in town visiting."

"Oh my," my mother says. "Neesha, how lovely to hear your voice."

"You, too, Mrs. Rossi."

"Gina sent me a picture of your family. Beautiful."

"Thank you."

"I wish I could be there to see you, dear. Promise me you'll come back."

"I promise, Mrs. Rossi."

We say good-bye to my mother. A police car driving in the oppo-site direction zooms by us. After a split second of silence, Neesha and I break into hysterical laughter. I am so out of control that I have to pull over to the side of the road. After we compose ourselves, Neesha reaches over and touches my arm. "This is what I missed most. Laugh-ing with you about the stupidest stuff. I'm sorry, Gina. I really am."

"I'm sorry, too," I say. "I shouldn't have given up so easily. I should have kept trying to contact you." I try to hug her, but my seat belt re-strains me, preventing me from reaching her. We laugh again. "I missed talking to you. So many times I thought, I really wish I could tell Neesha about this," I say. "You were the one person who under-stood me best. I could always be myself, and no matter what dumb thing I did or said, I knew you wouldn't judge me."

Chapter 29

The sound of Neesha's voice from the living room wakes me early Sunday. "I miss you, Jayda," she says. "I'll be home tomorrow afternoon." A few seconds later, she laughs. "Kisses for AJ, and be good for Daddy."

I pick up my phone from the nightstand, but I have no messages. I want to pull the covers over my head and go back to sleep. Even though Neesha is visiting, the weekend has sucked. I haven't heard from Ethan since we left the Chinese restaurant Friday night, and I can't say I blame him. If he told me someone had predicted he would marry a woman named Gina, I'd think he was nuts. Then there was Miss Minivan at Cooper's house. I wish I had never driven by. Oh God, why am I thinking about Cooper?

There is a knock on my bedroom door. "You up, sleepyhead?" Neesha asks. I remember when she slept over when we were kids, she'd be up by six making pancakes with my mother. Now she bursts into my room without waiting for a response. "I called Patty Ryan. She's going to show us the house at eleven."

"Did you tell Ashley you were looking at it?"

She grins. "I told him that in order to spread the ashes, I had to make an appointment with the Realtor for a tour. He told me not to get any ideas."

"Do you want to move back?" I ask, getting out of bed.

"Absolutely. The problem is Ashley's job." She shrugs. "But there is a Boston office."

* * *

Patricia Ryan is waiting in the Murphys' driveway as we drive up Towering Heights Lane. Out of habit, I park at my parents'. "You know what you're doing?" Neesha asks.

I nod. We reviewed the plan several times on the drive over. When Patricia shows us the basement, I will distract her, and Neesha will slip out the side door and spread the ashes under the rosebush. No matter what, I can't let Patricia go outside.

Neesha and I cross the street. "Neesha Patel," Patricia screams. "You are absolutely gorgeous!" They hug while I stand there awkwardly watching. "How wonderful to see you." Patricia glances at me and touches my arm. "You, too, Gina."

We follow Patricia up the walkway and wait while she opens the lockbox and then the front door. Neesha steps through the door frame and pauses. As she studies her surroundings, her eyes fill with tears. I put my arm around her. Slowly she walks up the stairs. "It looks the same but different," she says. Patricia shrugs, but I know exactly what Neesha means. The bones of the house are the same, but the Murphys have made many cosmetic changes through the years. They took down the blue and gray wallpaper and painted the walls tan. They ripped up the dark blue shag carpet that was covering the hardwood floors and replaced the old avocado-color kitchen appliances with stainless-steel versions.

Neesha runs her hand over the granite breakfast bar that replaced the Formica one that was there when she lived here. "We had a lot of laughs sitting here," she says.

I nod.

She turns to inspect the stove. The Murphys replaced the Patels' electric version with a gas five-burner. "Do you remember how my grandmother used to make us pudding after school in the winter?"

"Butterscotch." I picture Ajee at the stove stirring and asking about our day. "You two got in trouble in Social Studies for passing notes today, yes?" She seemed to know everything we did and everything we were about to do.

Neesha reaches into her bag. For a moment I think she's going to pull out the urn. Instead she grabs her cell phone and begins snapping pictures. "The kitchen is gorgeous now," she says. "Ashley will never believe it's the same room as the one in our photo albums."

From the kitchen, Neesha walks down the hallway where the bedrooms are located. She turns into the first room on the left, which used to be hers. When Neesha lived here, there was a constant pile of clothes on the floor. Open books and notebooks were sprawled out on her unmade bed, and bureau drawers were never closed all the way. Today, there are two desks with clean surfaces and a wall of bookshelves. Neesha stands by the window and looks out. "Perfect view of your driveway," she says. "When you were out, I used to watch for your mom's car to return and then run over."

Next she enters the bedroom next to her old one, which was Ajee's. "I swear, she spent countless hours with her ear pressed against the wall when we were in my room," Neesha says. "That's how she always knew what we were up to."

I stop to consider this. Maybe Neesha's right. It's what my mother has implied all along: Ajee knew the things she did because she made it her business to listen to conversations and watch interactions that were no business of hers.

Patricia, who remained in the kitchen talking on her cell phone, joins us in the master bedroom. Neesha rocks back and forth as she glances around. "Never spent much time in here after Mom died," she whispers.

"They redid the bathroom and added a walk-in closet," Patricia explains, either not hearing or ignoring the emotion in Neesha's voice. Patricia opens a door, revealing a closet three feet wide with racks of clothing. I peek inside the bathroom and notice a Jacuzzi tub. Neesha laughs when she sees it. "That's something my dad never would have added." Again she sends pictures to Ashley.

We are on our way downstairs when he responds. Neesha smiles as she reads his message and hands me the phone. *"I very much like this house,"* his text says.

Once in the basement, Neesha gravitates immediately to the area where Ajee conducted her readings. Nothing of her reading parlor remains, however. Instead the walls are lined with shelves filled with boxes of tissue, toilet paper, soap, paper plates, and plastic cups. "Looks like someone shops in bulk," Patricia says.

"Keep her distracted," Neesha whispers. Then she wanders up the stairs that lead to the side door that opens to the yard.

Patricia takes a step to follow Neesha, but I stop her by calling her name. "Have you had a lot of interest in the house?"

"I'll be honest because, you know, we're old friends." Patricia hesitates. "This is my first showing. The Murphys don't want an open house. Makes it hard." She shrugs.

Patricia continues on toward the door. I pull on her arm, and she stumbles on the stairway. "Gina, what are you doing?"

"Sorry. I think, I think Neesha's talking to her husband. Let's give her some privacy."

Patricia narrows her eyes. I wonder if she's remembering the time Neesha stole her dress from her gym locker so that she had to finish the school day in her sweaty shorts and T-shirt or some of the other tricks Neesha pulled on her. Now Patricia runs a hand through her hair. "Sure," she finally says, spinning on the step and heading back down.

I glance out the door and spy Neesha by the rosebush with the urn in her hand. It seems so wrong to spread the ashes on the sly. I'm sure that's not what Ajee had in mind. We should have a ceremony or at the very least offer up a prayer. I want to run outside and stop Neesha.

Patricia interrupts me from my thoughts. "Do you think you'll buy anytime soon, Gina?"

I love my apartment, but how nice would it be if Ethan wanted to get a place with me? He can't live with Jack forever, after all. Maybe if he doesn't want to get married right away, we could just live together. How great would it be to come home to Brady and Ethan every night instead of an empty apartment? I imagine telling my parents I'm moving in with Ethan. I can see my mother's frown. *"He won't buy the cow if he's getting the milk for free, Gina."* I think about what my father would say and make a mental note to ask Ethan if he plays golf the next time I speak with him.

"How are your parents?" Patricia asks. "Do you think they'll be selling anytime soon?"

"I doubt it." I fear they will, though. Each year they stay in Florida longer, and I wouldn't be surprised if they decide to live there year-round.

Several minutes later Neesha comes back inside to find Patricia and me sitting at the breakfast bar. She catches my eye and shakes her head. "Thanks for showing me the house, Patricia," she says. "Ashley and I are going to discuss it tonight."

She sounds sincere, and I think she may be telling the truth.

Patricia hands Neesha her card, and we all head outside. We say good-bye to Patricia and head across the street. In the distance, a jogger crests the hill. Neesha and I turn to watch him. The runner calls my name. I bring my hand to my forehead to shade my eyes from the sun. He waves. As he gets closer, I realize it's Cooper. When he reaches us, he bends at the waist and hangs his head. Why anyone would voluntarily run up Towering Heights Lane is beyond me. Neesha tilts her head and studies him carefully.

When he finally catches his breath, he looks up and smiles. Beads of perspiration drip down his beet red face. He lifts his green shirt to wipe the sweat away, showing glimpses of his six-pack abs.

"He's hot!" Neesha mouths.

"So this is where you grew up?"

I nod. "I can't believe you ran up that hill."

He pats his stomach. "Ate a lot of decadent food over the weekend." I picture him sharing dessert with the soccer mom and her brood of kids. I bet Cooper is excellent with them. "Did you spread the ashes?" he asks.

"No," Neesha says. "It seemed wrong to leave her by herself." Cooper studies her with that squinty look I love so much. "I know, it sounds weird," she says.

"Not at all," Cooper answers. "I'm Cooper, by the way."

"You're Cooper!" Neesha exclaims. He turns questioningly toward me. "Luci told me all about you. I'm Neesha."

Why would Luci tell Neesha about Cooper?

"Don't believe anything Luci says," Cooper answers.

Sweat is dripping off him onto the driveway. "Do you want to come in for some water?"

"No time," he says. "Got some people waiting for me at home." Miss Minivan and her kids. They're probably going on a picnic.

He waves and takes off down the hill. Neesha and I watch until he disappears from our view. "I think Ajee would like him for you," she says. "Even if his name isn't Ethan."

Chapter 30

Neesha's wandering around my apartment collecting her belongings: a jacket over the back of the kitchen chair, shoes by the couch, a book in the bedroom, shampoo in the shower, lipstick by the mirror. We were supposed to have left for the airport twenty minutes ago.

"I think I've got it all now." She fastens her suitcase and wheels it to the front door.

I scan the living room looking for anything she might be leaving behind. The only item that's not mine is the urn. Neesha plans to come back during the summer with Ashley and the kids to spread the ashes. Until then, Ajee's staying with me.

Once in the car, I can tell Neesha wants to say something important by the way she's studying my profile. Every time I turn to look at her, she quickly looks away. "Gina," she finally says. "I think Ajee got the third predictions wrong for both of us. Ashley can't leave his job, and I'm not sure about Ethan for you."

"Ajee never got it wrong." I put on my blinker and turn right onto the entry ramp for the Mass Pike.

Neesha turns the radio up. "This is Jayda's favorite song," she says, and she sings along to "Call Me Maybe." When the song ends, she turns the radio off. "Jayda," she says. "Ajee told me I was having a boy."

I glance over at Neesha. I can tell by the way she's pulling on the seat belt by her shoulder that there is more to this story. "Did she specifically say Jayda would be a boy or that you would have a boy someday?"

Neesha laughs. "You sound like Ajee now." She changes her voice to imitate Ajee's. "Ah, dear one, I only said that you would have a boy, I did not say that *this* baby would be the boy." She goes back to her normal voice. "But we all knew she was talking about Jayda."

"Was she, though, because soon after you had AJ." I step on the gas to put some room between me and a green Civic that is riding my bumper. "Why can't he just go to the left lane and pass me?"

Neesha turns to look at the car behind us, which has already closed any space I put between us. She points to the lane on the left. Instead, he turns into the right lane and gives Neesha the finger as he accelerates by.

We both laugh. "I bet that doesn't happen in Texas."

"It does, but usually it's me giving the finger."

In the airport I pull up to the curb as close to the terminal entrance as I can get. Neesha unfastens her seat belt and leans over to hug me. "It was so great to reconnect, Gina." A bus nearly sideswipes my car as it pulls in to drop off passengers; its exhaust chokes me as it idles in front of us. I pull away from Neesha to cough, and she gets out of the car. I pop the trunk.

When I am on the sidewalk with her, she takes my hand. "I know you've been waiting for Ethan, but I don't think you should rule out Cooper. Ajee might have been wrong."

"What did Luci say?"

Neesha squeezes my hand. "She didn't have to say anything. I saw the way he looked at you. I heard the lilt in your voice when you were talking to him."

"Lilt in my voice?"

A police officer approaches, pointing to my car. "Move it."

I hold up my index finger, indicating he should wait a minute. Neesha hugs me.

The police officer taps me on my back. "Time's up," he says.

I arrive at work at ten forty to find Peter sitting in my seat, which he has rolled over right next to Luci's. She's leaning back, laughing at something he just said. Their arms are touching, and Luci moves away from him when she sees me.

Peter gets up and pushes my chair back behind my desk. He blows Luci a kiss as he walks out. "What was that all about?"

"He's trying to convince me to come to karaoke on Friday night." She's chewing gum and blows a bubble. "Cooper and Jamie were looking for you."

I start my computer. Sure enough, I have a message from both of them. Jamie's e-mail instructs me to finish Gail Germain's report today while Cooper asks me to get his report back to him by five o'clock.

"How was the rest of your visit with Neesha?" Luci asks. "Did she like me?"

"What did you tell her about Cooper?"

"I just said it's a shame his name isn't Ethan."

Ethan and Brady are waiting on my steps when I get home from work that night. Brady leaps up on me, and Ethan grabs him by the collar. "He missed you," he says. I squat to pet the dog. Ethan places his hand on my shoulder. "I missed you, too."

I stand again. "Why didn't you call?"

He shrugs. "Leah called. I had to pick up Brady."

"I thought she was supposed to have him until next week."

Ethan hunches his back and stares at the ground. "Apparently that prick she's dating doesn't like dogs. She's giving me full custody."

I stop to consider this. A few weeks ago she was ready to cement the dog's paws in place so she could hold on to him, and now she's just handing him over. I guess she's serious about this guy. "Isn't that a good thing?"

Ethan takes a deep breath and lifts his head but doesn't answer.

"I told her about your friend's grandmother's prediction."

Luci would say he told her to make her jealous. To show her that he's moved on, too. I sit down next to him and pet Brady. "What did she say?"

"Not much." He sighs. "She wondered if you were only dating me because of my name." He stares into my eyes.

"Of course not," I blurt out, but as soon as the words are spoken, I wonder if they're true.

"Why are you dating me? What can I offer you?"

I touch his leg. "No one has ever affected me like you do."

"Great," he says. "You're in lust."

I shake my head. "That's not it, or all of it. I feel safe and loved when I'm with you. You make me feel wanted."

He strokes my face. "Who wouldn't want you?"

I turn to face him and slide onto his lap. We kiss on the stairs under the spotlight. "I do want to marry you," he says. "I just need time." I'm not thrilled by the idea of having to wait longer, but his statement makes me feel better than I felt on Friday night. "Can you wait?" he asks.

"Ajee told me I'd have to be patient."

He runs his fingers through my hair, and his kisses become deeper. We stay tangled up on the stairs as the sound of cars passing on the street and car doors slamming drifts into the backyard. Finally Ethan stands. One hand grabs Brady by the collar; the other takes mine. *It's going to turn out just as Ajee predicted*, I think as he leads me to my bed.

Later I cook dinner while he watches *SportsCenter* in the living room. The urn with Ajee's ashes sits on the coffee table just a few inches away. I wonder if seeing me and Ethan content like this would make her happy. Of course it would. Ethan yawns and stretches. He lifts his feet up on the table, and they brush against the urn, knocking it to the floor. He stands to retrieve it, but trips over Brady, banging his face against the coffee table.

Brady stands and barks as I rush into the room. "Are you okay?"

"It hurts." He covers the side of his face with his hand.

"Let me see."

He lowers his hand revealing his cheek. There's a small circular red mark with a deep scratch running diagonally through it. I can't stop staring at it because it looks exactly like the symbol for "no."

Chapter 31

The elevator stops on the second floor. Jamie boards. He's carrying a stack of folders and eyes Luci's and my empty hands. "Are you two prepared for this meeting?"

Luci points to her head. "We have it all in here. Don't you worry."

"I am worried," Jamie says. "They're thinking of outsourcing editing to India."

Luci and I laugh. "I'm pretty sure editing can't be outsourced to India," she says.

Cooper and I still have not come up with a way to speed up the editing process. The other executives are losing their patience, so Cooper called today's meeting to solicit ideas from Jamie and Luci.

The elevator reaches the fourth floor. The doors slide open. We follow Jamie down the hall into Cooper's office. He's sitting at the round table in the corner of the room studying a piece of paper with a half-eaten sandwich in front of him. He looks up and smiles, the two-dimple version that transforms his face. I'm so mesmerized by it that I walk into the bookshelf that's next to the door. I hit it so hard that the framed picture of Cooper with the beautiful dark-haired woman falls to the ground. Cooper leaps from his chair and rushes to my side. "Are you okay?" He puts his hand on my shoulder and leads me away from the door. I look up at him. He has that squinty look. I swear it takes my breath away. I notice a smear of peanut butter by the corner of his mouth, and I instinctively reach up to wipe it away. When I touch him, his grip on my shoulder tightens, and he lets out a small gasp as he exhales.

"Catherine Zeta-Jones," Luci says. She's holding the picture that fell to the ground. Cooper and I immediately step away from each other. "How did you meet her?" Luci asks as she places the photo back on the shelf and takes the last chair at the table.

"She is, or was, the spokesperson for one of the cellular companies I cover. Met her at a banquet."

Luci shoots me a smug look. I'm behind Cooper's desk about to roll his chair to the table. "Gina thought it was a picture of you and your girlfriend," she says. I wish I could make myself invisible. Instead I do the next best thing and sit down right there behind Cooper's desk. I can feel my neck getting splotchy. I slouch in my seat, wishing I could kill Luci. "I told her you don't have a girlfriend, but she thinks you do." Now, instead of killing her, I want to kill myself.

Jamie clears his throat, and Luci stops talking. I refuse to make eye contact with anyone and stare at the desktop. I can feel Cooper and Jamie both looking at me, though. Christ, it's suddenly a thousand degrees in Cooper's office. I think I might melt. I wish I could melt. I imagine turning into a big puddle on the floor.

Jamie slides a piece of paper with graphs in front of Cooper and Luci and then hands one to me. "These are our statistics for the past few weeks," he says. I have never been so happy to discuss work.

After five minutes of brainstorming, Cooper's computer buzzes, and an e-mail flashes across the bottom of his screen. The sender's name, Monique Harrington, catches my attention. I read the message: *"Can you take Tyler to baseball tonight?"* Well, the woman in the picture might not be Monique, but obviously she and Cooper are serious if he's involved in the kids' lives.

"Gina?" Jamie says. "Your turn."

We are all taking turns making suggestions. "Hire more editors," I say.

Jamie frowns. "Luci just said that."

"Yeah, well, it's worth repeating."

"Maybe we're going about this wrong," Cooper says. "Why don't you tell me about the reports you're able to edit quickly."

"Well, once . . ." Luci begins. I don't hear the rest because Cooper's e-mail flashes again. It's a second message from Monique. *"Steak tonight?"*

Do she and her children live with him? Does she have more than one kid? She must if she drives a minivan. I imagine Cooper in a Red

Sox cap, playing catch with a small boy. Then I imagine him and Monique sharing a candlelit dinner. Of course, I picture Monique looking exactly like Catherine Zeta-Jones. Then the image of the woman blurs, and when it comes into focus, it's me. Cooper is clinking a wineglass against mine. We each take a sip. He puts his glass down, reaches for mine, and places it next to his. He leans over and kisses me. Then he stands, picks me up, and carries me into the . . . *Stop it. Stop it right now. I have a boyfriend. A fiancé, practically. And his name is Ethan, just like Ajee said.*

I look back to the table. Jamie, Cooper, and Luci are all staring at me, clearly waiting for a response. Luci raises an eyebrow. "And that's my example of a time when I had to rush to meet an impractical deadline," she prompts.

And that is one reason Luci Chin is my best friend. She keeps me from getting fired. "Right," I say. "Last week, reports from Gail and Cooper were due on the same day. Hers was so bad there was no way I could finish it and yours," I say, looking at Cooper. Oh boy, I shouldn't have done that. I feel my chest heating up as I notice how plump his lips are. I bet they're soft.

"So, what did you do?" he asks.

I twirl a long strand of hair around my index finger and then unravel it slowly. "Truthfully, I edited hers and just lightly scanned yours. Hers was unreadable and couldn't go to the client as written; yours was okay."

"You sent Cooper's report to the client without editing it," Jamie repeats in a judgmental tone.

"I did."

"Gina, how could—"

Cooper cuts off Jamie. "That's it."

"What?" Jamie asks.

"The way to speed up editing. Comprehensive edits for those who need it, and cursory reviews for those who don't."

"Who determines that?" Luci asks.

"You and Gina." He scribbles something on a piece of paper. "You'll rate the analysts. Those with high scores get quick reviews, and those with low scores get the full treatment."

Jamie, Luci, and I file out of Cooper's office and head back to our own. We ride the elevator in silence. It dings when we reach the second floor. "Do the ratings right now," Jamie says before stepping off the elevator. "And I want an explanation for each one."

Luci salutes him. "Yes, sir."

"I mean it," he says as the doors slide shut.

Luci waits until we're back in our office to tease me. "Can't believe you thought Catherine Zeta-Jones was Cooper's girlfriend." She leans back in her chair with her hands interlocked behind her head.

I sigh. "I didn't recognize her."

"Obviously." She laughs.

"Okay, so it wasn't a picture of Cooper and his girlfriend, but he still has one, Monique. She e-mailed him during our meeting."

"Is that why you weren't paying attention? You were reading his e-mails." It's the same judgmental tone Jamie used earlier.

"It's not like I was snooping. They were flashing right in front of me."

"Anything juicy?"

"He's taking her son Tyler to Little League, and they're having steak for dinner." Luci starts typing as I speak. I'm not sure she's even listening anymore. "So I guess it's serious," I say. "If he's involved in her kid's life."

Luci nods. "His profile's off the dating site. Looks like you waited too long and lost your chance."

Waited too long. Story of my life. My heart beats faster. When I try to take a breath, a sharp pain rips across my chest. They're the exact symptoms I had when I fled the church for the emergency room. I'm having a panic attack because Cooper took his profile off a dating site. What's wrong with me?

"Are you okay?" Luci asks.

I tell myself to calm down. It doesn't matter what Cooper does, because I'm with Ethan. Just like Ajee predicted.

Luci watches me through narrowed eyes. "You don't look so good."

"I need some fresh air." I stand and head outside for a walk.

Chapter 32

On Saturday night Ethan and I are lying on opposite ends of my couch watching a movie. His legs are draped over mine, and my foot begins to tingle because it's at such an awkward angle. I pull it out from under him. His body weight shifts, but he says nothing. A few minutes later I hear snoring. I look over at him. His eyes are closed tight while his mouth hangs open. When I used to think about meeting Ethan, I imagined us going to fancy restaurants, plays, and concerts on Saturday nights.

My cell phone rings. I reach for it on the coffee table in front of me and see my mother's face flash across the screen. Ethan startles awake.

"We're leaving a week from Wednesday," she says.

Finally! This is the latest they've ever stayed in the Sunshine State. Usually they're home by early April, in time for the start of the golf league at Westham Country Club. This is also the first year I haven't visited them in Florida, so it's the longest I've ever gone without seeing them.

"That's great!" I say as Ethan stretches his arms above his head. I watch him pull out his phone and press a few buttons. I still haven't told my mother about him. I imagine what would happen if somehow she found out he is still married. "We raised you better than that!" I can see the veins in her forehead bulging. "Adultery is a mortal sin. You are going to hell. On the express elevator." She'd probably be crying. "Get out. Get out now. I never want to see you again." Yup, definitely best to wait until Ethan's divorce is final to tell her about him.

"Any news on the Murphys' house?" she asks now.

"No, but Neesha looked at it while she was here." Complete silence. "Mom, are you still there?"

"I'm here," she says. "Don't tell me she's thinking of buying that house."

"She's trying to talk her husband into moving back."

My mother sighs. "Hopefully, he has more sense than she does. She's only doing this because Ajee put the idea in her head."

It's useless fighting with my mom about Ajee. She will never give the woman any credit. "Well, I hope she does move back," I say.

My mother is silent. I picture her counting to ten. "Gina, even if she does, it doesn't mean you're going to meet and marry a man named Ethan."

"I met him." Oh crap. She goaded me into it.

"You met a man named Ethan?" The disbelief in her voice suggests I just told her Elvis is alive and well and living in Westham.

"He's here with me now." Ethan glances at me. "You can meet him when you're home. We'll all go to dinner." All that's coming from the other end of the phone is heavy breathing. Oh boy, did I just shock her into cardiac arrest? "Mom, are you all right?"

"How did you meet?"

I tell her the story.

"Well," she says. "I guess the odds were that at some time you would meet someone with that name."

"Unbelievable. You still refuse to give Ajee any credit."

She sighs. "Ajee was not psychic, Gina. She didn't know you were going to meet a man named Ethan."

"She didn't just say I was going to meet a man named Ethan. She said I was going to marry one."

Ethan's watching me intently now. He clenches and unclenches both fists repeatedly.

"So you and this Ethan have discussed marriage?"

"We've talked about it."

Next to me Ethan exhales loudly, stands, and heads for the kitchen. He opens the refrigerator. I hear a pop top snap open and turn to look at him. While my mother remains speechless on the other end, I watch him guzzle down a beer.

"I thought you'd be happy," I finally say to her.

"Oh Gina, I just wish Ajee had never—"

"Never mind, Mom. See you soon."

"Right," she says. "You and my future son-in-law."

"What was that all about?" Ethan asks. He's back in the living room, perched on the end of the sofa cushion, his back straight and both feet on the ground. His beer is already gone.

"My mother refuses to believe that Ajee got the predictions right."

Ethan taps his foot on the rug. "Gina—" he begins but is interrupted by his beeping phone. He pulls it out of his pocket, smiles, and then hands it to me. It's a text message with a picture of Brady asleep on a bed, his head resting on a pillow. The message is from Amber. It reads, *"Wore out our sweet boy today. Took him for a long run on the beach."*

He turns his back to me as he types a response to Amber's text. I rewind the movie to the scene we were on before my mother called. A few minutes later, his cell phone buzzes again. This time instead of sharing the message with me, he quickly shuts off his phone and slides it back in his pocket.

On Sunday morning, we walk the block to the bakery. The door is propped open, and the aroma of baking bread drifts out to the sidewalk, where the owner hurriedly sets out small round tables.

Inside a man sits at a table, sipping coffee and reading on a tablet. A few tables away, a woman pulls her hand off her laptop's keyboard to break off a piece of a donut.

I order a blueberry muffin and iced tea. Ethan gets a lemon pastry and coffee. We take our food outside and sit at one of the tables the owner has just set up. The sun beats down on us. After a few minutes, I'm so warm that I stand and remove my jean jacket. As I hang it over the back of my chair, a man, a pregnant woman, and a little boy pass our table. The boy stops to look at Ethan, who is wearing sunglasses that wrap around his head. "Hello," I say to the boy, crouching down to his height.

He points at Ethan. "Glasses," he says.

I nod as I stand and return to my seat.

The boy reaches up, clearly wanting Ethan to give him the glasses. Ethan glances at him and then turns away and bites into his pastry. The mother reaches for the little boy's hand. "Let's not bother these nice people while they eat," she says.

"Glasses," the boy screams, and now he's bouncing on his feet and waving his hand at Ethan, who continues to ignore him.

"Sorry, buddy," I say. "He needs his glasses."

The father bends down and lifts the boy, carrying him away from our table and into the bakery.

"Sorry," the mother says.

"It's no problem," I say, but she's looking at Ethan. He nods. It's so subtle, though, that I doubt she even notices.

As she starts to walk away, Ethan says, "I hate when people can't control their kids."

I glance up. The mother pauses in the doorway. We make eye contact, and then she keeps going.

"Why were you so rude to them?"

Ethan laughs. "How was I rude?" he asks. "I was trying to eat, and the kid wouldn't leave me alone."

"He was three. He doesn't know better."

"His parents do." I take a bite of my muffin. Ethan shrugs.

"Do you think our kids are going to behave perfectly all the time?"

"Whoa." He slams his pastry back to the table. "Now you have us married off with kids?"

"Yup, a boy and a girl, of course." I smile as I say it.

Ethan takes another bite of his breakfast and chews very deliberately. "I guess I should make it really clear. I don't want kids."

"What?" Above us, the sun disappears behind a cloud.

Ethan crams the rest of his Danish into his mouth before responding. "I'm too old and set in my ways now. Plus they're a financial drain."

I reach behind me for my jacket and wrap it around my shoulders. "So, is it that you don't want kids, or you think you can't afford them because I—"

"Gina," he says very deliberately. "This is nonnegotiable. I am not having kids." The couple with the little boy exits the bakery. I look at the mother's stomach. She's at least seven months along.

"You might change your mind." My mouth is dry, and I gulp down my iced tea.

"I won't."

In the distance, a horn from a train sounds, or maybe it's the alarm on my biological clock trying to awaken me. I am thirty-six years old and dating a man who doesn't want children.

Chapter 33

My windshield wipers squeak as I sit in gridlock on Monday morning. The noise irritates me, so I switch them off and watch the raindrops bounce off the window. The weather matches my mood. I have waited almost twenty-five years to meet Ethan, only to learn he doesn't want children. While Ethan slept peacefully next to me last night, I tossed and turned, weighing my options. Not wanting kids should be a deal breaker, a sign that he is not the right Ethan. I could break up with him, but then what? In four months, I will be thirty-seven years old. Does that leave me enough time to meet some-one else, fall in love, get married, and have kids? Probably not. My punishment for not listening to Ajee would be being completely alone. If I listen to her, I can at least end up with Ethan, with whom I have great chemistry and . . . I tried to think of things we have in common. The list was short. Just one item. Love of Mexican food. He doesn't read novels; he doesn't like movies; he doesn't like kids. That's what I kept coming back to.

The driver behind me blasts his horn. Guess he's mad that I haven't moved my car into the available two inches of space in front of me. The horn blasts again. I fight an urge to throw my car into Re-verse and accelerate backward.

My cell phone rings, and Neesha's face flashes on the screen. "There's an opening in Boston," she screams. "Ashley's putting in for a transfer today."

"Wait, what?"

"It's a great opportunity," she says. "I called Patricia. There are still no offers on my house. If he gets the transfer, we're making one."

Neesha's still talking, but in my mind I hear Ajee on that warm summer day when we were thirteen years old: *"You will move away before the start of high school, and you will not return again until you are an adult with children of your own. Yes, you and your family will own this very house."*

Of course Ashley's transfer will go through, and there's no doubt the Murphys will accept Neesha's offer. She's moving back to Towering Heights Lane just like her grandmother said.

I think about what Ajee said to me: *"You will get tired of waiting. You will doubt that he will come, but he will. You must wait. You must wait for Ethan."* Well, I *am* tired of waiting, but I guess I just need to be patient a little longer. Ethan will come through. He will change his mind about having children. He has to.

The traffic in front of me has crawled a foot forward, and the psycho in the car behind me is now leaning on his horn because I haven't moved. I shift into Reverse and turn to glare at him. The beeping stops. He motions with his arms as if to say, *What the hell are you doing?* I put the car back in Drive and inch forward.

"How are things with Ethan?" Neesha asks.

"They're great," I say, needing my words to be true.

I race into the building at 8:55. Today Luci, Jamie, and I are attending the 9:07 meeting to watch Cooper present our idea for speeding up the editing process. As I step off the elevator, Luci is about to board. She glances at her watch. "Hurry up." I run down the hall to our office, grab a notebook and rush back to Luci. We ride the elevator upstairs in silence and enter the executive boardroom at 9:05. Jamie and Cooper are the only ones there. Cooper nods at Luci and me while straightening his tie. Dressed in a suit and sitting at the head of the table in this large boardroom, he seems more like the TechVisions's Senior Vice President Cooper than the playful man I have come to know over the past few months.

At exactly 9:07, the other executives file into the room and take their places around the table, filling the remaining seventeen seats. Luci, Jamie, and I are sitting in a row of folding chairs set up to the right of the table, next to the windows. Our position in the room makes it clear we are not here to participate but to observe. "Good morning," Cooper begins. His voice sounds deeper than usual. "Today we are joined by the editing team: director of editing services, Jamie Welch, and his staff, Luci Chin and . . ." He looks over at me and pauses. "And . . ." My eyes widen in surprise. "And . . ." Luci elbows me. Unbelievable. "Gina Rossi," I say.

Cooper pushes his tongue against the side of his mouth so that his left cheek puffs out. "Gina Rossi," he says quietly.

"Over the past several weeks, Gina and I examined several possibilities for maximizing efficiencies in the editing process." He looks at me as he says my name. "We have determined the best opportunity to improve the turnaround time is to implement an analyst rating system." Here in this room he is slow-talking Cooper, the vice president who doesn't know me.

Luci glances at the clock and then bends toward my ear. "At this rate, we'll be here all day," she whispers. Jamie shoots us a look, and Luci leans away from me.

"The degree of editing a report receives will be determined by the analyst's rating." Cooper's tone is authoritative, and his colleagues are all turned in their chairs toward him. He goes on to describe the different levels of editing. As I listen to him speak and observe how the other executives are enraptured by his every word, I realize how foolish I have been to daydream about him. He is a well-respected senior vice president. I am a copy editor whose name he can't even remember. Of course, he isn't interested in me. I bet Monique is a doctor or lawyer or maybe even an engineer.

When Cooper finishes his presentation, the executives grill Luci, Jamie, and me about how we determined the ratings. Jamie answers all the questions. Every now and then, Luci clarifies something. I sit silently with my hands folded on my lap. I feel Cooper watching me and can sense his disappointment. *Say something, anything*, I imagine him thinking. When the questions are done, the vice presidents agree to take a few days reviewing Cooper's proposal before deciding whether to accept it, and the three of us are dismissed.

After Monday, the rest of the week drags. I don't see Ethan because he's redoing a kitchen for a house on Nantucket and is staying on the island. Cooper no longer calls or e-mails. I guess now that our project is over, he has no reason to. Even lunch is boring. Most days, Luci eats with Peter instead of me. They sit at a corner table in the cafeteria, talking nonstop and laughing as other employees cast sideways glances at them.

Neesha calls every day. She's definitely not as good at waiting as I am, because she begins each of our conversations with the same impatient whine, "We still haven't heard." Then she goes on to talk about renovations she's planning for the house, including a sunroom in the back.

We haven't heard back from the 9:07, and Jamie says it may be a week or so before we do. In the meantime, it's full edits for everyone as usual. Cooper hasn't submitted any reports this week, but Gail Germain has. Of course I'm stuck working on them.

Chapter 34

Luci and I are sitting at a high top in the lounge at Last Chance. When we got here just after five o'clock, we had the room to ourselves. Now, at almost six, all the tables are full, and there's a mob crowding the bar. Luci glances toward the door and then at her watch; she's been doing that since we got here. "Whom are you expecting?"

She flashes me a smile. "Pete—" She laughs before she can get his whole name out.

"Seriously, what's going on between you two?"

Luci leans across the table toward me. "I think you know exactly what's going on." She laughs wickedly, sits back, and flags down our waitress, a heavyset brunette with a hairy mole under her left nostril. Luci stares at the mole but doesn't say anything.

"What do you need?" the waitress asks.

Luci narrows her eyes. Here we go. She's going to comment on the mole. I know it. Finally, she looks into the waitress's eyes. "Another round."

"You got it," the waitress says. She takes Luci's empty martini glass, but I still have a third of my drink left so she leaves it.

Luci excuses herself to go to the restroom. I finish my drink, pull out my phone, and send a message to Ethan. *"What are you doing?"* He's still on Nantucket this weekend working on the kitchen. I imagine right now he's at a bar with the rest of his crew having dinner. A moment later he sends a picture of a mug of beer next to a plate of steamers. I snap a picture of my martini and send it to him.

"*Ciao,* Bella," a familiar male voice says. "Expecting a call?" I look up. Cooper is standing in front of the table.

I stare without speaking. Only Ajee has ever called me "Bella." "What did you just say?" He points to my phone, but I shake my head. "No, what did you call me?"

"Look, Gina, I'm sorry about what happened at the 9:07. I lost my train of thought." His cheeks turn bright red. "You looked so . . ." His voice trails off, and he studies me with that squinty look.

I looked so what? Out of place in a room filled with executives?

The waitress appears next to Cooper and places the chocolate martinis on the table. Cooper lifts his hand and swipes under his nose like he's trying to remove something on his face. He plants himself in Luci's seat and studies our drinks. "You girls don't mess around," he says, picking up Luci's glass for a taste while I take a sip of mine. "You could hurt yourself with this," Cooper warns, returning Luci's drink to the table. He's right. The martinis are dangerously good.

"So, what are you doing here?" I ask, imagining that Monique must be busy with her kids tonight.

Cooper blinks really fast. He points across the room where a bunch of our coworkers are sitting. When did they get here? Luci is standing at the head of their table laughing at something Peter just said. "It's karaoke night."

"Are you going to sing?" I ask.

"I might."

I take another swallow of my martini. "That I would like to see."

Cooper stands. "Well then, stick around."

He leaves me alone at the table. My phone buzzes with another message from Ethan. *"Don't do anything crazy."* As soon as I finish reading the message, my phone is ripped from my hands. "Who are you texting?" Luci shrieks. She studies the screen for a moment, gives me a look of disapproval, and powers my phone off. "Gina, don't always be so accessible to him. Make him work for it." She slips my phone into her pocket. "Let tonight be about having fun with your coworkers. Don't give him a second thought." She picks up her drink and tilts her head in the direction of the table where Peter and Cooper are sitting. "Let's join the others." She marches off, and I follow.

Two and a half hours later, I am sandwiched in a booth between Cooper and Luci. I have had three martinis, and the waitress places another in front of me. Luci must have ordered it. The waitress's mole looks bigger than it did at the start of the night. Cooper discreetly slides the drink in his direction and pushes a glass of water toward me. I have to admit I like that he is looking out for me. It makes me feel safe.

Peter struts around the makeshift stage doing a rap version of Billy Joel's "Uptown Girl." Throughout his performance, he points to Luci, who laughs while clapping her hands. When he's done with the song, he pushes himself into the booth next to Luci, forcing me to press against Cooper. His body is rock-solid. I flash back to the day Neesha and I saw him jogging up Towering Heights Lane. A vision of his six-pack abdomen pops into my head. I fight an urge to lift his shirt and touch his stomach. I feel myself getting hot and shift my weight away from Cooper toward Luci. She nudges me back toward Cooper. He leans sideways, so close his mouth is by my ear. I feel his hot breath on my face. He whispers, "Are you okay?"

I turn my head toward him. His face is so near that if I leaned a quarter of an inch closer, our foreheads would be touching. A piece of hair falls over my eye. He lifts his hand and pushes the hair behind my ear. I lick my lips and edge closer. His glance drops from my eyes to my mouth. He's going to kiss me. I want him to kiss me. I close my eyes. I pucker my lips. I feel his fingertip rub the corner of my mouth. I unpucker my lips and open my eyes. "Chocolate," he says. He slowly raises his finger to his mouth and sucks it off.

I jerk away from him. I have to get out of here before I do something dumb. I tap Luci on the back. "Let me out. I'm going to sing."

Peter and Luci both look at me in surprise, but they stand so that I can get out of the booth. Cooper grabs my arm. At first his grip is tight, but he immediately lightens it, and gently slides his hand down my forearm. "Are you sure you want to do this?"

What I want is for him to keep touching me like that. What is wrong with me? "Absolutely."

He releases my arm. "Break a leg."

My feet feel as if they are encased in cement as I walk to the stage. I take my time flipping through the playbook. The words appear to be jumping all over the page. I decide on Cyndi Lauper's "Girls Just Want to Have Fun" and tell the DJ. The music starts. I just stand there. Everyone watches me. I try to open my mouth. Nothing comes out.

Luci pushes Peter out of the booth and rushes to the stage. She points at the DJ. "Start again." He starts the music over. Luci puts her arm around me and sings. She sounds awful. The tune is so wrong that I wonder if she's ever heard the song before. I sing over her to drown her out. Peter and Cooper pump their fists.

Luci stops singing, but I keep going. Soon the entire room is clapping and cheering for me. I sneak another look at Cooper. He's turned in his seat so that he has a clear view of me. He's smiling. When our eyes meet, he gives me another fist pump. When I finish the song, Luci hugs me. "You were great."

"Thank you."

Cooper and my other coworkers are on their feet giving me a standing ovation while the rest of the people in the room remain seated but clap enthusiastically.

I laugh and bow. Karaoke makes it so easy to make a room of drunken people think you can sing. Just pick a song by a singer with a horrible voice. I mean, if I had chosen an Adele or Kelly Clarkson song, I would have been booed off the stage. But Cyndi Lauper? Anyone can sing better than she does.

Luci leads me back to our table. "Who knew you could sing?" Peter says. I'm not sure if he's talking to me or Luci. Before I climb back in the booth, Cooper stands to get out. "My turn," he says. He brushes against me as he heads to the stage.

I get settled in the booth while Cooper looks through the playbook. He clearly does not have the same karaoke strategy as I do. He chooses "My Way" by Frank Sinatra. The whole room goes silent. I swear to God, if I were to close my eyes, I'd swear ol' Blue Eyes himself were the one on stage crooning. When Cooper's done with his song, the entire room leaps to their feet. Peter starts a chant of "Encore, encore, encore." Cooper says something to the DJ, and then music that I instantly recognize begins to play. Nat King Cole's "When I Fall in Love." This is the song I always imagined Ethan and I would dance to at our wedding. I feel my eyes filling with tears as Cooper sings. I don't know if it's because his voice is so beautiful or because of the meaning I've always assigned to the song.

Before Cooper returns to the table, I go to the restroom to get ahold of myself. I don't think I'm gone that long, but when I return karaoke is over for the evening, and Cooper is alone in the booth. "Where's everyone?"

"They all went home." His eyes bore into mine.

"Where's Luci?"

"She left with Peter."

I stare at Cooper. I love the little wrinkles near his eyes. They make him look sophisticated. "She left?" I stammer. "She's my ride. My car is still at the office."

Cooper nods. "I really don't think you should be driving. I told Luci I'd take you home."

I can't go home with Cooper Allen. I don't trust myself to be alone with him. Oh God, what is wrong with me? "I'm fine. You can just take me to my car."

"Okay," he says. A wave of disappointment ripples through me. I expected him to put up more of a fight than that.

We walk out of the restaurant to Cooper's car. He opens the door for me.

When he pulls out of the restaurant parking lot, he turns left toward the highway instead of right to the office. "Hey," I shout. "My car is at the office."

"Gina, you had three martinis. You shouldn't be driving." He's using his I-know-better-than-you work voice, which automatically makes me want to argue with him.

"I'm not drunk."

"Maybe not, but why risk it?" He makes it sound so reasonable that it now seems pointless to disagree. Cooper Allen is taking me home. Cooper Allen, whom I almost kissed. Cooper Allen, who caressed me. Cooper T. Allen, a senior vice president. Cooper Allen, who forgot my name on Monday.

He catches me staring at him. "Where did you learn to sing like that?" I ask.

He shrugs. "I could ask you the same thing."

An image of me and Mrs. Patel sitting at the piano in the Patels' living room pops into my head. "I used to sing with my friend Neesha's mom when I was really small."

Cooper turns to look at me. He flashes his perfect smile. "Well, you have a beautiful voice."

I stare at him without speaking for a beat longer than is comfortable. He turns his attention back to the road. "Thank you. So do you," I finally say. And a beautiful smile and beautiful six-pack abs. Oh boy, I really must be drunk. Why am I having these thoughts about Cooper?

"So," Cooper says, "Luci and Peter. I would have never put those two together."

I sing the theme to *Beauty and the Beast*, and Cooper joins in.

"I'm surprised you know that song." Of course he knows it; Miss Minivan has kids. He's probably watched the movie with them dozens of times. I see him, a Catherine Zeta-Jones look-alike, a small boy in a baseball uniform—Tyler—and an unnamed little girl snuggling together on the couch. Cooper even made a batch of Jiffy Pop for the viewing.

He laughs. "It's my niece's favorite. I must have watched it with her at least five times."

The online dating picture of Cooper playing Candy Land pops into my head. "So, you like kids?"

"Sure," he says. "Who doesn't?"

Ethan, I think. *Ethan does not like children.*

"Why did you choose 'When I Fall in Love'?" The words spill out without me even knowing I was going to ask the question.

He glances at me. I can tell he's trying to decide whether he should tell me. He shrugs. "I don't know. I've always loved that song." He looks at me again. "I guess it's just something that I've always believed."

"What, that when you fall in love it will be forever?"

Small pink circles splotch his cheeks. He nods.

"So you've never been in love?"

He exhales loudly but doesn't answer. Maybe right now he's realizing that he loves Miss Minivan.

"Well, you've never been married anyway," I say.

"Marriage is something I intend to do just once," he says.

"That will be nice for your wife," I say. "She'll always know she was your first choice." I feel tears building behind my eyes.

"Gina, what are you talking about?"

"Never mind, I don't know what I'm saying."

"Hey, are you all right?" He pats my thigh.

A tear has escaped and is running down my face. I wipe it away and muster up the strength for a smile. "I'm fine." I switch on the radio. Pink is singing about punching someone. I'd like to punch Ethan. How can he not want kids?

Chapter 35

I wake up the next morning still dressed in my clothes from the day before. A glass of water and a bottle of aspirin are waiting for me on my nightstand. I have no recollection of putting them there. A blurred image of Cooper with his arm around my waist leading me upstairs to my apartment and into my bedroom forms in the back of my mind. He slowly lowered me to the bed and pulled my shoes off before pulling the blanket over me.

"I like that you look out for me," I whispered.

"I like looking after you," he said. He brushed his fingertips over my lips and gently kissed me.

I startle to an upright position and reach for the water. Surely that didn't really happen? It must have been a dream. I pop open the aspirin and down two. Now, I see Cooper placing them on my nightstand. "You are not going to feel good tomorrow."

"Well," I corrected. "I am not going to feel well."

"Actually," he said, "you are going to feel like hell." He left and returned with the wastebasket from the bathroom. "This might come in handy." He placed it next to my bed.

I look down now, and sure enough, the wastebasket is there. Could these be real memories and not recollections from a dream? Did Cooper really kiss me? I brush my fingers over my lips. Of course, he didn't kiss me. He's with Miss Minivan.

I get up and make my way to the bathroom. My reflection in the vanity mirror scares me. My bloodshot eyes are half the size as usual, and my skin has a distinctive greenish tint. A wave of nausea hits, and

I collapse in front of the toilet. I never drink martinis. Why did I drink them last night? And then it comes back to me. Luci promised they'd help me stop obsessing about Ethan. She was right. I barely gave him a second thought. I have to call him now. I force myself to stand and look for my phone. I find my purse and rifle through it, but my phone is missing. Then I remember Luci confiscated it. I can't even drive to her place to get it because my car is at work.

I will e-mail Luci and ask her to drive me to my car. I fire up my computer and log in to my e-mail. I have one message from Cooper. *"Make sure you drink plenty of water today. CA."*

It's so easy to write things in an e-mail you would never say in person. I type my response. *"Did you kiss me last night?"* I imagine the look of confusion on Cooper's face when he reads the message and then see his fingers flying across the keyboard. "Of course not. Why would I ever kiss you? I can't even remember your name."

On the other hand, what if he wrote, "Why, yes. I'm in love with you, Gina"? When it comes right down to it, isn't he better for me than Ethan? He has no ex-wife who still owns his heart. He wants children. He notices me. He looks out for me. He makes me laugh. I can't stop thinking about him. Should I rule him out solely because his name isn't Ethan? Maybe this is the one time Ajee got it wrong.

I delete my response and replace it with *"Thanks for seeing me home safely last night. Gina, the booze bag."* Then I send a message to Luci imploring her to return my phone and take me to my car.

She shows up two hours later. "I've never seen you look so bad," she says. She, of course, looks like her perfect self. Her eyes scan my apartment. "I thought maybe Cooper would spend the night." She winks. "You two looked pretty cozy last night."

I glare at her. "Did you spend the night with Peter?"

Luci laughs. "I never kiss and tell, Gina."

"Seriously, what's going on between you two? Is it serious?"

She plops down on the couch and sighs. "He makes me laugh. He's a distraction, and right now I need to be distracted." She stretches her legs across the coffee table.

I sit next to her. "What do you need to be distracted from?"

She exhales loudly. "Do you think this is how I planned my life? Do you think I want to be forty years old and single again? I'm supposed to be living in the suburbs with Kip and our kids, and now that prick is living my life with someone else." Tears spill from her eyes. She lets them roll down her cheeks without wiping them away. "He knocked up his ghetto gal pal. That's why he's marrying her."

I try to make sense of what Luci is telling me, but my head is pounding, making it hard to focus. He got his wife pregnant and divorced her; he gets his girlfriend pregnant and marries her? "Luci, that makes no sense. Are you sure?"

Now she glares at me. "Yes, I'm sure." She springs to her feet. "I'm starving. Let's go to that place around the corner."

The thought of food causes my stomach to churn, but I want to support Luci.

Fifteen minutes later, Sal Senior is leading us to a table. "So the beautiful girl has a beautiful friend," he says after I introduce him to Luci. "I'll send Tory over to wait on you. He always likes to see you, Gina." He pats me on the shoulder and then bellows Tory's name across the restaurant.

Tory races out from behind the counter. He's wearing a button-down shirt and dress pants instead of his usual T-shirt and jeans. Sal wraps his arm around Tory's shoulders. "He just came from a memorial mass for his mother, God rest her soul. He looks good, doesn't he?"

"Mmm," Luci says. "Handsome." She kicks me under the table.

Some other customers enter the restaurant, and Sal leaves to greet them. Tory remains where he is, with his hands in his pockets staring at me. "How have you been, Gina? I haven't seen you here for a while."

"I'm good. We're going to split a small pizza with peppers."

"I put it in the oven as soon as I saw you walk in." He moves to another table.

Luci watches him walk away. "You could work with that," she says. "Get him a decent haircut. Trash some of that jewelry. He's got potential."

"Can I have my phone?"

Luci unzips her purse, pulls out my phone and hands it to me without saying anything else. I push the On button, and the familiar music of the phone powering up fills the silence. After a few minutes the voice mail icon lights up, indicating that I have three new messages. The first is from Ethan. "I'll be home Tuesday night. I'll cook you dinner." It sounds like a dog barking in the background, but Ethan is on Nantucket and Brady is home. "Call me." He ends the message quickly.

The second message is from Neesha. As I listen, Tory returns to the table with our drinks. "Hey, soul sister, Ashley's transfer has gone through, and the Murphys accepted our offer. Westham, here I come."

"Oh my God." Luci and Tory both look at me. "Neesha is moving back. Ajee's third predictions are right."

"What does that mean?" Tory asks.

"It means Gina will be getting married soon," Luci answers.

Tory nods. "I could tell that guy really liked you. You two didn't stop laughing the whole time you were here." As he walks away, I realize he's talking about Cooper, and then as if to confirm this, Cooper's voice comes out of my cell phone. "Hello, Gina, I just realized you might need a ride to your car. I'm around. Call me if I can help."

Luci looks at me expectantly. "Cooper offering to give me a ride to my car."

"I'm sure he wants to give you a ride." She winks.

I put the phone down and look at Luci. "I think he kissed me last night."

"Finally! That's great!"

"It's not. I'm with Ethan. And Cooper has a girlfriend. Who has kids."

Luci uses her index finger to trace one of the squares on the red-and-white-checkered tablecloth. After several seconds, she looks up at me. "If Ethan had a different name, do you think you'd be with him or consider marrying him?"

I know I'm supposed to say "of course," but I can't make the words come out, especially knowing he doesn't want kids.

"Do you think that maybe because of Ajee's prediction, you're forcing yourself to be interested, forcing him to be the one?"

Tory arrives with our pizza, saving me from having to respond. I look up at him. "I'm sorry about your mom. I didn't know she had passed."

Tory blinks fast, places a piece of pizza on a plate, and slides it to me. "Thank you. We lost her five years ago. She would have liked you, Gina."

"Everybody likes Gina," Luci says, reaching for a slice as Tory turns to leave.

I take a bite of my pizza. The cheese burns the roof of my mouth. I immediately return the piece to my plate and grab my water.

Luci puts a napkin over her pizza and presses down on it so it soaks up some of the grease. "Look, Gina, just because some crackpot old lady told you that you would marry a man named Ethan doesn't mean that you have to do that."

"If Ajee's such a crackpot, how do you explain Neesha moving back to her childhood house?"

Luci peels the napkin off her pizza and wads it into a ball, which she pushes to the side of the table.

"What are you doing to that pizza?"

"I explain it the same way I explain your interest in Ethan. Neesha thinks that's what she's supposed to do. These predictions have become self-fulfilling prophecies for the both of you."

Chapter 36

E than's Jeep is in the driveway, but no one answers when I ring the bell. I try the door, but it's locked. Maybe he's in the shower? I sit on the stairs next to a whiskey barrel of lilies that wasn't here the last time I visited. I try to figure out whether Ethan or Jack is responsible for their appearance and decide on Jack. Frankly, though, I can't imagine that either of them is a flower guy.

I know Ethan didn't forget about our dinner because he called this morning to remind me. The woman whose kitchen he renovated gave him a Crock-Pot recipe for ribs, and he said that's what he's making me tonight. "You have a Crock-Pot?"

He laughed. "I'm borrowing Amber's."

Five minutes have passed. I get up and ring the bell again, thinking that maybe Ethan was in the shower when I first got here. Again there is no answer.

I sit back down. A few minutes later I hear a car driving down the road and then the rumbling of the garage door opening. Jack turns into the driveway and pulls into the garage. The car door slams, and he pokes his head out the overhead door. "What are you doing out here?"

"Ethan didn't answer."

"He's probably walking Brady." Jack motions for me to come in through the garage. As I make my way across the walkway, Ethan and Brady come into view down the street. A short, pudgy woman walks beside them. From where I'm standing, it looks like her body and

Ethan's are touching. Ethan says something, and the woman smiles and playfully pushes him. He grabs her wrists. She tries to twist away. They are both laughing. Ethan lets go of the woman, and she shakes her frizzy blond hair over her shoulder.

Brady sees me and barks. Ethan looks up at the walkway. "Gina, you're early."

"Not really." I walk to the edge of the grass to where they are now. I glare at the woman.

"This is Amber," he says. "The dog walker."

"I didn't realize you walk with her."

"Sometimes," Ethan answers.

"We had a good time today, didn't we?" Amber looks at Ethan while she crouches so that she's eye level with the dog. Brady licks her face. She giggles while Ethan watches them with a stupid grin on his face. Finally she pushes Brady off of her and brings herself to her full height.

"See you soon," Ethan says.

"You're not rid of me so quick," she says. She places her hand on his arm and runs her index finger down toward his elbow. "My sweatshirt is inside, remember?" Her voice is two octaves lower than just a moment ago. Ethan looks at me, but glances down when we make eye contact.

When she's out of sight, Ethan pulls me into his arms. "Missed you, babe." He kisses me hard. He tastes like a cigarette, and I pull away quickly.

"Were you smoking?"

He wipes the back of his hand across his mouth. "The guy I was with on Nantucket. Always had a cigarette in his mouth. Realized I missed it. The only reason I stopped was Leah."

I didn't know he used to smoke. I guess that explains why his teeth are so yellow. "Well, you should stop again."

His only response is a frown.

By the time we arrive upstairs, Amber and Jack are sitting in the kitchen, and Jack is speaking in a harsh tone. He stops speaking as soon as he sees me. Amber's open purse sits on the table in front of her. I can clearly see a pack of Marlboros. Ethan breezes by me and fills Brady's water dish at the sink. I remain standing at the threshold of the kitchen door facing Amber. Her eyes travel up and down my body. I stand perfectly still, feeling awkward and wishing I were wearing a more figure-flattering outfit or were more like Luci, who would definitely call Amber out for this.

Ethan turns from the sink and heads downstairs with Brady's bowl. Amber rises from her seat. "I'll just get my sweatshirt," she says. I watch her walk down the hallway. She looks at me over her shoulder as she saunters into Ethan's bedroom. A moment later she comes out carrying the sweatshirt. I swear to God, she smirks at me.

The smell of the ribs simmering on the counter is overpowering. I feel nauseous. My legs shake, and I lean against the wall to steady myself. I feel Jack watching me. I lift my head to look at him. I think I see sympathy in his expression. Amber struts back into the middle of the room, pauses, turns the sweatshirt right side out, and pulls it over her head. The sweatshirt looks new. It is red with big white letters that say NANTUCKET.

Ethan appears at the top of the stairs. Amber kisses his cheek. "See you soon," she says in the same low tone she used with him before. He turns and watches her descend to the front door.

I make my way to Ethan's room. The bed is unmade. A musty scent fills the air.

Ethan appears in the doorway. "What are you doing?"

"Why was Amber's sweatshirt in your room?"

Ethan crosses his arms across his chest. "What?"

"Amber went into your room to get her sweatshirt."

"So?"

I walk toward him. "What was she doing in your room?"

He unfolds his arms and rubs the stubble on his jawline. "What exactly are you asking, Gina?" He grits his teeth and leans toward me.

I hold my ground. "I'm asking what she was doing in your bedroom."

He punches the door frame. "I can't believe this," he shouts. "Jack doesn't like Brady in the house. You know that. The only places he's allowed are the garage and my bedroom. When Amber got here, I had him in the room with me."

I look away from him. Am I being paranoid? His explanation makes sense. Then I think of the way Ethan and Amber were playing around as they walked down the street, the way Ethan watched, practically aroused, as Brady kissed her face, the way Amber touched him, her smirk as she emerged from his room, her inside-out Nantucket sweatshirt, the stench of cigarettes on his breath and the pack in her purse, the way he watched her as she descended the stairs. I look back at him. "Where did she get that sweatshirt?"

He shakes his head. "I got it for her for watching Brady. I got one for you, too." He stomps across the room, pulls a similar sweatshirt out of a bag, and throws it at me.

I fling it on the bed. "When did you give it to her?"

He bites his lip. "Last night. When I picked up Brady."

"So she wore it over here today. Why did she take it off?"

He lets out a deep breath and takes a step toward me. "Why don't you just ask me what you want to know, Leah?" I stare at him with wide eyes, waiting for him to correct his mistake. "Go ahead, ask me. Ask me if I banged her!"

I shake my head and push him out of the way. He grabs my arm. "Don't," I scream.

Jack appears at the end of the hallway. "Everything okay?"

I shake my arm free. "I was just leaving."

I calmly walk down the hallway. I don't look back at Ethan. When I get to the stairs, I hear his bedroom door slam. "I'm sorry, Gina. Really, I am," Jack says. And somehow I think his apology is for the answer to the question that I wouldn't ask Ethan.

I shake with rage on the drive back to Clayton. It's one thing to put up with Ethan's unresolved feelings for his ex-wife, but his cheating, or at the very least flirting, with the dowdy dog walker, no way. Did he really cheat, or am I being paranoid? My cell phone rests in the cup holder. I keep glancing at it as I drive, expecting him to call. *"Sorry, I lost my temper, Gina. I understand it looked bad, but of course nothing happened between Amber and me. I would never do that to you."*

I turn onto my street. My cell phone has been silent. A landscaping truck is parked in my spot, and two deeply tanned men are loading mowers into the back. I wait for them to finish. It's like they're moving in slow motion. I beep my horn. The larger of the two men puts his hands on his hips and stares at me. I step on the gas and drive around the block. By the time I return, the pickup is pulling out, and I take the vacated spot.

Once inside, I call Luci. Peter answers. I hang up without saying anything, which is really stupid because Luci has caller ID. Sure enough, two minutes later, Luci calls back. "Why did you hang up on Peter?"

"I didn't want to interrupt."

She laughs. "Don't worry. We weren't doing anything uninterruptible."

"We could be," I hear Peter yell in the background.

I plop down on my couch and stare at the urn with Ajee's ashes. I notice a bunch of DVDs strewn across the coffee table: *Goodfellas*, *Saving Private Ryan*, *My Cousin Vinny*. They are all Ethan's. "I think Ethan is cheating on me with the dog walker."

"Why would you think that?" she asks me, and she whispers something to Peter.

I explain why. The line is silent. I hear Luci swallow. "I'm sorry, Gina."

"So you don't think I'm being paranoid?"

She breathes loudly as I stack the DVDs into a neat pile. "Is that what you want me to tell you?"

"I want you to tell me what you really think."

"In a minute, Peter," she yells. "I think you should trust your instincts."

I look at the urn and then the stack of movies. "All his stuff is still here. How will I get it to him?"

"Just throw it away," she answers. "You don't owe him a thing."

"She's not even pretty."

"Who?" Luci asks.

"The dog walker. She's short and fat. Has a flat face."

Luci says nothing.

"I mean, I could understand if she was pretty, maybe, but . . ."

"Gina, don't try to understand. It doesn't matter why he did it, or who he did it with. What matters is that he did it."

I pick up the urn with my free hand. "I know you're right."

"Do you want me to come over?"

I smile. "No, but thank you."

After Luci and I hang up, I go into my bedroom. Ethan's Patriots sweatshirt hangs over the back of the rocking chair in the corner of my room. I pick it up and bury my face in it. It smells like pine and sawdust. I march to the kitchen, get a paper bag, fling the sweatshirt in it and then the DVDs. I head to the bathroom. His razor, shaving cream, and toothbrush sit on the corner of the sink. I dump them into the bag. I lean into the shower and remove his soap and all-in-one shampoo and conditioner. I head back to the kitchen. I place the bag next to the garbage can.

I walk past the coffee table on the way back to my room. I glance at the urn, and an image of Ajee nodding pops into my mind.

I can't sleep that night. Maybe I'm overreacting. Maybe it really happened like Ethan said it did. On the other hand, maybe he's been cheating all along. I think of all the times they texted each other when we were together. Does he love Amber? Did he ever love me?

Somehow I manage to fall asleep, because I wake up to my alarm buzzing. I like waking up to music, but Ethan needed the buzzing sound to get out of bed so I changed the setting. Now I change it back. I will not start my day with an abrasive sound ever again.

When I get to work, there is a vase of sunflowers on my desk and a card. Luci is not in the room, but her computer is on and the office smells like hot sauce so I know she's around. I hold my breath as I tear the small envelope open. Ethan is apologizing. The card will explain that nothing happened between him and Amber. I pull out the card and read: *"Sorry, I got it wrong about Ethan. Ajee from Beyond."*

"It's a little funny, right?" Luci asks. She's standing in the doorway watching me. I look at her, and tears run down my face. "I hate crying," she says, rushing to me. She pulls me into a hug. "I hate hugging, too. Get yourself together."

Luci's hug lasts for all of five seconds before she pulls away, reaching for my purse. She unzips it and removes my cell phone.

"What are you doing?"

I watch her press a few buttons. "Deleting Ethan's contact information. There will be no drunk dialing or texting." She presses a few more buttons and hands me back my phone. I scroll through the contact information. Ethan's name is gone. I look through my log of calls and texts. All the ones from Ethan have been deleted. I try to recall his number, but I never memorized it. I programmed it after he called the first time and then just scrolled to his name and pushed ENTER.

"I really don't know his number."

"That's the point," Luci says. She's back at her desk looking at her monitor. "Trust me, you'll thank me for this later." My cell phone rings in my hand. "Oh Christ," Luci mutters. I look at the screen, hoping it's not Ethan and praying that it is. It's Neesha's name and picture that I see.

"Our closing is on July twenty-eighth."

"That's great."

Neesha hears the flatness in my voice. "What's the matter?"

I tell her about Ethan and Amber. She clicks her tongue. It is the same exact noise Ajee used to make. "Looks like Ajee got this one wrong," she says.

"I guess it had to happen sometime."

Chapter 37

Thursday is a crazy day at TechVisions. In the morning we learn the 9:07 has accepted our proposal to speed up the editing process and released the analysts' ratings. The irate e-mails and phone calls from analysts demanding better grades begin at nine thirty. After Gail Germain visits our office and screams at us for seventeen minutes straight about her F rating, Luci and I lock our door and stop reading e-mails and answering the phone. At noon, we slip out the loading dock door and head to lunch. As we sneak around the building to the parking lot, I see Cooper standing on the curb talking to a dark-haired woman. The minivan is parked in front of them, and from where Luci and I are standing, I can see three small heads. I elbow Luci and point. "Cooper's girlfriend and her kids."

She brings her hand to her forehead to shield her eyes from the sun. One of the kids in the van screams out the window, "Please come with us, Uncle Cooper."

"Uncle Cooper," Luci repeats. "I wonder if she has her kids call all her boyfriends that."

"Probably just the serious ones," I say as Luci and I trample across the flower bed leading down to the parking lot.

"Well, Cooper's a good catch. If you don't mind short men. If she's smart, she'll hang on to him."

I take a last look over my shoulder to study Monique. She looks smart. Well, she has a short, sensible haircut and flat shoes anyway. Damn.

Luci drives to Last Chance. We sit in the same booth we were in last Friday when I thought Cooper was going to kiss me. "You know," I begin, "I almost cheated on Ethan with Cooper." Kissing is cheating. Not as bad as what I think Ethan did, but still.

Luci puts down her menu. "But you didn't."

"Maybe he's telling the truth about Amber. Maybe it just looked bad."

Luci picks up her menu again. We sit in silence until the waitress comes to take our order.

"He wants to meet. To talk," I say after the waitress leaves. He has sent a few texts asking if we can get together.

"I don't think you should do it," Luci warns.

"We're meeting on Saturday."

Ethan is positioned in the booth so that he is facing the door. He stands when he sees me. My chest squeezes when I notice he's wearing the blue shirt I love. I slowly walk to the table, noting it is the same one we sat at the morning I learned his name, and I wonder if he intentionally chose it.

"Hi, Gina." He smiles. I focus on his uneven yellow teeth and not his beautiful blue eyes or the cleft in his chin. He steps toward me. I recoil, thinking he's going to hug me, but instead he reaches for the bag I'm carrying, places it on the seat, and pushes it toward the wall. "Didn't realize I had so much stuff at your place."

Not trusting my voice, I nod and sit on the side of the booth Ethan sat on when we first met. He sits across from me. All around us, diners are eating and conversing, but Ethan and I just stare at each other. I look away from him and notice a twenty-something couple a few tables away that may be as miserable as we are. The man's reading something on the screen of his cell phone while the woman works the keypad on hers. *"Put your electronic devices away and talk to each other,"* I want to shout.

Ethan clears his throat, and I turn my gaze back to him. Our eyes meet. I swear his are watery. "Look, Gina," he begins, but before he can say anything else, the waiter who served us the first time we were here approaches our table. Today, he is sans nose ring and apparently in a better mood. "Good morning," he says, filling our coffee cups and handing us our menus.

"Good morning," I reply, surprised there is no quiver in my voice. Ethan says nothing. He folds his arms across his chest and waits for

Mr. No Nose Ring to leave before speaking again. "Thanks for meeting. I wasn't sure you would show up."

"I said I would, and I usually mean what I say."

He either doesn't realize I'm taking a dig at him or he chooses to ignore it. "Well, I thought you might bring reinforcements. Luci with a baseball bat or Neesha with some black magic." He laughs. I keep my face rigid. I never liked that he laughed at his own jokes. "So, how are Neesha and Luci anyway?" he asks.

Mad I'm here with you. "Fine."

The waiter returns for our order. I don't feel like eating, but I get the french toast anyway. Ethan decides on blueberry pancakes and a side of bacon. "We're known for our home fries. You have to try them," the waiter says. I stare up at him, thinking that maybe he is the talkative twin of the waiter who was our server the first time we were here.

"No thanks," Ethan says.

"You're missing out," the waiter says.

I watch him walk away. "He's a lot happier without the nose ring."

Ethan turns to look at the waiter. "That guy has a nose ring? Are you sure? He doesn't seem like the nose ring type."

Obviously he didn't choose the booth on purpose. "I'm sure."

He reaches into the bowl of sugar. I know he's going to pull out four packets. He opens them one by one. I count as he empties them into his coffee: one, two, three, four. I wonder if he's learned any of my preferences or if any part of our relationship was memorable to him. "Do you know you called me Leah that day?" I ask.

Confusion passes over his face. He stops stirring his coffee. I swear he's going to ask which day. He sighs. "I'm sorry, Gina." He emphasizes my name. "I know you don't believe me, but nothing happened that day between Amber and I."

Inside my head, I scream *"Amber and me!"* To Ethan, I say, "I don't believe you." And then I wonder why he qualified his statement with "that day."

He lets out a deep breath and looks down. "I don't want to fight."

"Why did you want to meet?"

"I just wanted to explain."

A group of boys dressed in baseball uniforms charges through the door, capturing my attention. Ethan turns to see what I am looking at. "I thought that ball was headed up the middle," a boy with the number two on his uniform says. "But then you were there, stepping on second and throwing to first. Game over." He high-fives with number seven.

"You really don't want kids?" I say to Ethan.

"Nope." He sips his coffee.

"I so badly wanted you to be the man that Ajee told me about that I tried to turn you into him," I admit.

He sighs. "Maybe I was trying to turn you into Leah. That's what Jack thinks, anyway."

I guess I knew that all along, but to hear him say it out loud makes it hurt even more.

The waiter interrupts me from this thought by sliding a plate in front of me. "I brought you a complimentary dish of the home fries," he says. "I guarantee you'll order them next time." I stab a potato with my fork and slide it into my mouth. It's cooked just the way I like it, crispy on the outside and soft on the inside. Salt and spicy flavors explode in my mouth. "They've got a kick," I say, pushing the plate toward Ethan for him to try, but he declines. I pull the plate back to my side of the table. "Thanks," I say to the waiter. He smiles and disappears to help another customer.

"I think that waiter likes you," Ethan says.

I wish he sounded jealous, but he sounds matter-of-fact. "Maybe I'll leave him my number."

Ethan reaches for the syrup without responding. I open a packet of butter and spread it through the confectioners' sugar topping my french toast. I wait for Ethan to finish with the syrup. When he does, he puts it down. I reach across the table and then flood my plate with it.

"So, you were going to explain," I say.

He finishes chewing. "I'm just not strong right now, and I have to focus on getting stronger." He stuffs a large bite of his pancakes into his mouth.

I look at his tan arms and his bulging biceps. "What are you talking about?"

He drops his fork so that it clanks against his plate. "I was with Leah for most of my life. I only know myself as part of the couple Ethan and Leah. Leah and Ethan. There was never one without the other. I have to get used to being on my own and get to know myself as me. Do you know what I mean?"

He watches me, waiting for a response. I shift uncomfortably in the booth. The crazy thing is that I do know what he means, because in the few months Ethan and I spent together, I started to think of myself as part of a couple and I lost a piece of myself. I want it back. I nod. He picks up his fork again and resumes eating his pancakes. I break off a bite of french toast with my fork and drag it through the ocean of syrup on my plate.

"I just need some time on my own right now," Ethan says. "Time to do what I want, when I want. The last thing I want is a commitment, and you had this entire life planned out for us." He takes another huge bite of his pancakes.

I push my plate away. "So that's why you slept with Amber."

I watch his Adam's apple move up and down. He leans back in the booth, casually spreads one arm across the back of the bench seat. "I already told you. I didn't sleep with her." His eyes are trained on a spot an inch above my head.

I think back to our first visit here, how I was sure my future was finally starting. I even stopped to buy an issue of *Brides* magazine on the way home. All because his name was Ethan. Idiot.

"I'm sorry I got you into my mess. I'm in no way ready to date."

I laugh. "It's a little late to figure that out, don't you think?"

A large, uncomfortable silence screams at us. It is the type of silence that was comfortable when things were going well. "You know, Gina, you're a great girl. Lots of fun. I like you. A lot. I really do." He pauses. "If I'd met you at any other time . . ."

I thought the silence was uncomfortable, but this is worse. I push the plate of home fries away from me. He pulls it toward him and takes a forkful. "These are good."

My phone rings. I have never been so happy to hear its ringtone. I scramble through my purse and pull it out. My mother's face lights up the screen. I click on ANSWER.

"We made it. We got back late last night."

"You made great time."

"Your father was determined to play at the tournament at Westham Country Club today." She laughs. "When am I going to see you? I'm making meatballs and gravy."

"I'll come now."

I end the call and stand. "I have to go," I say to Ethan. "I guess this is it."

He stands and reaches for me. I fall into his arms. "Just give me some time, Gina. Time to get myself together. We can try again. It will be . . ."

I pull away. "The thing is, Ethan, I'm done waiting. For you or anyone." He blinks fast. I walk past him, leaving a wide berth, and make it out of the restaurant without looking back.

Chapter 38

There is a woman standing in my parents' door waving at me as I pull into the driveway, and it takes me a moment to realize that the woman is my mother. Each year when my parents return from Florida, I'm a little shocked to discover the toll the five months have taken on their appearance. The change in my mother this year is more drastic than in past years because her hair, which was jet-black when she left, is now mostly gray.

"Mom, your hair!"

She pushes open the door, descends the stairway, and meets me on the walkway. "I missed you," I say.

"Why didn't you come down to see us this year?" She pulls me into a tight hug, and I start to cry. First silently, but then loud sobs escape.

She pulls away to look at me. "Gina, what is it?"

"I missed you."

She hugs me again while rubbing my back. "Tell me what's wrong."

My mother has always been able to tell when I'm lying, so I decide to try to distract her instead. "Why did you stop coloring your hair?"

"You don't like it?"

"It's not that. It's just . . . different."

"I've decided to grow old gracefully." She shrugs.

She breaks away, then leads me up the walkway and into the house.

Inside it already smells like tomatoes, basil, and garlic. I enter the kitchen and see a pot simmering on the stove.

"It never comes out right in Florida," my mother says, taking the lid off and stirring the gravy. "I think it's something to do with the stove there." She pulls the full spoon from the pan and extends it toward me with her hand cupped underneath. "What do you think?" I taste the sauce. It's as good as ever. "Too much garlic?" she asks.

I shake my head.

"Sit down." She points to the kitchen table, and I take my usual spot.

She grabs two rolls and fills them with meatballs that she extracts from the gravy. Next she goes to the refrigerator for provolone cheese and places it over the meatballs. Finally she drowns the contents of the sandwich in tomato sauce.

She carries both plates to the table and sits down next to me. "Now, tell me what's going on."

Even though I just ate, there is no way I can resist my mother's meatballs. I pick up the sandwich and bite into it. My mother watches me chew. "It didn't work out with Ethan," I say after I swallow. I can feel the tomato sauce smearing above my lip.

My mother hands me a napkin. "Ajee's third prediction is coming true for Neesha, but not for me." I get up, go to the refrigerator, and return to my seat with two glasses and a bottle of sparkling water. My mother watches me pour.

"I think it's worse that it almost came true. You know? Like it was supposed to work out, but I did something to ruin it." I look up at the ceiling. Then I look at her again and swallow back my tears. "I really thought it was going to work out."

"Oh Gina. I'm sorry."

We eat in silence for a few minutes. "I think maybe you were right," I finally say. "Ajee was wrong about me marrying someone named Ethan."

My mother bites into her sandwich and doesn't say anything for a minute. "I know you think Ajee was psychic, Gina, but she was just very observant."

I shake my head. "I don't know what you mean. She certainly didn't see that woman kidnap Matthew. She was in Maine."

"A few weeks before she left, she told me that she suspected Mr.

Colby was having an affair. You know I never like to gossip, so I didn't ask for any of the details."

"What about Neesha moving and us going to Italy and me breaking my arm? How did she know those things?"

My mother sighs. We are done eating, so I clear the table and put the dishes in the dishwasher. She waits until I'm sitting again to continue speaking. "I've told you this so many times. She knew Dr. Patel had been interviewing for the position in Texas, just like she knew your dad and I were discussing a trip to Italy." She pauses. "And, Gina, the way you rode your bike down the hill with your hands in the air above your head. I told you a million times you were going to hurt yourself. You didn't think I was psychic when you finally did."

Three hours later, I pull out of my parents' driveway and make my way down Towering Heights Lane. In the distance, I see a man and a woman jogging up the hill with three small kids on bikes in front of them. Even from a distance, I know it's Cooper. As I get closer, I see he's wearing a TechVisions's T-shirt. I'm almost upon them, and I slow down and move to the right. Cooper stares into the windshield. I raise my hand to wave, but I pass before he has a chance to respond. I glance in the rearview mirror and see the woman looking back at my car.

She must be living with him. The french toast and meatball sub shift in my stomach. I'm afraid I'm going to be sick. I think about turning around and racing back to my parents' bathroom, but I don't want to pass Cooper and his happy, healthy instant family again. I open the window and stick my head out, breathing in the fresh air. My stomach settles down, and I drive home much faster than usual.

Chapter 39

My mother and I are in the kitchen making pasta when we hear the moving truck rumbling up Towering Heights Lane. My mother uses her apron to wipe the flour off her hands and heads to the living room window. I follow a few feet behind. We watch the truck groan to a stop across the street. Shortly after, a black SUV with Texas plates climbs the hill and turns into the driveway. The passenger door swings open, and Neesha Patel Davidian steps out onto the driveway of the home she left twenty-two years earlier, almost to the day. She turns toward our house and brings her hand to her forehead to shade her eyes from the sun. A moment later, she lifts that same hand high above her head and waves like she's in the midst of a huge crowd trying to catch the attention of a rock star on stage.

"Dear God," my mother whispers. "For a moment, I thought it was Jayda standing there."

I race out the front door and across the street. Neesha is leaning into the backseat of the minivan, removing her son from his car seat. Her husband and daughter walk around from the driver's side. The girl, dressed in a green sundress, has a long black ponytail and large, inquisitive eyes. She could very well be Neesha at age eight, if Neesha wore dresses, that is. "Hello," I say.

She studies me cautiously before responding. "Hi."

"I'm Gina."

"I know. My mom told me to call you Aunt Gina." The movers roll a dolly with a bureau strapped to it past us and up the driveway. "I don't know why she wants me to call you that. You're not really my aunt."

I nod. "You don't have to call me Aunt Gina if you don't want to."

"Oh yes, she does," Neesha's husband says.

I extend my hand to him. "Gina Rossi."

He removes his Texas Rangers baseball cap, revealing thick, black wavy hair. "Ashley Davidian." He ignores my outstretched arm and instead steps toward me and pulls me into a tight hug, crushing his cap against my back. "Thrilled to finally meet you, Gina. Neesha has talked about you for years."

"I'm so happy you two are finally meeting," Neesha says. I pull away from Ashley to embrace Neesha and Ashley Junior, whom she is holding.

AJ studies me with his dark eyes but says nothing. "He's a little shy," Neesha says. "Say hi to my friend Gina."

"No." He buries his head in his mother's chest.

"That's the effect I usually have on males." I mean it as a joke, but it makes me think of Cooper, who has pretty much been avoiding me since that night he gave me a ride home. Luci thinks it's because he's getting serious with Miss Minivan and I am a temptation. Me a temptation. That's pretty funny.

"He just has to get used to you," Neesha says apologetically, handing him off to his father.

Across the street, I hear the screen door open and shut and then watch my parents make their way down the lawn and across the street. Neesha rushes to the end of the driveway to greet them. My mother's eyes fill with tears as she pulls Neesha into a tight embrace. They hug in silence. Then my mom steps backward so that she can see Neesha's face. "You look exactly like your mother," she says.

Jayda has made her way to the edge of the driveway. She takes Neesha's hand. "Mommy, what's wrong?"

Neesha squeezes Jayda's hand. "This is Mrs. Rossi," she says. "She was my mom's best friend."

"You knew my grandmother?"

"I did," my mother says.

"I'm named after her," Jayda says. "And I've seen pictures of her."

"She was very beautiful," my mother says, "just like you and your mom."

My father has made his way up to the garage entrance, where the movers have placed a golf bag. "Nice clubs," I hear him say as he pulls out a pitching wedge and inspects it.

"Any challenging courses nearby?" Ashley asks. A few minutes later I hear them talking about handicaps.

AJ has made his way to the edge of the driveway. Neesha lifts him into her arms. "Say hi to Mrs. Rossi."

AJ gives a small wave. "Your children are beautiful," my mother whispers, reaching for AJ.

He goes straight to her. No crying or hiding his face like he did with me. He grabs a handful of my mother's newly gray hair. "Ajee," he says.

"She's not Ajee," Jayda says.

"But her hair is the same color as Ajee's," Neesha says.

"Ajee," AJ repeats.

"No, AJ," Jayda whines.

"Why don't you call her Grandma Rossi," Neesha says.

Grandma Rossi? My heart misses a beat. Is Neesha suggesting this because she doesn't think my mother will ever be a real grandmother? It's been six weeks since I last saw Ethan, and I'm still getting used to the idea that he wasn't the man Ajee was talking about all those years ago. On this day especially, it's hard for me to admit that her third prediction for me was wrong.

My mother smiles and nods. "I'd like that."

Chapter 40

The clouds drift in, covering most of the sun. Only one beam of sunlight shines down, and it illuminates the urn cradled in Neesha's hands. To me, it looks like the container is glowing from the inside out, and I wouldn't be at all surprised if the light coming from it is Ajee's smile. She'd be thrilled to see us standing in this semicircle around the rosebush in Neesha's yard, spreading her remains.

Neesha scoops a spoonful of ashes from the urn with a silver sterling utensil that she bought specifically for this occasion. "A waste of money," Dr. Patel said when he saw it a few minutes ago. Now Neesha uses it to sprinkle the ashes over the bush. "Good-bye, Ajee. I hope you know how much I loved you," she says.

She passes the urn and spoon to my mother, and as soon as they're in my mom's hands, she sneezes. Three violent nose eruptions that echo through the backyard. Dr. Patel pulls a handkerchief from the pocket of his suit coat and hands it to my mother. In return, she gives him the urn and spoon and then sneezes two more times. I had been looking forward to hearing her say something nice about Ajee, but it looks like she's found a way out of it.

Dr. Patel slips the spoon into his coat pocket, reaches into the urn, and pulls out a fistful of his mother's remains. Neesha crinkles her nose. He extends his hand, and the ashes sift through his slightly parted fingers, falling into the mulch below the bush. "Ashes to ashes," he says. His face is beet red from the heat, and I'm wondering if he regrets wearing a suit.

Dr. Patel passes the urn to Sanjit, who looks like he's melting. His sideburns are wet, and his yellow golf shirt is drenched in sweat. "Thank you for helping raise me." He, too, uses his hands to distribute the ashes. "I know it wasn't always easy." He passes the urn to me and wipes his dripping forehead with his arm.

The spoon is still in Dr. Patel's pocket. I glance at him. His head is bowed, and his eyes are closed. I tilt the urn slightly and sprinkle a few ashes over the bush. "Thank you for making my childhood interesting." Out of the corner of my eye, I see my mother raise one of her well-groomed eyebrows.

I pass the urn to Jayda. She stares into it. Before anyone realizes what she's doing, she turns it upside down, dumping out all the remaining contents. As the thick black ashes fall to the ground, the wind gusts. A cloud of dust smears my sundress. I try to wipe it off, but I only make black streaks on the coral-colored fabric. "Ajee looks good on you," Sanjit whispers, sounding more like the prankster he was than the cardiologist he is today.

Jayda hands the now-empty urn to Ashley. "Why don't we all recount some of our favorite memories of Ajee?" he suggests.

Neesha smiles. "I have too many good memories to choose a favorite, but I will always remember how after my mom died she pointed to my heart and said, 'She will always be with you, dear one, right there.'"

"My favorite memory is her saving Matthew Colby," I say. "I didn't think we'd ever see him again."

Sanjit laughs. "After I got a D in AP Bio, she told me not to worry, that I was going to be a fine doctor one day. Until that moment, all I ever wanted to be was a policeman."

"I liked it when she took me for ice cream," Jayda says. She turns to her father and says with a smile, "She always let me get a large, but she told me not to tell."

"Ice cream!" AJ yells.

"My favorite memory of Ajee is actually the first time I met her," Ashley says. "I came to pick up Neesha for our first date. I had a Mustang. The car had no muffler and was really loud. I loved driving it fast, and I came racing down the street. I brought the car to a screeching stop at the bottom of the driveway and blew the horn a few times. Ajee came running out of the house and reprimanded me for not coming to the door or showing her granddaughter the proper respect. She practically dragged me inside by the waistband of my baggy jeans, but just before we entered the house, she stopped. 'This can't be,' she said, and she sounded angry. 'What?' I asked and she glared at me. 'You will be the father of my great-grandchildren.' She went inside shaking her head, leaving me on the landing."

Dr. Patel shakes his head. "I don't know how she did it, but she was never wrong."

She was wrong once, I think.

In the distance, bolts of lightning appear, and then thunder booms. We all dash through the side door and make it inside just before the heavens open up.

The inside of the house smells like garlic. A bowl of salad, a basket of bread, pans of lasagna and chicken parmigiana, and stacks of paper plates and plastic silverware are arranged on the breakfast bar. We all stand in line making up dishes.

"I made this with Grandma Rossi," Jayda says as I scoop a piece of lasagna out of the pan and onto her plate.

"She was a big help," my mother says, smiling down at Jayda. In the six weeks that Neesha has lived here, my mother has become best friends with Neesha's kids. She is their one and only babysitter. She watches them once or twice a week. Sometimes I can't help but think the entire reason Neesha moved back is so that my mother can be a surrogate grandmother to her kids. Maybe Ajee somehow arranged it because she blew the prediction about Ethan.

Across the room, my father, who just arrived moments ago and is still dressed in his golf attire, including a Callaway baseball cap, has Ashley pinned in a corner. I hear my father say, "Made a birdie out of the sand trap." Ashley pats him on the back. Usually they play together on Sundays. My dad refers to Neesha's husband as his adopted son-in-law.

I should be happy that Neesha and her family are giving my parents what I can't, but seeing them all interact makes me feel more alone than ever. I carry my plate to the dining room table and sit down by myself. I watch everyone talking and laughing in the kitchen. A few minutes later, Jayda starts whining that she wants ice cream. "Have a piece of cake," my mother suggests.

"I don't like it," Jayda cries. It's a rum cake. I don't much like it, either.

"Stop whining," Ashley warns.

Sanjit enters the dining room. A piece of lasagna falls off his over-flowing plate onto the table as he pulls out the chair across from me. "Mine never cry like that." He wipes off the spill with his napkin. "They're about a hundred times louder." He laughs and takes his wallet out of his pocket. He hands it to me so that I can see pictures of his children. He describes each of his three kids and tells me about his wife, Jenny. As I listen to him speak, I find it hard to believe that this distinguished man is the teenage boy who used to moon Neesha and me at the bus stop. He stuffs a large forkful of lasagna into his mouth. "We don't get food like this in Texas," he says. I watch him chew, thinking about how his and Neesha's lives have changed since they left here. On the other hand, my life has basically stalled while I've been waiting for Ethan.

Sanjit looks at his watch. "Whoa, it's late." He stands. I look at my watch. It's five o'clock. "Better get to the airport."

While Neesha and Ashley take Sanjit and Dr. Patel to the airport, my mom and I stay with the kids. My mother reads AJ a story, and Jayda convinces me to take her to the Westham Creamery.

While much has changed in Westham over the past twenty-five years, one thing that has not is the Westham Creamery. Since the Calpin family converted their barn to a small restaurant in the 1970s, the place has served grilled cheese sandwiches, crinkle-cut french fries, and nineteen flavors of ice cream. In the winter, the place can comfortably seat only twelve or so at a time. In the summer, the family sets up row upon row of picnic tables on their grassy acre, and that number jumps to a hundred.

When Jayda and I arrive on this warm September night, there are three long lines at the takeout counter. Jayda takes my hand and directs us to the one in the middle. To me it looks the longest. "It will move the fastest," she promises. I make note of who is at the end of the other lines, a family of four to our left and two women in biking gear to the right.

We stand behind a teenage boy and girl. She is wearing short jean shorts and a shirt that showcases her belly ring. He has a tattoo of a snake that coils around his right shoulder. Every few minutes Tattoo Boy pulls Belly Ring Girl into his arms and kisses her. Each time he does, Jayda points and laughs.

After about fifteen minutes, Jayda and I reach the counter. I turn around to check out the location of the people who were at the ends of the other lines. The women bikers still have four parties in front of them. The family of four has two people before them, but what captures my attention is the five people now at the end of the line: Cooper, Miss Minivan, a young girl, and two small boys. Cooper sees me at the same time I see him and waves. I wave back. Miss Minivan has been watching, and she waves, as well. I don't want her to be friendly. I don't want to like her.

I'm vaguely aware of Jayda placing her order, cookies and cream with rainbow sprinkles in a waffle cone. "Aunt Gina"—she taps me on the back—"what are you getting?" I turn back to the counter and order black raspberry chip with chocolate sprinkles in a sugar cone.

When we get our ice cream, I take Jayda by the hand and turn in the direction opposite Cooper. I lead her to a free picnic table in the middle row and position myself so that I have a clear view of Cooper's back. Miss Minivan turns around, looks at me, and then says something to Cooper. He glances over his shoulder. They talk for a few seconds. Then Cooper grabs one of the boy's hands, steps out of line, and heads toward Jayda and me. We've only had a few bites of our ice cream, but I have to get out of here. I do not want to meet Cooper's girlfriend and her kids. "What do you say we take the ice cream home?" I stand as I ask Jayda this.

"I like it here," she says.

Cooper and the boy are upon us now. I sit back down. "Mind if we join you?"

"Where's your ice cream?" Jayda asks the boy.

"My mom's getting it."

I study the kid. He has dark hair and dark eyes. Is it my imagination, or does he look like Cooper? The boy notices me staring and smiles. A dimple appears in each cheek. He is definitely a mini Cooper. Why does Miss Minivan's son look like Cooper? Exactly how long has he been dating her?

"This is Tyler," Cooper says.

"Hi, Tyler. I'm Gina and that's Jayda."

Jayda says hello as Tyler sits next to her. Looks like I'll be eating ice cream with Cooper and his girlfriend.

"Hi, Jayda. I'm Cooper." He reaches across the table to shake her hand. I laugh at his formality, but Jayda is very serious in her greeting.

"We spread Ajee's ashes today," she announces and then takes a lick of her ice cream.

"How was that?" Cooper asks.

Jayda shrugs. "It was okay. Did you know her?"

"I didn't," Cooper answers.

Jayda stares at him as she eats. Across the field, I see Cooper's girlfriend and her other kids making their way over to us. Perfect.

"I thought she knew you," Jayda says.

Cooper shakes his head. "Never had the pleasure."

The rest of his party has arrived at our table. Miss Minivan hands Tyler a cone of cookies and cream and Cooper a dish of something chocolate. "This is Brendon and Clare," she says, "and I'm Monique."

"Nice to meet you," I lie. "I'm Gina." I don't extend my hand, but only because it's sticky with ice cream.

Monique sits down next to Cooper. She has a bottled water but no ice cream. Ha! That's a point for me. Cooper likes women who eat, especially dessert.

"So, Gina," Monique says, "I've heard so much about you." Cooper, who was bending toward his dish, sits up straight. Why would he talk about me with his girlfriend? "He really enjoyed working on that project with you. Talked about some of those late nights as if they were dates." Cooper's ears turn bright red. Monique pats him on the back.

Across the table, Brendon and Tyler are pushing each other. "Knock it off," Cooper says. I think he's addressing them, but if Monique's embarrassing him as much as she is me, maybe he's talking to her.

Brendon leans against Tyler so hard that Tyler falls off the bench. He picks himself up and punches Brendon in the arm. Cooper starts to say something, but Monique cuts him off. "Your dad is going to be here tomorrow, and if I tell him how bad you were . . ." The boys immediately stop their horseplay. I guess Monique's ex is pretty scary.

Monique touches Cooper's arm and leans toward me. "He is going to be so happy when we're out of his hair."

Jayda and Clare move from our table to a narrow strip of bare grass, where they take turns doing cartwheels.

"You said two weeks, it's been close to four months," Cooper says.

"We're having a house built in Pennsylvania," Monique tells me.

"It's been one thing after another. My poor husband is down there by himself in a tiny apartment."

Her husband? I suddenly notice a gold band on Monique's left ring finger. Monique is not Cooper's girlfriend. I feel like joining Jayda and Clare in cartwheel alley.

"I have to go to the bathroom," Brendon says.

"Me, too," Tyler says.

Monique stands. "I'll take you."

Cooper and I eat our ice cream in silence for a few minutes. "So, Monique's your sister," I finally say.

He nods. "Luckily they're leaving soon," he whispers.

I can't stop smiling. Miss Minivan is Cooper's sister! Cooper smiles at my smile. "It's really not funny, Gina. The kids whine constantly, and my sister's a slob—and loud. And she doesn't stop talking. Ever. You noticed. I know you did."

"She's not that bad." Not as bad as when I thought she was his girlfriend.

"She is. I'll tell you about it sometime."

I don't want to wait for some unnamed time that may never come. "How about tomorrow night?" The question pours out of my mouth so fast that it sounds like one long, unintelligible word.

Cooper uses his spoon to push around the ice cream in his dish. "Are you asking me on a date?"

I've started down this path, and I'm taking it to the end. "Yes, I am." Somehow I don't sound scared.

He puts his spoon down and turns to face me. I realize I'm kicking the leg of the picnic table and stop my foot from swaying. I look up at him. He reaches toward my face and tucks a strand of hair behind my ear. Then, right there at a picnic table at the Westham Creamery, before our first date even, Cooper Allen kisses me. This time I'm sure this kiss is my last first kiss. As it goes on, the future flashes through my mind: Cooper meeting my parents, Cooper down on one knee, Cooper and me standing by an altar, me holding a baby with Cooper looking over my shoulder. It's a future I've never been more certain of.

Chapter 41

Peter pulls Luci's nameplate out of the slot on our door, hands it to her, and slides in her new one: Luci Corrigan. Luci snaps the old one in half and gives the pieces back to Peter. "It's a bloody shame what happened to that Luci Chin lassie," she says in an Irish brogue. "May the new Mrs. Chin fare better." Peter laughs, pulls her toward him with one arm, and kisses the top of her head.

Unlike Cooper and me, they don't care if everyone at TechVisions knows they're dating. They commute together and eat lunch in the café at a table for two tucked away in the corner. It's hard not to notice them, because their laughter echoes around the room. With Luci's influence, Peter has swapped out his burgers and fries for salads. He's lost about forty pounds. He's dressing better these days, too, well-fitting Dockers and golf shirts instead of baggy jeans and T-shirts. Peter's been a good influence on Luci, as well. She is less bitter about Kip and is even thinking about sending his newborn an outfit.

As Luci walks back into our office, she looks at me. "Soon we'll be replacing your nameplate with one that says Gina Allen." She winks. I pick up a pen and practice signing "Gina Allen" on a scrap piece of paper. I've never been good at cursive Ls. I might have to work on that, because things are going extremely well with Cooper. We've been dating for just over a month now. Last night he asked if he could meet my parents. Who asks for that? When I called my mother this morning to tell her Cooper wanted to meet her, she was thrilled and invited us to dinner tonight. She's going to have to wait, though, because Cooper, Neesha, Ashley, Luci, Peter, and I are going to Last Chance. Neesha really wants to do karaoke, so Luci and I are going to sing Jayda's favorite song, "Call Me Maybe," with her. We actually spent the last week practicing. It didn't help. Luci is tone-deaf and loud, and Neesha can't sing a verse without laughing.

There is only one empty table when Luci, Peter, and I arrive at Last Chance. It's in the back right corner as far away from the makeshift stage as possible. I race across the floor and fling myself into a chair, narrowly beating out a group of women who were heading to the same spot. The smallest of the ladies stands beside me with her hands on her hips, glaring down at me. "Sorry," I say just as Luci and Peter arrive and slide into the seats across from me.

"What are you apologizing for?" Luci asks. She smiles at the woman. "You were just a step too slow." She shrugs and waves her hand like she's shooing away a fly.

The waitress with the mole on her face approaches our table. Luci asks for a chocolate martini. There is no way I'm drinking those again. Instead, I get coconut rum and pineapple juice. Peter orders a beer for himself and one for Cooper, who is stuck at work on a conference call with a client on the West Coast.

A man carrying a piece of paper heads to the stage and picks up the microphone. "Listen up. We have a bunch of people who want to do karaoke tonight, so if you want to perform, make sure your name is on this list."

I get up and make my way across the sticky floor to add our names to the list. There are at least twenty people in front of us.

A few minutes later, Neesha enters the room with Ashley trailing behind, holding his phone. He sits and places it in the center of the table. "Jayda insists I record this. Don't let me forget."

The man on the stage calls out the name Kathy. A skinny brunette wearing a short sequin dress takes the stage. She sits on a stool, and the piano intro of Adele's "Someone Like You" begins to play.

Kathy begins to sing. Her voice screeches. Peter holds his hands to his ears. "Make it stop," he says. Three excruciating minutes later, Kathy is done. The crowd gives a mock cheer.

Next up is a group of young women celebrating an upcoming wedding. The tallest of the five is wearing a white veil. As they choose their song, the waitress drops off our drinks. They settle on Carrie Underwood's "Before He Cheats." They laugh as they sing, but hearing the bride-to-be sing that song depresses me.

Cooper arrives as the fifth group exits the stage. He sits next to me and kisses me hello. Then he extends his hand to Ashley, who is sitting next to him. "Cooper Allen." He nods at Neesha. "Nice to see you again."

The next group of singers hits the stage and consults the playbook.

"How did your call go?" I ask Cooper.

He picks up his beer. "Not good. I overestimated iPad sales and had to explain why." He takes a large swallow.

"How many did you predict would sell?" Luci asks.

Cooper grimaces at her word choice. "I forecast sales of sixty-one million." He emphasizes the word *forecast*.

"How many actually sold?" Ashley asks.

"Just over fifty-eight million."

"Damn, you were close," Peter says, saluting Cooper with his beer mug.

The music starts. "I'm a Believer."

"Clients don't pay me to be close," Cooper says. "They pay me to be right."

We are all silent as we listen to the group singing. They sound more like The Monkees than Smash Mouth.

"Hey," Neesha says, reaching behind Ashley to touch Cooper on the back. "My grandmother made the most accurate predictions of anyone I've ever known, and even she got it wrong sometimes."

Luci nods. "And it's a good thing she was wrong sometimes, or Gina wouldn't be sitting with you right now."

Cooper gets that squinty look. "What do you mean?"

"Never mind," I say.

Luci, of course, won't let it go. She tells Cooper about Ajee's prediction that I would marry a man named Ethan.

Cooper lets out a slow breath and very quietly says, "My name was supposed to be Ethan."

"It wasn't." But even as the words are coming out of my mouth, I know he's telling the truth.

He takes my hand and squeezes it. "Swear to God. I was named after a friend of my father's who passed away right before I was born. Ethan Cooper. My dad even wrote Ethan on the birth certificate, but when my mom saw Ethan Allen written down, she changed her mind.

She said she didn't want her son being named after a historical figure and a furniture store."

The entire room goes silent. Maybe it's just our table. I'm not sure. Luci and Neesha stare at me. I shift my body and pick up my drink.

Ashley's phone rings then. A picture of Ajee appears on the screen. It's the exact same picture as the one from the obituary. I look at it and then look up at Ashley. "Jayda has Ajee's old phone. Like an eight-year-old needs a phone." He shrugs. "Hey, Jayda," he says into the phone. "No, no, they haven't gone yet. They're still waiting."

But he's wrong. My wait is over. This was the final sign from Ajee. I know it. *Cooper is Ethan*, she is saying. *You have waited long enough.*

CPSIA information can be obtained at www.ICGtesting.com
Printed in the USA
LVOW11s0254030816

498765LV00007B/126/P